THE LEGACY SERIES

SERIES TITLES

What We Might Become
Sara Reish Desmond

The Silver State Stories
Michael Darcher

An Instinct for Movement
Michael Mattes

The Machine We Trust
Tim Conrad

Gridlock
Brett Biebel

Salt Folk
Ryan Habermeyer

The Commission of Inquiry
Patrick Nevins

Maximum Speed
Kevin Clouther

Reach Her in This Light
Jane Curtis

The Spirit in My Shoes
John Michael Cummings

The Effects of Urban Renewal on Mid-Century America and Other Crime Stories
Jeff Esterholm

What Makes You Think You're Supposed to Feel Better
Jody Hobbs Hesler

Fugitive Daydreams
Leah McCormack

Hoist House: A Novella & Stories
Jenny Robertson

Finding the Bones: Stories & A Novella
Nikki Kallio

"Garcia's stories are clear-eyed snapshots of people from a wide range of backgrounds attempting to navigate the choppy seas of daily life. Whether the tale take place in Kandahar or San Francisco, whether the main character is a veteran suffering from PTSD or an Afghan refugee adjusting to life in the U.S., all are laced with a skillfully restrained compassion that makes them moving but never manipulative."

—RICHARD LANGE
William Saroyan International Prize Finalist
author of *Joe Hustle* and *Dead Boys*

"J. Malcolm Garcia shows himself to be a master at the use of small, everyday events to open windows into the very souls of his characters. Garcia's granular, impressionistic style is somewhat reminiscent of Raymond Carver, though the language is richer and the imagery more vivid. He has developed his own distinctive voice for telling a story, and in the process he is doing the writer's work, which is to reveal the world as it is truly lived."

—DONALD LYSTRA
Midwest Book Award Winner
author of *Season of Water and Ice*

A DAY DOESN'T GO BY

WHEN I DON'T HAVE REGRETS

J. MALCOLM GARCIA

CORNERSTONE PRESS

UNIVERSITY OF WISCONSIN-STEVENS POINT

Cornerstone Press, Stevens Point, Wisconsin 54481
Copyright © 2025 J. Malcolm Garcia
www.uwsp.edu/cornerstone

Printed in the United States of America by
Point Print and Design Studio, Stevens Point, Wisconsin

Library of Congress Control Number: 2025944788
ISBN: 978-1-968148-18-8

This is a work of fiction. Names, characters, businesses, places, events, and incidents are either the products of the author's imagination or used in a fictitious manner. Any resemblance to actual persons, living or dead, or actual events is purely coincidental.

Cornerstone Press titles are produced in courses and internships offered by the Department of English at the University of Wisconsin–Stevens Point.

DIRECTOR & PUBLISHER
Dr. Ross K. Tangedal

EXECUTIVE EDITORS
Jeff Snowbarger, Freesia McKee

EDITORIAL DIRECTOR
Brett Hill

SENIOR EDITORS
Paige Biever, Eva Nielsen, Reilly Crous

PRESS STAFF
Karlie Harpold, Lilly Kulbeck, Samantha Bjork, Sophie McPherson, Madison Schultz, Autumn Vine

For Charles W. "Scott" Hope.

STORIES

Searching

Six of us were in the water holding hands, forming one long line while Ernesto's mother paced on the beach. Sometimes she stopped and raised her hands, framing her face and the open O of her mouth in the black shadows of her palms, her lips arching back like the steady drag of the undertow, stretching into hysterical grooves in her cheeks, exposing gums and protruding teeth like a horse braying in a barn fire, grotesque and wild, and we heard her screams and continued looking.

The surface of the water was warm and we could see the warbling reflection of our faces lined in a row staring up and pale white stomachs, goose-bumped where the warmth of the sun had not penetrated, cold and dark green, but we could not see our legs, and only knew they were there because of the cold soft sand gripped between our toes.

One of us pointed,

Look! Over there!

but then shook his head,

Nothing.

Nothing but the wet blink shimmer of the reef exposed to the sun and the huge withdrawn hoop of sky above us, so clear and blue without low hanging clouds. We couldn't even pretend to reach up with our hands and hope someday to touch it.

Fisherman who had been dragging for hours now began approaching us on their return to the beach, rowing through small white-capped waves, the flat smack-smack of water slapping against the hulls of their empty boats and we imagined drivers parked outside the closed beach, leant out of windows of idling cars or standing up on bird-poop-spattered hood, squinting, peering.

Nothing.

We tried to remember what our legs looked like. We tried to remember what Ernesto looked like but all we could recall were his black, thick-lensed glasses. We tried to remember the last moment we saw him. We remembered Señora Rivera calling, Okay boys, it's getting late. Time to come in, and Ernesto pleading, Oh, Momma. But maybe that was not Ernesto. Maybe that was Victor, (Oh, Señora Rivera, please! Five more minutes!) Or Rafi or Miguel or Carlos or who knows? we thought, as a wave raised all six of us up off our feet and we no longer felt the sand between our toes, nothing, but balanced uncertainly between the unreachable sky, the waiting beach, the warm surface of the water and the dark green cold beneath the warmth.

On Deck

Although he had allergies, my father mowed the lawn every Saturday, weather permitting, and the flying specks of cut grass and dandelions would always set off a discordant mix of sneezing that left him gasping.

The ozone and pollen levels are supposed to be very high this weekend, my mother would warn frequently on Friday nights. Let the lawn go. We can hire someone to do it.

My father always ignored her. In the contest of wills that ran the gamut of their forty-year marriage, she had long since conceded defeat but remained hopeful on occasion for a surprise victory. He would rather suffocate than listen to her, she said.

They had been introduced by mutual friends during the war when he was stationed in Puerto Rico; she was a nurse then in San Juan. They would stroll to the lobby of the Agua Caliente Hilton after an evening of dancing and watch the ocean roll onto the beach. The sea breeze tugged at their clothes, the sounds of crickets mingled with the whir of ceiling fans, and they sipped tequila sunrises and shared wet kisses in the shadows. My mother's perfume lingered on my father's shirt. They held hands and planned for the future.

He used to tell me about running laps on the deck of his ship, the USS Collins, during calisthenics. He remembered the precision of the drills, the bow of the ship angling into waves and the huge, gaping troughs that now and again concealed the ship, dipping and rising as the wind whipped the sea into foam.

Mowing the lawn was not a matter of mere recalcitrance on my father's part. He approached the yard as a test of physical endurance and would not be dissuaded by his doctor, whose constant harping, he said, was worse than my mother's. If the doctor had his way, my father declared, he wouldn't let me take one step out of the house.

His preparations were methodical. He responded to the six o'clock clatter of his alarm clock with weary obedience. Posting himself in front of the bathroom mirror, he would silently weigh the multiple complaints of his body. His bladder was full. His mouth tasted awful. His feet were cold against the tile floor.

He quickly brushed eight hours of accumulated odors from his mouth before stepping up to the toilet to relieve himself. Within fifteen minutes he was showered, shaved, and dressed in a frayed woolen sweater, a pair of old corduroys, and sneakers.

After drinking a glass of orange juice and reading the sports page, he would drag the lawnmower out of the garage, balancing a box of plastic trash bags on the handlebars.

Almost immediately his face would scrunch up and he would begin sneezing. As he started cutting, his sneezing seemed to take on a life of its own, exploding against the morning stillness as thick flecks of clipped grass clung to his dew-dampened shoes.

By the time the grass was cut, he could barely breathe, but in autumn the job wasn't finished. Leaves covered the driveway and needed to be raked. He would work his way from one end of the driveway to the other, scooping the leaves into a pile. Digging around in his pocket for a book of matches, he would roll a section of newspaper into a long tube and bury it in the leaves with only the tip showing.

One morning my mother looked out the kitchen window and saw my father coughing beside a pile of burning leaves. He's going to kill himself, she said.

Jerry! she shouted tapping the window, Jerry!

She turned to me.

Go and tell your father to come in, please.

I ran outside and heard leaves snapping and saw white clouds of smoke envelop my father. I stood beside him and started coughing too, doubling over.

Mom said to come in, I gasped.

My father gently steered me back toward the house.

I'll be in in a minute, he said, his voice hoarse.

Only when the leaves were reduced to a pile of ash would he collapse into a lawn chair making loud, snuffling noises. Dandelion heads of plucked Kleenex bounced across the terrace. He swallowed two antihistamine tablets he kept tucked in his hip pocket, took a deep breath, and closed his eyes.

One Saturday when he had regained his breath and stood up, he noticed a young woman wearing a tight green nylon running outfit jogging down the block. A soft breeze lifted the woman's thick black hair. He watched the rhythm of her arms and the jiggle that ran through her breasts with each deliberate stride, her face full of color.

She stopped abruptly and walked in a circle taking deep breaths. Her chest rose and fell and he continued staring at her. I watched him as I practiced driving the car, repeatedly backing out of the garage and turning it around slowly in the driveway.

I imagined he was remembering those hot afternoons in Puerto Rico.

Under the shadows of the big guns his arms pumped steadily at his sides. Sweat gathered in the grooves of his forehead and he thought of my mother in her swimsuit on the beach, her long hair, tossed carelessly behind her shoulders, catching the sun. He remembered holding her the night before, her breasts pressed hard against his chest. Sunlight sparkled, skipped across the water. The sea rocking the ship.

A twitch in his nose interrupted his reverie, ballooning from nothing into a small temblor.

The rest of that day he spent doing chores. He washed the car, bought tools at the hardware store, and fixed the dryer. He helped my mother make dinner but his mind roamed. He looked out the kitchen window toward the spot at the edge of the driveway where he had seen the woman jogging.

That night with the lights out and the timer connected to the living room lamp ticking methodically, my father lay awake in bed, absorbing my mother's muffled snores in his shoulder.

He rolled over and swung his legs out of bed. My mother's head dragged off his shoulder to the fitted sheet. He sat slumped at the edge of the bed, picking at his pajamas. He pulled one of her gray hairs off his shoulder and reached for his robe and slippers.

Tiptoeing into the hall, he crept downstairs, delicately balancing the moans of the wood floor with the sighs of the house as it settled into night.

He opened the garage door and cringed at the raspy hinges. Walking past our station wagon and stepping over the lawnmower, he walked out to the driveway. The night air brought a shiver to his spine. A familiar weight asserted itself against his chest.

He wrinkled his nose and sneezed. He jogged forward slowly, steadily. He sneezed again. He continued jogging. His sneezing increased. He jogged in a circle around the driveway, gradually tightening the circle and bringing himself back closer and closer to the garage. His breath came in harmonic wheezes. A few feet away from the open garage he pushed himself into a sprint and, throwing up his arms, collapsed at the foot of the door.

He cleared his throat and spat and cleared his throat again. He raised his head and pushed himself over. Sand he had tossed over oil stains stuck to his pajamas and robe. A full moon cast the sun's reflection across the sky, splashing a wave of blue light over him. He felt the heat ripple through his chest and, feeling it, sat up and rested his head between his knees and breathed a little easier.

Strangers

Six thirty, evening, still light but the cloudless sky is beginning to pale, blue diluting to gray. Eight-year-old Pablo González rides his bicycle in the gravel driveway of his house while his mother, Elvira, observes him from the window above the kitchen sink. His father, Alberto, has just come home from work. He waves at Pablo as he pulls into the garage.

What are you doing? he asks as he gets out of the car.

Nothing, Pablo says.

How was school?

OK.

Undoing his tie, Alberto walks into the house. He shouts, Hello!, and Elvira shouts back, Hello! He drops his briefcase on a chair at the breakfast nook table where Pablo has left his backpack, opens a cabinet door, and reaches for a bottle of Scotch. He mixes two shots with soda in a tall glass. Elvira comes up behind him and he turns and they exchange a routine, home-from-work kiss. She returns to the window. He sips his drink.

How was your day? He asks.

She speaks of long lines at the Jewel-Osco and as a result she is cooking dinner later than she had planned. Alberto takes another sip of his drink.

Did you hear me? She asks.

Yes, he says.

I'm making chicken and rice.

Tell Pablo he shouldn't just drop his pack in the breakfast nook. He should take it to his room.

We have ice cream for dessert.

Did you hear me about Pablo?

Yes.

Alberto loosens his tie and walks into the living room to watch Fox News. Elvira empties the dishwasher and begins slicing a chicken breast, glancing up now and again to watch Pablo. He wanted to ride with his friends on the street but she told him he was too young.

Mom! he whined.

Don't Mom me, she said.

Glancing past Pablo, Elvira notices her neighbors, Martin and June Dean, walking and holding hands. Their son, Drew, is riding his bicycle and stops to speak with Pablo, and across the street another neighbor, Jan Harvey, gets out of her car and waves at someone Elvira can't see. A truck drives by and blocks her view. When it passes, an uneven quiet settles over the street. But then Dulce, González's poodle, charges the living room window, barking at sounds only she can hear, and Elvira chases after her, clapping her hands for her to stop.

Pablo rides his bicycle back and forth in long, looping figure eights. Growing bored, he stops at the edge of the driveway and turns, facing the garage. Then he races toward it. Just feet away, he brakes and spins hard to his left and comes to a noisy stop. Looking over his shoulder, he beams at the long, crooked skid mark that stretches behind him through the gravel, and beyond the line at the edge of the driveway he sees a man on the street watching him.

Hello, the man says.

Strands of dark hair hang across his forehead and he pushes them back with the back of a hand. He wears a grass-stained T-shirt and mud-spattered blue jeans. His sneakers have holes. He looks up at the sky and squints. His skin shines with sweat. He turns his head as if he is expecting something to emerge from the trees on either end of the street. He tells Pablo his name is Miguel and rests his hands on his protruding stomach.

What's your name?

Pablo.

Really, Miguel says. You're *guero*.

What?

White. Do you speak Spanish?

No, Pablo says.

Why not?

My dad's father is named Pablo.

Does he speak Spanish?

I think so.

Well, then why not you?

Pablo shrugs. Miguel laughs.

Pablo just started the third grade. On the first day of school, his teacher, Miss Brinker, had asked him if he spoke Spanish. He told her no and for the rest of the day she called him Paul. He reminded her his name was Pablo. During recess, he wrote *Paul* and *Pablo* on a piece of paper and compared them. They had a lot of the same letters. He wondered why he couldn't be one or the other, Pablo or Paul, all the time in both languages. That afternoon, he asked his mother. It just isn't, she said.

How long have you lived here? Miguel asks.

Since I was born, Pablo answers.

How old are you?

Eight.

Miguel nods. He considers the two-story homes up and down the street, how some have tennis courts while others have pools and still others have both. He comments on the large size of the houses and asks Pablo what people did to afford such big homes.

I don't know, Pablo said.

How many bedrooms do you think are in each one? he wonders.

Pablo shrugs.

Do they need anyone to work on their yards?

I don't know.

How about your parents? Do they?
Pablo shrugs again.
Maybe I'll find a job here and then I can teach you Spanish.
OK, Pablo says.
Show me what you can do on your bike.
Pablo smiles, peddles over to Miguel, and spins around.
Watch me, he says.
He races toward the garage and brakes with a screech. He turns around; Miguel raises his hands.
Bravo! he shouts. Again!

After calming Dulce, Elvira returns to the kitchen and removes the last plate from the dishwasher. She glances outside but doesn't see Pablo. She leans forward peering through an open window above the sink, turning her head from one side to the other, and she almost shouts his name when she hears him enter the kitchen from the garage. He tells her a guy on the street just offered to teach him Spanish. But he needs a job first. Would Dad hire him?
Elvira wipes water off the counter. She faces Pablo.
What are you talking about?
Some guy, he says.
Some guy what?
He said he'd teach me Spanish.
Who was he?
I don't know.
Elvira looks out the window but sees no one.
Is he still here?
He left, Pablo says.
Where?
I don't know.
Pablo reaches for the cookie jar, but his mother swats his hand away.
This is serious Pablo, she says. How many times have I told you not to speak to strangers?

She calls for Alberto. He comes into the kitchen with his drink. Pablo knows his father doesn't like being interrupted when he watches the news.

What is it? Alberto says.

Elvira tells him about the stranger and how he said something about meeting Pablo to teach him Spanish. He didn't say meet me, Pablo wants to correct her, but it's too late. His father looks at him and he knows he's in trouble. It surprises him how fast his day has changed. One minute, he is showing off on his bike to Miguel and the next his father is mad at him. He wishes he could go back outside and come in again, and this time not say anything to his mother about Miguel.

Have you seen this man before? Alberto asks. Do you know him?

No, Pablo says.

What else? his father insists.

Nothing, Pablo says.

Did you tell him anything about yourself? Where you go to school?

No.

Alberto sets his drink down. Pablo hears the ice clink.

Well, I don't like it, Alberto says. How many times have we told you not to talk to strangers? Will you ever listen?

He talked to me first, Pablo said.

I don't care, his father snapped. You should have come inside at once.

I think we should call the police, Elvira says.

You start listening to us or you won't be allowed to play outside ever again, do you understand? Alberto said.

Alright, Alberto, Elvira says.

Don't alright me, he snaps. I did not come home so we'd have to call the police.

Elvira reaches for her purse on the counter and searches for her phone.

I don't want to hear about you talking to strangers again, Alberto says. Not today, not tomorrow, ever. Do you understand?

Pablo stares at the floor and nods. His father tells him to turn on the porch lights and close the living room curtains. Pablo hurries out of the kitchen. Dulce follows him. The last hours of the afternoon have turned gray. A sparrow lies on the stone terrace, its beak opening and closing, wings splayed. It probably flew into the glass, Pablo thinks. His parents would never let him put it in a box and bring it inside. It's full of germs, his mother would say. He worries a cat might get it. He watches the bird and then closes the curtains and walks into the front hall and flips on the porch lights. He goes back into the living room and looks at the TV. A woman stands in front of a map with all sorts of twisting lines and talks about the weather. It will be cold tomorrow and hot the day after. He hears a car pull into the driveway and Dulce starts barking. Red flashing lights sweep the house. After a moment the doorbell rings.

Alberto ushers the police officer into a dining room adjacent to the front door and offers him a chair. Elvira and Pablo follow them and Elvira asks if he would like a glass of water. No, thank you, ma'am, the officer says. Light from a chandelier shines down on them. The officer sits and hunches forward and his shadow casts a dark pond beneath him. Pablo notices he has big hands and his uniform fits snugly on body. He opens a small notepad and asks Alberto to spell his last name.

G-O-N-Z-Á-L-E-Z.

The officer repeats the spelling. González, he says, pronouncing the name with a hard *a* in the first syllable so that it sounds like, *Gane-zalez.* Alberto corrects him. The officer repeats, *Gane-zal-ez.* No, Alberto says. The officer scowls.

And your first name is Albert?

Alberto.

You go by Alberto.

Yes.

Not Albert.

Yes.

The officer turns a page.

So, you had a prowler? he says.

Not exactly, Alberto replies.

He explained Pablo's encounter with a stranger outside their house. Sometimes, the officer takes notes, his writing cramped to keep the words within the narrow lines of his notepad. Every so often, he looks up at the chandelier as if a thought has occurred to him. Turning his head, he sees a candelabra on a cabinet and then he glances down the front hall where a table holds a sterling silver flatware set, and past the front door to a guest bedroom, dark with the shades drawn.

You've done well, the officer says. You don't often see that.

What do you mean? Alberto asks.

The officer looks out a window at the front yard and the manicured beds of impatiens illuminated by the porch lights.

Who does your lawn?

I hire people, Alberto answers curtly, why?

Mexicans right? the officer says. Maybe this Miguel knows the people who cut your grass.

I don't know about that, Alberto says.

Well, they're mostly Mexicans, the officer continued, probably illegals, and this Miguel, he's probably Mexican too, and illegal. I mean, what does the name tell you?

He jots something down in his notepad.

The people who do your grass, they may have told this guy a few things, he continues looking up from his notes. They may have said you have a lot of money. He may be a little jealous that you hired his friends but not him. He may be jealous of you. Like, hey, how come this Mexican is doing so well and the best I can do is cut his lawn and he won't even hire me?

We're not Mexican, Alberto says.

Not at all, Elvira joins in, far from it. Our parents are from Spain.

This Miguel character wouldn't know that, the officer says. All he'd know is your name, assuming the people who do your yard told him. Did you know the O'Malleys? Alberto shakes his head.

No.

Ah, the officer said. Well, they lived around here. A good family. Must've been before your time.

He considers Alberto. Alberto looks back at him.

What? he asks.

The officer clears his throat.

I have to say … well, what I mean is, I'm surprised. I wouldn't expect your name to be Mexican. You could be an O'Malley. I mean you look, well, you know, I wouldn't have guessed is all I'm saying.

Well, we're not Mexican, Alberto says, unable to hide his irritation.

How'd you come to live here? the officer asks.

I grew up around here.

Like I said, it was mostly Irish families.

Well, we're not Irish, Alberto says, and I'm sure this Miguel person wouldn't have cared if we were.

I'm sorry, the officer said. You're right. I was just curious.

Alberto watches the officer and feels his anger mounting. He stares at his hands. Who is this man to question him? He provides for his family. He donates to charities. He meets all his obligations to his family and the community. Who cares who works on his lawn? Mexicans, Cubans, Puerto Ricans, it doesn't matter as long as they do the work. He pays them well. He resents being confused with them, lumping him in as if he is some common laborer, as if there is no distinction between his accomplishments and their work. He has no relationship with these people. If they have the determination of his parents, they may be equally successful.

His parents had immigrated from Madrid to Chicago before he was born. They did not speak English when they arrived. They took jobs in supermarkets, and Alberto's father went to school at night. He learned English and put himself through college and earned a business degree. He found a job with a branch of Continental Bank as a teller. He never left. Over the years, he received one promotion after another, eventually becoming vice president of client services.

Alberto was an only child. He grew up in a house surrounded by elms on Chicago's north side, near where he and his family now live. His parents never spoke Spanish to him. We came here for a better life, his father liked to say. We are no longer Spaniards. We're Americans now.

After graduating from Northwestern University, Alberto went on to graduate school and earned an MBA. His father helped him get a loan to buy a small furniture business whose owners wanted to retire. He worked hard, married Elvira, and expanded the business so that now branches of the González Furniture Store operate in Chicago and three suburbs. He makes no excuses for owning a big house on almost an acre of land. Sometimes, just like this officer, people would comment that he didn't look like a González. He would laugh away these comments. What else could he do? Talk about Spain? He knew nothing about it, had no connection with it other than his name, which was just his family name and nothing more. No one ever questioned him because of his last name.

I expect you to do your job and protect my family, Alberto tells the officer. His speaks slowly, steadily, but his hands shake as he struggles to maintain his composure. That's what I want. I don't want this Miguel person lurking around and talking to my son. He has no connection to me.

Of course, the officer says. I don't's think we're at the point where anyone needs protection, but I do want to understand what happened tonight. That's why I'm here.

Elvira excuses herself and walks into the kitchen. She finds the policeman's attitude so infuriating she just had to step away for a moment. Confusing them with Mexicans, my God, of all things! She was born in Madrid and came to the United States as an exchange student and met Alberto at Northwestern. They married and she became a citizen. Every few years they travel to Madrid to visit her family. After their return to Chicago, she's caught herself speaking Spanish as if they were still in Spain. Sometimes, she will dream in Spanish and see herself speaking to her family. The words come out of her mouth like a song, the tip of her tongue dancing against the roof of her mouth as she rolled her R's, and her hands rise in flight, animated, the words taking on a physical presence.

Elvira spoke Spanish to Pablo after he was born but Alberto would grow impatient with her because he did not understand what she was saying. I'd like to know what you're telling my son, he would say, so, she stopped. Over time she learned to muzzle that part of herself until the next trip to Spain.

When they first began dating, Alberto didn't have a car. They rode buses and Elvira would often listen to Mexican house-keepers and janitors talking in the back seats. She noticed the puzzled, agitated expressions of passengers who did not speak Spanish, and they would nod imitating the reproachful looks as if they, too, disapproved, and then she would laugh because no one suspected that this young white woman understood Spanish. They thought she was one of them, and Alberto too. And in a way they were and in a way they weren't, which lent an air of tension and subterfuge that Elvira enjoyed. What happens if we're found out? she wondered. Nothing, she knew. Still it was exciting. It was her secret. And then to think that tonight of all things a police officer has the gall to suggest they have something in common with this Miguel person and here is Alberto who can't even speak Spanish.

She wishes he would ask the officer to leave. He is as coarse and common as they come, and couldn't be ruder if he tried. She will certainly let the police chief know about his behavior. The O'Malleys, really. She's never heard of them. A McDonald family, yes, down the block, but not O'Malley. She doesn't know the McDonalds, either, just waves when they pass by. She and Alberto have as much a right to be here as they do. This Miguel person is the problem, not us, she thinks. Alberto's father used to get so worked up about illegal immigrants, how they needed to wait their turn and come over as he had. He complained that they never spent their money in the United States but instead sent it back home to pay for more of their families to come over. The officer knows nothing of her family. He makes her uneasy. It's not them he should wonder about.

About what time did you see Miguel? the officer asks Pablo.

My mom wanted me to be inside at six thirty for dinner, he answers. My dad just came home.

So, it was about that time, six thirty? the officer says.

Yes, Pablo answers.

His mother comes back and sits beside him. He watches the officer make a notation. He will tell his friends all about tonight at school tomorrow, but he would have to be sure he got everything right, that he didn't mess up like he did one Saturday afternoon when Drew came over. They played on a jungle gym in the backyard and then Alberto took them out for ice cream and gave Drew a ride home. Drew asked Alberto if Pablo had been born in Spain. Alberto laughed and said no. Drew said Pablo told him he had.

Well, it feels like I was, Pablo said hurriedly, almost desperately, because my dad and mom are always talking about it, isn't that right, Dad?

 Can he speak Spanish, Mr. González?

Drew asked the question as if Pablo wasn't there.

No, Pablo's father answered.

Pablo squirmed and he felt his face turning red. He had told his friends he spoke Spanish.

Liar, Drew whispered to him.

After they dropped Drew off, Pablo's father told his mother about what Drew had said and they both laughed.

What a thing to tell your friends, his mother said. Why would you do that?

Pablo didn't answer. He didn't know. His friends thought it was neat. They asked him about Spain and he told them stories his mother had told him. He knew a little of the language because his cousins, Ricardo and Victor, lived in Barcelona and when they would visit, he would listen to them speak Spanish and over time he picked up a few words. After they left, his mother would speak Spanish to Pablo and then cut herself off and laugh. I'm sorry, honey, she'd say before continuing in English. Pablo had worried that Drew would tell everyone he wasn't from Spain but when he saw him the next day at school, he didn't say anything. Maybe he thought no one would care because Pablo wasn't one of the popular kids. None of his friends ever wanted him on their teams when they played basketball because he sucked at it. Drew was good at everything. Pablo never mentioned Spain to his friends again.

And you're sure you didn't hire this Miguel to cut your yard? the officer asks Alberto. Or, maybe one of his friends?

It's possible I hired him or one of his friends, I don't know, Alberto replies. I'd have to see him to know, but what does that matter? Working for me or anyone else, he shouldn't be wandering around talking to children.

Agreed, agreed, the officer says. We'll look into it. I'll drive around when I leave but I didn't see anyone on the street when I came in. When I get back to the station, I'll suggest we send a cruiser through here tomorrow. Do you have any questions?

No, Alberto says.

Okay, someone will follow up. Call if you need us.

He closes his notepad with a flip of his hand. Alberto pushes back his chair. The officer stands and Alberto and Elvira walk him to the door. Pablo follows.

You do have a beautiful house, the officer says. Have a good night.

Good night, Alberto and Elvira say together.

They hear his footsteps on the walk and listen to his car as he backs out. The headlights of the squad car illuminate everything. When he turns down the street, it gets quiet and dark again.

Elvira, Alberto, and Pablo walk into the kitchen. Alberto makes another drink. Elvira asks him for a glass of sherry.

We're going to have a late dinner, Elvira says.

That's fine, Alberto says.

I'll get the chicken cooking, and I have to put on the rice.

That's fine.

The way this officer spoke to us, goodness, it's just inexcusable. I'm going to call the police chief in the morning.

No, don't, Alberto says.

Why not? Elvira says.

Alberto sighs. As far as he is concerned, no one considers him to be anything other than who he is—a husband, father, and successful businessman. His authority as a father and the officer's authority as a policeman combined to impress upon his son the importance of caution, a point that in his mind pushed aside everything else that had sidetracked their conversation. He didn't want trouble. What one officer thinks doesn't matter. No reason to antagonize the entire department.

Just don't, he tells Elvira.

We don't look like Gonzálezes? Elvira says. Who do we look like?

He didn't say that, Alberto says.

He may as well have. How stupid can he be?

Elvira, please.

I was already late with dinner because of the lines at Jewel. Now, we'll eat even later.

That's fine.

No, Alberto, it's not fine.

Pablo is hungry and wonders what time they'll eat. What does his mother mean by late? How late? His mother stands by the stove, her back turned to Pablo's father who slumps in a corner across from her, arms folded against his chest. Pablo decides not to ask when they'll eat. His parents are angry and he doesn't want them angry at him. He goes into the breakfast nook and retrieves his math book and a notebook from his shoulder pack. He has a little homework. He didn't tell his mother because he knew she wouldn't let him ride his bike until he finished it. He hopes she doesn't notice now or he'll get in trouble again.

He wonders if he'll see Miguel again. He wasn't afraid of him. He imagines school tomorrow. A policeman came to my house, he says out loud as if he is talking to his friends. He can just see them crowding around him, asking, What happened? There was this guy named Miguel and he talked to me and my parents thought he was like a criminal and they called the police but I wasn't afraid. Drew might say he was lying. He wouldn't be and could prove it but then Drew might say how Pablo really wasn't from Spain. He did make that up. Still, he decides not to say anything about tonight, and when he goes to school tomorrow he will tell Miss Brinker that it's okay to call him Paul. He doesn't understand why it should matter but it does.

Walking into the living room, Pablo peeks out from behind the curtain. He doesn't see the sparrow. He hopes it felt better and flew away. Pablo shuts the curtains and walks to his room, sits at his desk and sets his backpack by his feet. Leaning back in his chair he thinks how everything is a little different now. He closes his eyes and sees the officer sitting across from him and his parents and how he would turn his head and look at each one of them when he asked a question. Sometimes, he stared past them out a window and Pablo had followed his gaze but he never saw anything other than the officer's reflection in the glass and that of himself and his father and mother.

Touring

I was on a tour bus from Guatemala City to Quetzaltenango, a town in the western highlands against a backdrop of dormant volcanoes. An Australian woman about my age, mid to late fifties, plopped down in the seat beside me. Her shoulder pack slipped down her left arm and smacked into my leg and she apologized. I shifted over and said not to worry. She stuck out her hand and introduced herself: I'm Laura. I took her hand and squeezed it.

She wore a large, floppy hat and a loose T-shirt and baggy jeans. Her gray hair fell to her shoulders and a necklace of seashells hung from her neck. I told her she looked like a hippie and then apologized. I had no business saying that. Not to worry, she said, and laughed and I laughed despite myself.

When the bus reached Quetzaltenango, Laura and I wandered its narrow, stone streets, pausing to view the baroque colonial facade of Espiritú Santo Cathedral. We walked through the restored Municipal Theater and the Ixkik Mayan Costume Museum, marveling at the bright colors of indigenous clothing as a guide described how various designs were associated with this or that tribe.

Women sold carpets, clothing and trinkets in the plaza. Laura bought an orange scarf after I told her I liked the strands of blue filtering through it. We stopped at Restaurante Tertulianos for a glass of white wine and sat on the patio in the shade of a broad-leafed tree, and birds called from its branches.

A waiter brought us red tamales stuffed with tomato sauce, chilies, raisins and pork. As we ate, Laura said that according to her travel guide, centuries-old churches still stood in many nearby villages. Among these, she read, the town of San Andrés Xecul has a striking yellow church with an intricately painted facade. The oldest church in Central America stands in another town, Salcajá.

I'd like to check it out some day, I said.

Laura suggested we do it together, but I could not. In the morning I was leaving for San Cristóbal, a highland town in the southern Mexican state of Chiapas. Next time, Laura said. Yes, next time, I agreed.

When we returned to Guatemala City that evening Laura suggested we exchange emails and phone numbers. Then she surprised me with a hug and a kiss on the cheek. I held her and she remained in my arms. When I let her go she draped the scarf around my neck and told me to keep it until we met again. In my room, I pressed it to my face and faintly smelled her perfume.

I left the next morning to San Cristóbal. The bus ride took ten hours. I thought of texting Laura but decided to wait and see if she'd text me first. I stared out the window at lines of laundry strung above the apartment courtyards and at the stooped-shouldered men prodding overburdened donkeys. I held my phone but it never buzzed with a message.

The bus reached San Cristóbal at night. I checked into my hotel and went directly to bed to the sound of mariachi music drifting from cafés. In the morning, I looked at my phone. I had no messages. After coffee, fruit, and a croissant, I strolled the *andador*, a pedestrian-only street. Dozens of overpriced sidewalk cafés, restaurants, and shops selling wine and designer clothes filled the narrow sidewalks. Young musicians played outside with open guitar cases sprinkled with pesos from tourists.

Stopping in a coffee shop, I asked for a latte. As a waiter took my order, I noticed a boy running about the *andador*. A young woman in a loose tank top picked him up and passed him to one of her friends, another young woman, and she held the boy and then set him down and patted him on the back shooing him away. He scampered into the coffee shop where he sat and fist-bumped the waiter.

Let me clean some glasses and then we can play, the waiter told him. Turning to me, he said, I am twenty-four. What do I know of children?

Outside, the boy's mother stood beside a cart selling *esquete*: corn on the cob smeared with butter, mayonnaise and picante. She worked every day until midnight, the waiter told me. He had never seen her until he took this job. He once worked as a chef in a French restaurant but the pressure to cook exquisite meals became too much and he quit. He enjoyed making coffee drinks because it required little effort. Stand, pull levers, add milk, pour.

Taking a plastic car from his pocket, the boy rolled it across the floor. It bumped my shoes and flipped over. I pushed it back and the boy picked it up and hurried to the waiter, who chased him out the door. The two women who had played with the boy minutes before sat across the street at another coffee shop and watched. The waiter noticed them and smiled. After a few minutes, he returned to his post behind the counter and the eager look on his face told me he hoped the women would come over. The boy ran back in giggling and the waiter grabbed him.

Here! he said and thrust him toward me.

I pulled him to my chest and patted him on the back. An image came to me of when I was small and my father would come home from work and swoop me off the floor toward the ceiling, so I hefted the boy above my head and he laughed. I lowered him to the floor, and he ran to the waiter again but he was staring out the door at the two women and ignored him.

Looking dejected, the boy shuffled outside to his mother and she embraced him, pressing his head against her stomach. She reached for some blankets bundled beneath her cart. Holding him with one hand, she unfolded the blankets on the sidewalk for him to sleep. He lay down and she massaged the blankets around his body. Raising her head, she noticed the two women who had drawn the waiter's attention get up from their table and walk toward her. She stood perhaps hoping they wanted to buy *esquete* but they did not stop, so she returned her attention to her son and stroked his face until he fell asleep.

The waiter asked me if I wanted another latte, but I declined. He slouched in the door and folded his arms and stared out at the *andador* and at the empty table where the two women had sat. I checked my itinerary on my phone. I had a walking tour in the afternoon and a museum with a lecture in the evening. In the morning, I would leave for San Miguel Allende, a thirteen-hour bus ride. I had not arranged any tours there and wondered what I would do, when it occurred to me to call Laura. She may know San Miguel Allende as well as she did those Guatemalan villages with the old churches. I dialed her number. The phone rang once, twice, three, four, five, six, seven times and I lingered in the empty space between rings before finally hanging up. I should return to my room, I thought, but remained seated and dialed her number again.

Rebel

Mahmoud sat in a chair in his shop. Dust covered the warped, sparsely filled wood shelves holding a few boxes of crackers, some soft drinks, sacks of rice, and dried fruit. Tracks from scuttling cockroaches were evident as soft lines in the dust. The concrete walls held the winter cold and Mahmoud crossed his arms, watched his breath plume from his mouth. Looking out the door he noticed men standing in the ruins of a school, smoking and jostling to stay within narrow circles of sunlight, an illusion of heat. A faint sound caught his attention. Within seconds, he recognized it as an approaching plane. He ducked under the front counter and the men outside ran, cowering under the broken ceiling of a classroom where a math equation still remained on a blackboard. Soon enough, the droning of the engine peaked and began to wane, and they understood this plane wasn't a threat, and they crawled out from beneath what little shelter they had found, raised their heads, and watched it vanish.

The day before, three rockets had struck Mahmoud's apartment building when rebel forces attacked government troops. Government jets soon arrived to provide air support. Mahmoud ran to the front door of his apartment, understanding something bad had happened but not fully comprehending what, and as he opened the door his wife, Adelmira, jerked him back inside and slammed it shut. An explosion knocked them to the floor and a large piece of metal sliced through the door above their heads. Shrapnel struck their house like rain. Mahmoud counted one hundred explosions in an hour.

When the fighting subsided, Mahmoud and Adelmira got into their car and drove across the city to his brother's house. Shattered balconies. Broken glass. Ruined fountains. A charred ambulance shone in the sun. Dead fathers, mothers, and children, arms thrown wide, inside wrecked cars. The only boy in the Hassan family lay on the street. His face bloody. Eighteen years old. Engaged to be married. Yet, palm trees stood untouched. Cats emerged from the rubble and walked among the dead, proceeding in silence, emerging through scrims of dust like something untethered from the bodies around them. The wind carried pleas: Help me, help me. Mahmoud paused but could not tell where the voices were coming from, and he continued on. Adelmira stared out the car window. Mahmoud tried to think of something to say but could not. He felt empty. He wished he could cry. He felt himself shaking but he had no tears. He compared the rebel offensive to bad weather, something he was powerless to control. Nothing limited the slaughter, yet he survived time and time again while others died. Adelmira saved him today whereas another wife might not have reacted as quickly. Why? Fate, if not Allah, was on his side. A part of him found the will to rise above his helplessness by not caring and he wondered if that indifference had made him impervious to death, as if death did not want a man whose passion for life had all but been exhausted before it could claim him.

Mahmoud's brother, Samiullah, was standing in driveway when he reached his house. They embraced for a long time. His brother's wife, Casilda, led Adelmira into the house and Mahmoud drove back to their neighborhood. People stood in the ruins of their flattened homes, picking through debris, their eyes vacant, their faces immobile. They took small steps, first one way and then the other, as if they were toys functioning on dying batteries. The bright blue sky above them filled with small birds that made no sound other than the noise of their flight.

Mahmoud took as many people with him as he could fit in his car and drove back to Samiullah's house. A man squeezed into the back seat holding a small boy on his lap. He told Mahmoud he worked as a carpenter and lived alone with his son. His wife had left him. They had an arranged marriage and she had been unhappy. She paid a smuggler to take her to Turkey. One day, while he was pushing his son on a swing a kid sauntered up to him. He thought he was one of the boys he had seen playing fútbol earlier in a park. The kid wore green fatigues too large for his thin body. He told the carpenter that his commanding officer, General Hidari, had given him a message to deliver to all shop owners in a twenty-block area: they had to pay the general $300 a week to keep their shops open to help fund the war against the rebels. That includes you, the kid, said. The carpenter laughed. How could he take this scrawny boy, not even a teenager, seriously? It must be a joke by one of his friends, a bad joke. The kid did not react to his laughter. He turned around and walked away without another word and the carpenter assumed that was the end of it and started pushing his son on the swing again. Then, a day later, he looked out his front door at the cemetery across the street and saw the same kid shoot another man. Made him kneel. Fired a pistol into the back of his head. The kid saw him watching. You don't pay the general, I'll kill you too, he said. The carpenter left with his son that night, embarrassed that a kid had so intimidated him but what could he do? He had seen him shoot a man. He did not have what it took to stand up to him, let alone this General Hidari. Call him a coward. He just wanted to live and protect his son, but in his dreams he imagined killing him. He felt his fists connect to the kid's face, felt bones breaking beneath his knuckles. But he knew enough to know that he was not the man in his dreams. He hoped his son would understand when he was older why he had taken him from their home. He had been staying with a friend when the bombs started falling. He ran from that too. His friend also fled, both of them stumbling out of the house, the carpenter gripping his son against his chest. He didn't know what happened to his friend. He refused to dwell on where he might be because he might be nowhere other than where the dead go. The carpenter cared only to live and see his son grow up.

Mahmoud returned to his neighborhood three more times, taking more and more people to Samiullah's house. What do you want me to do with all of these families? Samiullah shouted at him. Do I look like a charity? You are family, they are not! He threw rocks at them to chase them away, and Mahmoud grabbed him and held his arms down. Stop it, stop it! he shouted. They are my neighbors! Samiullah relented and said they could stay in his yard. When it started to rain, he let the children inside but they cried for their mothers so he allowed them in, and then he threw up his hands and waved their husbands inside too, and everyone hunched together on the living room floor smelling of wet clothes and sweat, clutching suitcases and bags. The men slept on one side, the women on the other. In the middle of the night, Mahmoud heard the carpenter whispering to his son, Did you take it? Did you take it? Yes, the boy said, and started crying. That was for us to eat tomorrow, the carpenter snapped. Mahmoud's heart went out to the boy; he sounded so frightened. He was just hungry. It may have been nothing more than a piece of bread. The carpenter raised a hand to slap him, and Mahmoud sat up and cleared his throat. Whatever he did in his own home was one thing but this man, a stranger whom Mahmoud had chosen to help, could not hit his son in Samiullah's house. He was a guest. This was not his home to do as he wished. The carpenter turned and stared, and Mahmoud stared back. He wanted to say something but no words came. The carpenter dropped his arm, cursed, and stormed outside. Papa! The boy called. Some of the other families began to stir. Shh, it's nothing, Mahmoud said.

He stretched out again. After a few minutes, he heard the front door open and turned to see the carpenter walk back in. He unfolded some blankets on the floor and sat beside his son. He wiped tears from the boy's face until he stopped sniffling and wrapped him in the blankets, tucking the edges around his body.

He glanced in Mahmoud's direction. Mahmoud watched him. The carpenter looked away, saying nothing.

The next morning, everyone thanked Samiullah for his hospitality. They rolled up the blankets he had provided and stacked them in a corner. None of them really knew what to do, where to go. Their lives no longer had balance. They were like people who had just stepped off a boat, their legs wobbly. Some of them thought they could find their way to another city. Others would seek out family. Still others decided to find an abandoned house and live in it until they came up with a better plan. Mahmoud offered to give them rides to wherever they wanted to go. But since they had no firm ideas, they chose to walk because it was the one of the few things left within their control.

In the following days the fighting moved to other areas of the city. Two to three times a day, distant explosions interrupted the quiet. Mahmoud and Adelmira moved into a deserted apartment near his brother's house. The furniture remained. Plates were on the table with forks and knives and uneaten food. Stuffed animals in a cradle. Photos on the walls watching Mahmoud and Adelmira moving through the house with gentle steps as if they were at a wake.

Mahmoud sat in the kitchen most mornings not saying a word, the back of a hand against his open mouth, knuckles against his teeth. Adelmira made tea and sat with him. Her mind, she said, sometimes flashed to images of dead bodies and everything would turn dark, and she could no longer see for seconds at a time as if she had gone blind. Her needs and anxiety became a ringing in his ears he could not rid himself of, and he would erupt into a rage,—stop talking!—reducing her to tears.

In his dreams he remembered driving the narrow road from his shop to his home, the road twisting uphill between cinder-block homes gray beneath the shadows of cedars. He would turn into the narrow alley, lines of laundry stretched across balconies above his head, and he continued driving uphill until he stopped at his house at the end of the alley. He looked forward to nothing more than walking through the front door and greeting Adelmira. They had married months before the fighting started. During the day, she would visit him in his shop on her way to the bazaar and speak to him in an almost businesslike way behind the mask of her burqa as if he was not her husband but a stranger behind the counter, and the older men lingering about with their cigarettes took no notice of her or she of them. But at home, away from the formality of moving about in public, she took off her burqa revealing a face wreathed in an eager smile, and her body, Mahmoud thought, in the longing in which she presented herself, was something magical, arousing in him a hushed roar.

He would awaken from this sweet dream in the middle of the silent night without energy or will. Looking at Adelmira, he would roll out of bed without waking her and stand outside and pace back and forth beneath the stars, pausing only to light a cigarette. In the shadows other restless men lingered, their presence exposed by the glow of their cigarettes, and they spoke to one another from the isolated corners of desolate buildings, solitary burrows they used for these few moments to hibernate from the war and the responsibility to their families, their weary voices flat, wounded, broken.

The situation is not so dangerous now, one man commented, but we can't eat. There is no gas or electricity to cook.

Rebels call this a liberated area, another man said.

A combination of laughter and coughing followed his remark.

When there is shelling, my children hide and get sick, a voice said in the darkness.

We can't work like before, someone else commented.

Mahmoud listened but did not speak. He thought of Adelmira alone in the house with her visions of death and he felt he should go to her, but the weight of the voices of the men around him and their droning despair, on and on left him immobile. Seized by frustration, he hurled his cigarette butt to the ground, grinding it with the heel of his right foot long after it had stopped burning, twisting, pressing down with all of his weight as if he meant to choke it.

The following morning, a rebel commander knocked on their door. Mahmoud and Adelmira answered. The commander wore sneakers, sweatpants and a winter green coat over a turtleneck sweater. A Kalashnikov rifle hung from his right shoulder. Mahmoud guessed the commander to be in his late twenties, about his age, maybe older but not much. The commander explained that he and his men were in control of this part of the city. You will need to stay elsewhere, the commander told Mahmoud. My men and I will occupy this building for our barracks. Do you have some place you can go?

I have a shop, Mahmoud said.

Good, the commander replied. Is this your wife?

Yes, Mahmoud said.

She will remain here to cook for my men. I am sorry for this. With good luck, the fighting will be over soon. Of course, you can visit her. I'll let you know about those opportunities.

I don't understand, Mahmoud said.

The commander gave him a matter-of-fact look.

What don't you understand?

Mahmoud shook his head.

Three days ago, I sent fighters to storm a government armory, the commander said. We captured mortars and a big gun, Russian made. From the beginning of the fighting, no one gave us ammunition. We use what we take, but our best weapon is Allah. We shout Allah is the greatest, and the enemy becomes afraid because they know we are about to attack. This will be over soon. You should join us. If you die, you will be a martyr and forever live in paradise.

I am a shopkeeper, Mahmoud said.

Then go to your shop, the commander snapped, and support us with your home.

He told Mahmoud to take what clothes he needed and to be gone within the hour. Do not worry about your wife, he said without looking at Adelmira.

The commander turned and left. Young men on the street with their rifles similarly slung over a shoulder followed him. Gravel crunched under their feet. Mahmoud shut the door. He listened to the sound of them walking away. The visit was so unexpected that only after it ended did Mahmoud began to consider his timidity and what he could have said. No, you cannot have my apartment. What then? The commander's fighters would have dragged him out. What then? That would have been a worse humiliation than the one he felt now. He thought of the carpenter and the kid who had threatened him. What can a man do in such a circumstance?

He began to shake. It was as if all the emotions he had tried to bury suddenly rose up inside him and demanded to be felt until he became so furious that he raised his arms and shook his fists at the ceiling and screamed. He wiped tears from his eyes before he turned and went into the bedroom. Adelmira stood by a closet packing a bag for him. He watched her. She stared at the floor, sparing him her thoughts. Her humble acceptance of their situation served only to increase his sense of inadequacy and further infuriated him. He walked up to her, lifted her chin and looked in her eyes and saw nothing but his own weakness. His shame rose within him until his face burned red and he raised a hand to hit her, and she looked at him without fear, without feeling of any kind. He reached past her, grabbed the bag, and rushed out of the room.

The next morning, the commander stopped at his shop and shouted for Mahmoud. Mahmoud came out of the backroom where he had been lying on a cot staring at the ceiling. He had not slept. His neck felt as stiff as tree trunk. He smoothed his hair with his hands.

You were asleep? the commander scolded.

I'm up, Mahmoud said. He noticed four rebel fighters standing by the door eating nuts from one of his baskets of almonds.

Your wife Adelmira, if I may, is a very good cook. The men are happy with her.Mahmoud looked at the floor.

Tell me you are happy for this, for her work. In one small way or another we are all supporting the revolution.

Mahmoud opened his mouth to speak but closed it without uttering a word. He swallowed and tried to speak. Clearing his throat, he tried again.

I want to talk to you about my wife, he said quietly.

Yes?

I don't like this arrangement.

I didn't expect you would, the commander said. It's not about liking. It's about doing what's necessary.

Mahmoud felt his heart fill his chest with his unease. He had been awake all night imagining this moment, what he would say, and now he could barely get the words out.

The revolutionary guard youth group hands out two bags of flour to the poorest families, the commander said. Since you are here alone, I will tell its commander to bring you some flour. You can cook here?

Mahmoud nodded, looking at the floor.

The commander dug into his pocket for a pen and wrote a reminder to himself on his palm and then returned the pen to his pocket.

May I assist you with anything else? the commander said.

I have very little to sell and no one has any money. My wife and I need bread at least just to live.

The commander made a face.

You don't have to worry about your wife.

Yes, I do. She's my wife. I will worry about her! Mahmoud snapped. He stumbled backward, off-balance. His outburst surprised him. His body shook and he shoved his hands in his pockets to steady himself.

The commander sat in a chair. He cocked his head toward Mahmoud as if he was a kind of specimen that had aroused his interest. He tapped his feet on the floor.

Nine months ago, I became active in the revolution after the government arrested my father in our home for participating in protests, he said. Five black cars surrounded our house. I was in the back, my father in front. Run, run, he screamed to me as they dragged him outside. I ran out the back door with my mother and sister. The soldiers threw him against one of the cars. He is still in jail. I was a math teacher until that day. I taught in the small grades.

The commander slapped his knees. Mahmoud jumped.

Are you listening?

Yes, Mahmoud said.

Then look at me when I'm talking to you! How long have you been married?

Almost a year, Mahmoud said.

And no children! C'mon, man!

The commander laughed. Mahmoud pressed the heels of his palms against his eyes until they hurt. His racing heart made his chest ache. He had trouble breathing.

I was engaged but when the fighting started it was no time to marry, the commander said. My fiancée's family left, and she stopped calling me. Or maybe she didn't. The phones are shit now with the fighting.

He jerked his shoulder to keep his rifle from sliding down his arm.

I didn't want any of this. Perhaps if my father had not protested, I wouldn't be talking to you now, and you and Adelmira would be home trying to make children. It's impossible to say. But my father did protest and here we are, and your wife is with me. As a teacher I didn't have time to pay attention to the government. As long as it left me alone, I was indifferent. I spent many hours after school working with the slower students. Now, I don't care who is slow and who isn't. I just need fighters. If they die, they are martyrs. They are happy with this thought and so are their families. Very little explanation is needed. It's much simpler than teaching.

He waved a hand at the baskets filled with nuts and at a shelf sagging with three sacks of rice and boxes of cookies.

You do not look like you are doing badly with all of this. At least you have some things on your shelves. Some shopkeepers have nothing. I know this is not much but it's more than most. Unfortunately, I must take it for my men. I'll send someone this afternoon to pack it up. I'm sure your wife will make good use of the rice. I can see why your parents chose her for your wife. I don't know how long this arrangement will last. The fighting could go on for a long time, but she will be safe.

The commander extended his right hand.

You will receive the bags of flour. That is enough for you.

The commander's hand hovered between them. A cry tore from Mahmoud's throat and he stepped forward and slapped the commander across the face with such force that the commander stumbled sideways and dropped to one knee. The fighters by the door stopped eating, mouths open. Mahmoud felt their stunned stares. He heard himself inhale and exhale. Steady breaths, slowing, his body spent and relaxing now. A narrow ledge of silence separated this moment and the rush of angry shouting and the beating that would follow. The part of him that no longer cared was all of him now. The commander pushed himself off the floor and Mahmoud saw Adelmira's face in his eyes like a mirage. He watched aware and unafraid as the commander and his fighters rushed toward him.

Dependents

Bibi Sarwari and Earl Taylor met at an airport coffee shop in San Diego in the humid summer morning. The rising heat of the day pierced the city. Ceiling fans spun slowly as the two embraced, Earl swallowing Bibi in his big arms, squeezing him against his chest. After a moment, Earl released him and they sat, grinning. Bibi ordered tea; Earl asked for house coffee. Earl had a three hour layover, so Bibi took some time off work to meet him.

How's it going, brother? Earl asked.

Good, good, Bibi said. So good to see you.

Likewise.

Likewise, Bibi repeated, and laughed. In Afghanistan, Earl always said likewise. On patrols in Khost province when the Taliban attacked, Earl would drop to one knee jerking Bibi down with him and fire rounds from his M4 screaming, likewise, motherfuckers!

Bibi had arrived from Kabul six months earlier with his wife and four daughters. A Catholic Charities resettlement worker placed them in a two-bedroom apartment in South Park, a neighborhood not far from the airport. She called him Mr. Sarwari and never asked about his life in Afghanistan. She was not friendly, but she was not unfriendly. She was efficient. She helped him find a job working as a janitor at an athletic club. A month later, he made a down payment on a battered SUV with 175,000 miles from a used car dealer she knew. She gave him furniture from the donation room next to her office. Another room held trash bags filled with used clothing he and his family wore. This morning, he put on a red plaid shirt that hung off his shoulders and baggy blue jeans he rolled at the cuffs. He looked at his living room and the furniture in it, a couch and two armchairs, and wondered who had owned them and why had they donated them to Catholic Charities. He passed his case worker's office on his way to the airport and thought of stopping in to tell her he was meeting an American soldier he had worked with in Afghanistan as an interpreter. He's going to give me copies of my credentials, he would tell her. I earned them for my good work with American soldiers in the 503rd. My boss will see I'm not just a refugee. That's nice, he could hear her say. That would be helpful to show your work experience and to have recommendations from Americans. Now, I don't have much time, what do you need? He *needed* his parents and in-laws he'd left behind in Kabul. He *needed* a bigger apartment, a job that would support his family, and a car that wasn't close to a break down. He *needed* to feel at home and many other things he knew she'd not define as needs. I'm sorry you miss your family but I'm focused on you and you should be too, she often said to him. She'd pause and he'd look at her and then past her, staring out her office window at an AMC theater across the street. The large red letters of the sign made him think of the Bollywood movies he'd watched in Kabul, and for a moment he was no longer in San Diego. Or he'd glance in the direction of the North Park Farmers Market and recall the bazaars in Share-e-Naw and how he had walked between vendor stalls with his wife.

The clipped words of his resettlement worker would bring him back. Be grateful for what you have, Bibi, she'd say. Not every asylum seeker is so fortunate to have what I've gotten for you. I'm providing you with stepping stones. The rest is up to you.

He thought of her stern look, the tone of her voice like that of a teacher to a naughty boy and how he could feel his heart pound with anger as he swallowed his humiliation and shrank before her, head down. Once he showed her his credentials, she'd understand. She'd appreciate who he had been and who he could be again. She'd be embarrassed by the way she'd treated him, talking to him like a child. With his credentials, he would find a good job and not need her.

A waitress put a cup of tea and a cup of coffee on a round tray and carried it to their table. She gave Earl the tea and Bibi the coffee. They said nothing but smiled at each other. After she left, they switched drinks.

Fucking tea, Earl said.

Fucking coffee, man, Bibi said.

They laughed.

How was your flight?

Good, Earl said. Nothing to write home about, but not bad.

May I see my credentials? I want to show them to my worker.

Earl glanced down at the table, raised his head, and looked past Bibi. Yeah, I received them as attachments on WhatsApp, Earl said.

I've been asking you for them. You said you'd send them.

I forgot.

Earl flapped his T-shirt against his chest. Bibi could tell there was something on Earl's mind. He was trying to decide how to say it or maybe he was trying to pick the right time to say it.

Is everything all right, Earl?

It's hot, he said, still flapping his shirt.

Did you print my credentials? Bibi asked.

Not yet. I told you I forgot.

You can forward them to my phone and I'll print them, Bibi said.

Earl took out his wallet and offered Bibi five $20 bills.

Here, to make up for the hours you're losing at work to see me today.

No, no, my friend, it's OK.

Take it.

Earl extended his right hand, his thumb pressing down on the five twenties drooping from his fingers. He had been sending Bibi money ever since he arrived in San Diego. America was too expensive, he would complain to Earl over the phone. Can't argue with you, Earl would say. Bibi called him his big American brother but in many ways he was like his second resettlement worker, someone he turned to for help. They were friends, but Earl had all the advantages of an American. In Khost, Earl needed him, but here Bibi had nothing to offer.

Take it, Earl said again.

His insistence had an edge to it almost as if he was angry. Bibi made a face, took the money and shook Earl's hand and thanked him and promised to help him should he ever ask for it but nothing he said relieved the sense that Earl would never need him.

Earl had been a reservist assigned to the 1st Battalion, 503rd Infantry Regiment when he met Bibi at Forward Operating Base Salerno in Khost. Bibi worked security with him at the front gate, translating for carloads of destitute families requesting food and medical assistance. He taught Bibi how to play poker and Bibi showed him the Afghan card game, Teka. Bibi always allowed him to win. You are a guest in my country, he would explain, I cannot take your money.

This is hell, Earl thought when he landed in Khost. He had never experienced such heat. The land had the appearance of a brown wasteland speckled with scrub and in constant motion from sandstorms. He'd joined the reserves to pay for college, not to fight in Afghanistan. Shrapnel to the left hand sent him home to Chicago before the deployment was over. Gave him a chance to get his MBA. He wanted to start an employment agency for refugees in the U.S. *To help motherfuckers like you*, he told Bibi in an email. This morning, he was on his way to Phoenix for a three-day conference on start-ups. He'd reached out to Bibi when he bought his plane ticket.

Bibi said, my wife wanted to cook a big meal for you, Bibi said. Kabuli pulao, mantu, chicken beef kabobs.

Jesus, how much does she think I can eat?

Bibi laughed. Americans, he noticed, always swore using their God's name.

Another time, maybe, Earl said.

It would have been good for her. She is too sad. She misses her family. I'm sad too. My parents are in a refugee camp in Pakistan. Too many people in my old neighborhood in Kabul knew I worked for the Army. They were scared that someone might report them to the Taliban.

I'm sorry.

I try to send them money. My family thought I was a very important man translating for the Army. Here, I am struggling. I am just a refugee.

You're an asylum seeker.

What's the difference?

I don't know but I think being an asylum seeker is better.

We have an expression, Bibi said. Afghan men cry on the inside. Women cry on the outside.

It will get better, Earl said.

Inshallah, I hope so.

Inshallah. How's your apartment?

It's small. We have bunk beds for the children. In the living room, we have a big carpet and we eat on the floor in the Afghan way. On the wall, I will put my credentials and pictures of my parents and my wife's family. It will be our Afghan room, inshallah.

There's something I need to tell you, Earl said, strumming his fingers against the table.

Yes? Bibi said.

A man and a woman walked into the coffee shop and put their suitcases on the chairs of a table next to them. They placed an order and waited. They tapped text messages on their phones. When their drinks were served, they returned to the table. Cheers, the woman said, tapping the man's glass with her own. Watching them, Earl raised his glass to Bibi.

To better days, he said.

Inshallah, Bibi said. To better days.

Earl slugged down the rest of his coffee and took out his wallet.

That money I gave you was enough?

Yes, yes, of course, Bibi said.

It's no problem.

Bibi shook his head.

No, no, please, Earl.

Earl closed his wallet and put it back in his pocket.

What is it you wanted to tell me? Bibi said.

Bibi had earned seven hundred dollars a month as a translator, more than the Afghan government paid its own generals. He made twice that much at the athletic club but his salary was not enough to support his family. He started work at seven in the morning and stayed until three. Then he drove for Uber until eight when he took a dinner break to eat with his wife and children. At nine, he began picking up fares again. He used to go home at midnight, but by the time he ate a snack, brushed his teeth, washed his face, changed for bed, kissed his daughters good night while they slept, and did the same with his slumbering wife, asleep or passed out from anxiety meds—he never knew—it was time to get up and leave for the athletic club. To get more rest, he started sleeping in his SUV in the gym parking lot until his shift started.

Bibi had left Afghanistan just before the Taliban retook Kabul. He listened to news reports as the insurgents occupied nearby Nangarhār and Logar provinces. Neighbors warned him that Taliban fighters were already in Kabul seeking information on anyone who had worked for U.S. forces. He took his family to a friend's house and then left for another friend's house to keep ahead of anyone who might inform on him. He sent Earl a WhatsApp message with photos of his English language degree from Kabul University, certificates from The International Security Assistance Force and the U.S. Army Corps of Engineers in Kabul, with whom he had also worked as a translator before he joined the 503rd. Additional photos showed his army ID badges and letters of commendation from the commanding officer. These papers are very important to me, Bibi told Earl when he sent him the photos. This has been my work. It's my life. I understand, Earl wrote back. Once he confirmed receipt of the images, Bibi deleted the photos from his phone and all messages to Earl. Then he burned his documents. If Taliban fighters found him and searched his belongings they would find nothing connecting him to the Americans.

The CO recommended Bibi for an expedited U.S. visa, and the American Embassy in Kabul granted the request. However, the visa would apply to his family only and not his parents or in-laws. Bibi didn't understand. They're extended family, Earl told him in an email. What does that mean? Bibi asked. They're not part of your immediate family, Earl replied. But they're family, Bibi insisted. I'm sorry, Earl said, I don't make the rules.

Bibi debated his next move. If he stayed in Kabul, he would never be able to leave the house and feel safe, and he would need to move repeatedly for the safety of his family. How would he support his family under such circumstances? He slept little. He prayed. He cursed. His neck and the veins in his temples pulsed with stress. His indecision drove him mad. Finally, he called Earl and told him he would accept the conditions of the visa. You have to contact the embassy, not me, Earl said. I'm telling you because you are my friend and my heart is broken, Bibi said. That night, he told his wife of his decision. You cannot leave your parents and my family, she said. I'm sorry, Bibi said, but we have no other choice. She walked into the kitchen and closed the door. He listened to her cry. He went outside and covered his face with his hands and shook as he struggled to hold back his own tears. He stood like that for some time, the cool evening ruffling his clothes, before he regained control and returned inside.

A woman's voice came over the airport public address system and reminded passengers not to leave their luggage with strangers and to report any suspicious behavior.

What is it you have to tell me? Bibi asked again.

Earl glanced at his watch.

Do you have to go? Bibi said.

No worries, Earl said. Listen, I was thinking. There's something called humanitarian parole. It allows people like your mom and dad and your wife's folks to come to the states for being under threat because of the work you did for the Army. Do you know about that?

No. How long does it take?

I don't know.

I spoke to an immigration lawyer but he wanted $1,500 a day. This humanitarian parole, what does it cost?

I think it's like six hundred dollars for each person.

For each person!

Yeah, I know, it's a lot.

How can I pay for this?

I'll help you.

Please, Earl, Bibi said. You are helping too much.

In the gym parking lot, Bibi would notice other people who stayed overnight. They would sit in lawn chairs smoking cigarettes and talking. He would offer them water or fruit. They thanked him, spoke in low voices as if they did not want to disturb the quiet night and they stared out at the street or up at the sky and he would do the same, and they spoke as if they were back home in their yards in Texas, Arizona, Colorado, wherever they were from. Bibi told them he was from Afghanistan. He and his mother had stood outside their house when the Northern Alliance began its assault on Kabul about a month after 9/11. They watched the Taliban firing back, the sky lit up with anti-aircraft fire, a big flash followed by an explosion that pushed them to the ground. The Americans are here to help the mujahedeen, people shouted on the street. Everyone was happy, Bibi recalled, and a peaceful time followed.

He told them about studying English at Kabul University and becoming a translator for the Americans. His mother told him it was too dangerous and his father agreed. I'm going, he insisted. You're a young man, his father said, but still a man. I'm telling you not to, but it is up to you. On his first visit home, his parents arranged his marriage to a neighbor's daughter. He had known her since they were children and did not love her, but his father was good friends with her father so he promised that he would learn to love her. After they married, he returned to Khost and did not go home again for six months. After twenty days, long enough to impregnate his wife, he flew back to Khost. His wife said nothing, but his mother wept and begged him not to go. He told her it was fine, no problem. He did not mention the firefights and how they frightened him because he did not have a gun to defend himself. He surprised his parents and his wife with money he had saved from his salary.

Every other night he and Earl left the base on patrols with a platoon of U.S. and Afghan National Army soldiers. He recalled the lines of armored vehicles and the American soldiers wearing headphones and listening to music so loud that Bibi could hear it. He watched them mouth the lyrics, faces scrunched, bodies rocking as if they were seized with convulsions. They would leave at 20:00 hours in pitch dark. The stars and moon spread a pale glaze over the desert and Bibi would think that those same stars flickered above his home in Kabul. The platoon would reach its destination at 03:00 and search villages.

We're here to help, Bibi would tell the village elders. They led him and the officers into a hut built with mud bricks and lined with carpets, kicked off their sandals and offered them tea. They sat in a circle and burqa clad women lit candles and left. They returned almost immediately with tea and a plate of cookies and raisins, then retreated into the shadows before vanishing. These Americans are here to kill us, the elders would tell Bibi after they poured the tea. They spoke calmly, confident their assertion was beyond dispute. Their faded prayer shawls slipped off their shoulders as they stroked white, tobacco-stained beards, the rigor of their lives revealed in impassive faces lined with age and fatigue. They raised their cups of tea to their mouths and waited for Bibi to translate. No, we're here to build hospitals and schools, Bibi insisted, speaking for the lieutenant in charge of the patrol, but the elders lifted their hands for him to be quiet. You are no longer Afghan, they told him.

One time, a Taliban fighter shot at them from behind a wall in the village of Spin Boldak. Shrapnel struck Earl in his left hand. Blood sprayed onto Bibi's shirt, and he fell to the ground convinced he had been shot. Likewise, motherfuckers! Earl screamed, firing his weapon. I've been hit, Bibi shouted. Earl dropped beside him and felt his chest and arms before he noticed his hand and wiped it clean. Shit, man, he said, that's my goddamn blood.

Bibi laughed at the memory.

Well, that's it, he said to the men and women seated around him in the parking lot. That was my life. But now I am here because the Taliban came back and I could not stay, and now I have very little money and nothing in my apartment is mine.

They nodded without comment and then a man started talking and became lost in the tale of his own derailed life. I work at a warehouse, he said, but I don't make enough to pay rent. We're on Social Security, a couple said, interrupting him. Our landlord increased the rent and we had to leave. I had problems with my boyfriend, a young woman joined in. As the night progressed some of the people drank and grew loud and argumentative. A man called Bibi a fucking Arab. He was so drunk Bibi barely understood him. Okay, okay, Bibi said, and returned to his SUV.

What could he say to this crazy man? I am Afghan, not Arab. He knew a drunk would not understand the difference but he tried not to judge him. His wife took pills prescribed for her by a doctor at a San Diego clinic to help her cope with the absence of her family, and Bibi had learned not to argue with her no matter how she provoked him under the influence of the pills. She stayed in bed except when she cooked their meals. Bibi told her she must stop taking the pills. You sleep too much, he said. She glared at him, walked into the bathroom, uncapped a plastic bottle, and shook out a small, round tablet. Dropping it in her mouth, she swallowed it without water, without taking her eyes off him.

I will never forgive you for bringing me here, she said putting the bottle back on the sink. There will be no paradise for you.

Earl stood to get another cup of coffee.

You sure you don't want another tea? He asked Bibi when he returned to their table.

No, thank you.

Earl sat. He looked at Bibi, glanced at the floor.

What? Bibi said.

I have to tell you something, Earl said.

He paused.

What? Bibi said again.

You know when you sent me the photos of your credentials?

Yes.

Well, you deleted them before I downloaded the attachments.

He showed Bibi his phone, tapped his contact link on WhatsApp and scrolled to his message: *Here are my certificates. This is my work. It's my life.* Below it Bibi saw the word, *deleted,* for each image he had sent.

What are you telling me? Bibi said.

I mean I don't have them. I didn't know I had to download them. I thought they'd stay on my phone like any other texted photo. But when you deleted them, they were deleted from my phone too. I wanted to tell you, but you had enough problems getting out of Afghanistan. I'm sorry.

I don't understand.

When you deleted them they were deleted from my phone too.

But you said--

I don't have them. They're gone.

Bibi looked down at the table. He saw himself in his apartment staring at the empty living room wall. His Afghanistan room! Such a fool he had been to think anything here could be like Afghanistan. He grabbed Earl's phone and threw it on the floor. Earl jerked back from the table and stood. The couple beside them stared wide-eyed, got up, and hurried away. A girl behind the cash register jumped, covered her mouth. Bibi felt everyone watching him. His head pounded. He closed his eyes, took deep breaths.

Bibi, Earl said. I didn't know.

Bibi dug into his pocket for the money Earl had given him. He wanted to throw the bills on the table and shout, Keep your money. I don't want it, but he didn't. He needed the money. He needed Earl. He wasn't angry with him. He wasn't angry with anyone. He was just angry. He wanted to leave, to run from here, but where? Home? He didn't have a home. At night, he dreamed of Kabul and then he woke up stiff-necked in his car.

He noticed the cashier talking to a security guard and pointing in his direction. He pressed the heels of his palms against his eyes. Shaking his head, he looked at the skylights above him, squinting against the unrelenting glare.

I'm sorry, he said, turning to Earl.

Likewise, Earl said. Bibi stood.

The security guard stopped at their table. What's going on here? he asked.

Nothing, Earl told him. My friend got some bad news and just got a little upset.

The security guard looked at Bibi suspiciously. Bibi had seen that look before, in the eyes of Earl and the other American soldiers when Afghans approached the gates of FOB Salerno.

I do not want trouble. I only want my life, Bibi said, his voice drowned out by an announcement over the PA system.

What? the guard asked. Then a sudden rush of travelers, all bound for destinations of their choosing, streamed past. Bibi felt the damp trails of tears on his cheeks as he faced the guard, unable to say more.

Carpet Deals

When his former driver, Firash, entered his office, the aid worker glanced up from his desk and the drought report he had been reading, his face wreathed in sweat from an unrelentingly hot summer afternoon—did a double-take, and then collected himself and stood, a look of surprise spreading into a forced smile; he stuck out his right hand, and Firash, with his own tight smile, shook it. Then he bowed, placing his right hand over his heart. The aid worker did the same.

As-Salaam-Alaikum, Firash said.

Wa-Alaikum-Salaam, the aid worker replied.

It's good to see you.

And you.

The aid worker, an administrator for a Washington-based humanitarian organization he and his colleagues referred to as "the agency," pointed to a chair that held a heap of papers ready to topple.

Give those to me and sit, please.

Firash passed the papers to the aid worker, who set them on the floor by his chair.

Please, he said again.

Thank you, Firash said and sat stiffly.

How is your family?

Well. Yours?

Well.

Since the aid worker had last seen him, Firash had cut his gray hair so short his scalp showed, and he had allowed his beard to grow down to his chest. Perspiration gathered in the tanned, wrinkled valleys of his forehead, and his blue eyes were clear and mirrored the aid worker's face.

Your beard, you look like Taliban.

It is for my security.

Security?

Yes, of course. In Kabul, you never know who you're talking to. Maybe Talib, maybe not.

No one says safety here, the aid worker thought. It's always security. He ran a hand through his hair. He was thirty-three but felt much older. He'd attended college to be a teacher, but a friend pursuing a social work degree encouraged him to switch majors, so they would be in the same classes. A job fair his senior year connected him with the agency. He moved to Washington and helped administer farm programs in Iowa, Illinois, and Nebraska. Within five years, he was named director of the Midwest region. He anticipated further promotions that he hoped might lead to work within the executive director's office, but in his sixth year the agency sent him to Kabul to organize a new agriculture project funded by the United Nations and the World Bank—a temporary assignment, he was told. He studied the Qur'an and Dari, the language of northern Afghanistan. Five years later he was still in Kabul. He had long since given up understanding the opaque verses of the Qur'an, although he had memorized a few stanzas, and except for one or two expressions, mastering the guttural sounding words of Dari was beyond him.

There is no need to say anything about the Taliban other than to remind ourselves to be cautious, Firash said.

Of course.

How was Seattle? Your home, sir?

Yes. It was good, thank you, but too much rain as always. I got back last week.

Yes, I know this, Firash said.

The aid worker didn't ask how Firash knew. One of the gardeners may have told him, or one of the women who mopped the office floor every morning, the hems of their blue burqas wet with soapy water. All the nationals who worked for the agency seemed related in one way or another, the aid worker thought. Cousins, nieces, it was hard to keep track. Any one of them could have passed along news of his return. He patted sweat from his forehead with a prayer shawl and dabbed dust off his desk. A ceiling fan whirred and clanked above his head, and behind him, through an open window, he heard the sounds of traffic in the still air and the shouts of boys playing soccer in an empty lot among the remains of a mortared bank. Concrete blast walls now cordoned off the area, intensifying the warmth from the sun, and the noise of donkeys braying and roosters crowing and the calls to pray mingled into a cacophony that buffeted him with its commotion. Despite his time here, he continued to feel the culture shock of his first days.

Who drives for you now? Firash asked.

Mahmoud.

You like him?

Yes, why not?

Firash shrugged.

Better than me?

I didn't say that, the aid worker said.

The aid worker met Firash his first day in Kabul, when Firash picked him up at the airport. Over the course of their time together, the aid worker learned that he had survived the Russian occupation, the civil war that followed the Soviet withdrawal, the five-year Taliban rule, and now the Americans. He told the aid worker stories about Taliban officials whipping him when they suspected he had trimmed his beard, and about a militia leader who would not help his son, injured by a mine and in need of urgent care at a hospital controlled by the commander's militia, unless Firash agreed to let the warlord marry his daughter. Firash agreed. His son survived. The commander took his daughter that night, but he died two days later in a mortar attack and Firash's daughter returned home, no longer a virgin but legally wed and eligible for a war widow's pension. Praise Allah, Firash had told the aid worker. He lived a life in which he learned to fear men in power and use his wits to live one day to the next and trust in God.

His instincts for self-preservation had led Firash to quit the agency when U.S. soldiers burned one hundred copies of the Qur'an in a detention center outside Kabul. Local workers found charred copies among the ashes at an incinerator, touching off several days of rioting and protests with demonstrators shouting in Dari and Pashto, Death to America! The aid worker had been vacationing in Seattle when the news broke and his email filled with updates on the violence. His supervisor told him the furor prevented Western staff from leaving the agency compound. Firash and others, he continued, had stopped coming to work. Only a few nationals had not quit. These goddamn Afghans, the supervisor wrote. We spend all this money on them and they leave us when we need their help!

The aid worker had heard him make similar statements under much less stressful conditions. He had made them himself. All the Western staff had. The farmers who came to the agency never seemed appreciative of the help they received; they only asked for more. More this, more that, it was never enough. The national staff was no different. When the value of the dollar declined, they demanded raises to make up the difference. It was as if the agency had become an alternative to the failing government in Kabul, from which the farmers and national staff expected support for every aspect of their lives. Their dependency, the aid worker thought, had reduced them to spoiled, sullen children.

He had not always been this cynical. When he first arrived in Kabul, wearing slacks and a white polo shirt with the agency logo embroidered over the breast pocket, he had felt truly important. At a meeting, with maps of Afghanistan sprawled over a table, he leaned in, examining each one, imitating the serious looks and the deep-throated voices of his more senior colleagues as they discussed projects and budgets. They never asked the national staff their opinions, except those who had lived in the States, had returned to Kabul after 9/11, and now held positions in government and business.

Through the office windows the aid worker would watch farmers waiting in line for a case worker. Farmers did not participate in planning discussions either, although their perspective would have provided useful information, given their intimate knowledge of the land. They also might have asked pertinent questions: How would any of these plans work, given a years-long drought, the ravages of which they experienced daily and that appeared to have no end in sight? Where would the irrigation water come from? How would it be channeled to the farms? And how would cultivating wheat, maize, barley, and rice be better than growing the poppies that needed little rain and were much more profitable because of the demands of an illicit drug trade that supported the Taliban?

Over time, as he raced with a security escort through Kabul to endless meetings, to stare at countless maps and read dozens of memos, the aid worker realized that his colleagues had the same questions but had learned, as he did, not to ask them. Securing grant money was the end goal—implementing a project to its successful conclusion was secondary. The agency needed to show just enough progress to convince U.N. and World Bank representatives to not just continue their support but increase it. Among other things, this entailed a schizophrenic spending strategy. Use money sparingly at the beginning of a fiscal year and spend lavishly at the end, so not a dime was left. A surplus would mean less funding in the next budget cycle. Like the farmers and the national staff, the aid worker concluded, the agency always wanted more. In time so would he.

I think Kabul is peaceful again now, Firash said. Every day people complain that Afghanistan is in the deep shit, every day there is a bombing or a protest, but every day I wake up and my life continues, and I am not dead.

That's good, the aid worker said.

Yes, inshallah, but I have no job, Firash said.

I'm sorry, but I understand you quit.

For my security.

I understand.
I worked for you a long time.
Yes, but you quit.

The aid worker wished he could rehire Firash. Mahmoud made him uneasy, but he was certain his supervisor would disapprove. Mahmoud had been pleasant enough when he fetched him at the airport last week, formal and courteous like every Afghan he'd worked with, including Firash, but he was also agitated, hyped up as if he had drunk too much coffee. After Mahmoud put his duffle bags in the back of the agency van and then hurried around to the passenger side and opened the door for him, the aid worker asked him about Kabul. How were things? Had the city returned to normal after "the incident"—as his supervisor had instructed him to call the Qur'an burnings. You don't want to rile people by mentioning Qur'an and burning in the same sentence, he had been warned.

Despite this caution, the question released a passionate response from Mahmoud, and he answered with a simmering animation he could barely contain. Until recently, he said, there had been tire fires throughout Kabul and men marched, shouting, Jihad against America! No Westerner could go outside. All the agency people stayed in their offices. They were so scared. Mahmoud laughed, and he turned to the aid worker with a derisive look. I myself denounced America for burning the Qur'an, he continued. After all this time in Afghanistan, why is it I wonder, that the Americans still don't understand Afghan people? Why is it they insult and defile the holy book? Why is it there are no jobs except with NGOs? Why is it there is still fighting? Because America doesn't care for Afghan people and abuses us. We had security under the Taliban, and everyone understood the teachings of the Qur'an. Why is it the Americans do not? What has America done for us?

The agency director, Mahmoud went on, asked him to bring food for the staff and he refused because it was too dangerous to be seen entering the compound, but really, even if it had been safe, he would not have helped them. His duty was to Allah first, not the infidel, although he understood the agency staff had not burned the Qur'an. Still, they were all Westerners to him, just as Afghans were all Afghans to them. He had heard U.S. soldiers call Afghans "fucking hajis." No one separates the good from the bad. Why should he?

I am sorry for this, Mahmoud told the aid worker.

But you still work for us, the aid worker said.

Yes, of course. Your American president Obama apologized for burning our holy book, and I need my job.

Mahmoud took a smoke from a pack on the dashboard and offered one to the aid worker. He refused and stared out the windshield at the tumult of cars on the road and the rush of people on the crowded sidewalks navigating among the glut of vendors, their wares strewn across blankets on the ground, the bearded men and burqa-clad women resembling biblical figures, and he felt stunned as he always did when he returned to Afghanistan. Just twenty-four hours earlier he had been in Seattle. It seemed so long ago.

Mahmoud lapsed into silence, except when he cursed a driver who cut in front of him. The aid worker rocked in his seat with the stop-and-go traffic. The summer heat pressed down, and the aid worker thought of the farmers who would line up outside the agency when he arrived, to plead with him to let them join the agency's agriculture program. Mister please! The thought exhausted him. He could envision the year-end report on his desk, Giving the Afghan People the Means to Achieve Their Own Aspirations—The Good Book, as he and his colleagues dubbed it, filled with page after page of data listing the numbers of families assisted with "soil nutrients" (fertilizer), "crop initiators" (seed), and "agricultural enhancement aids" (hoes, shovels, rakes, mules). Then there was the "additional assistance" category—that included everything from distribution of clothes to bus tokens to food for starving families, unable to coax even a sprout from the dry soil.

Some services had no heading other than miscellaneous. Collected into this statistical rabbit hole were the "internally displaced" people. ("Someone who is forced to flee his or her home but who remains within his or her country's borders": Section 10, Page 220, Paragraph 4), people who had no farms, no homes, no anything, and nowhere to go, and who had turned the agency courtyard into a homeless encampment. The aid worker anticipated that when he reached his office, he would walk past these men, women, and children, as he had every day before he left, and they would reach out to him, their thin arms stretched upward, palms exposed, a grimace of silent pleading on their faces. They were no longer anything but lives disrupted by the circumstances that had led to and followed 9/11, reducing them to supplicants of the post-Taliban order, just as they'd had been supplicants in the post-Russian order and in the post-civil war order. Farmers who raised a good crop received more assistance the following year whether they needed it or not because the agency was reliant on them for *positive statistical outcomes* to offset the internally displaced and other bad numbers.

However, it remained a constant battle to tabulate positive data. Those families whose crops failed were discharged from the program and categorized as "unfavorable statistical outcomes," joining the families encamped in the courtyard. They were no longer eligible for the agriculture program but still in need. When Mahmoud pulled into the agency, they swarmed the van. Wading through the throng, the aid worker, his head barely above the outstretched hands, pushed his way toward his office like a drowning man struggling toward shore.

Ayan has been asking about you, Firash said. You know, the carpet merchant.

I know.

He asked if you're back.

You saw him?

Yes. He asked if you had his money.

The aid worker nodded and then looked toward the open door of his office as one of the gardeners knocked, another man following closely behind him. The aid worker recognized the gardener but did not know his name. The man beside him was quite thin, and his clothes were stained and dirt-smeared.

What's up? he asked.

Sir, this man wants to thank you, the gardener explained. His son got a job with the tailor you recommended.

Tailor? the aid worker thought. He looked at the man, who grinned at him. Tailor? He frowned, thinking. Oh … wait. Wait a minute. Yes, yes-yes, the tailor. Christ, that was before he left for Seattle. He remembered now. He had taken a jacket to a tailor in the Shar-e-Naw shopping district to have the zipper repaired. The tailor spoke a little English and told him that he had so much business he needed to hire an apprentice. He was an older man and did not want to be in his shop every day but instead at home, playing with his grandchildren. The aid worker mentioned him to a case worker responsible for the families living in the courtyard. Maybe she had a client who could help the tailor. She said she'd ask around. He had not expected anything to come of it.

Really? he said. That's good, isn't it? I mean, tell him congratulations.

This man wants to know if you can help him with money for food, the gardener said, looking down.

To hold the family over until his son gets paid? Yes, I understand.

Firash cleared his throat.

I'm sorry, sir, but an apprentice won't earn more than two, maybe five U.S. dollars a month, he said. I was an apprentice at one time. To a cobbler.

So, he's going to need money—today and tomorrow until whenever—is what you're saying?

Yes, sir.

It doesn't matter his son has a job.

Maybe a little. He is only a boy. When he is older and has his own tailor shop, then he can help his family.

The aid worker strummed his fingers against his desk and didn't look up for what seemed a long time.

Of course, he said finally. What happened to our food pantry? Don't we have anything?

No, we are waiting for a bread delivery, the gardener said, still looking down.

The aid worker opened a drawer and took out a small metal box that held petty cash. A few Afghan coins and bills. He took two dollars' worth and handed them to the gardener, who gave them to the man.

Tašakor, they both said and bowed.

You're welcome, the aid worker said.

He watched them leave. An internship. A successful outcome. He jotted it down in a notebook. Firash sat quietly as he wrote. The aid worker finished, put down his pen, leaned back, and faced the ceiling, rolling the stiffness from his neck.

OK, where were we? What were you saying? About Ayan?

I saw him in the bazaar. I said I'd not seen you.

And now you have.

What do we do?

We?

Firash stared at him.

We, he said again. I work for you. He will hold me responsible. You left owing him money. If he thinks you're not here, he will say I have to pay him.

Worked for me, the aid worker reminded him. You worked for me. You left.

My family.

He won't harm your family. You just tell him you don't work at the agency.

He won't care. This is about my security, sir. I have to answer to this man.

The aid worker spun around in his chair and stared out the office window, annoyed. Why does everything have to be so complicated? he wondered. He noticed Mahmoud washing the van, his agency polo shirt wet and hanging off his body, small rainbows shimmering around the wet bumpers. When he stopped for lunch, Mahmoud would put on a salwaar kameez and sit with the other national staff, who would also have changed into their traditional clothes, beneath trees near the cafeteria where the aid worker and his colleagues ate. It occurred to him that, when the national staff was off duty, they understood they were nothing more or nothing less than the farmers, dependent on this job provided by Westerners. They were not colleagues of their employers, but like them reliant on the needs of Afghans more desperate than they. He wondered what Mahmoud and the other nationals talked about. Had they found the fear Westerners felt during the riots amusing? Empowering? Maybe. Probably. He wasn't going to ask.

What do we do about Ayan? Firash asked again.

Why do we have to do anything? the aid worker asked, resting his chin on the steepled tips of his fingers.

I have to answer to him, Firash said again.

No, you don't.

The day before he left Kabul for Seattle, the aid worker had asked Firash to take him to Ayan, who had sold him carpets since he'd first arrived in Kabul. He got them for no more than one hundred, sometimes two hundred dollars a piece, and sold them for much more than that in Seattle. He had room in two spare duffle bags for six or so five-by-seven carpets, depending on their size and how tightly he could fold them. If, as usual, they sold for no less than twelve hundred dollars each, he'd make more money than he had on any previous trip home.

Firash pulled up in the agency van outside his office, and the aid worker got out, eyes adjusting to the bright sunlight, hands up waving away flies swarming around the open passenger window. He and Firash greeted one another—As-Salaam-Alaikum, Firash said; Wa-Alaikum-Salaam, the aid worker replied—in the monotone voices and expressionless smiles of men who had fallen into a habit of addressing one another the same way morning after morning no matter their mood.

Turning out of the compound, Firash drove toward Chicken Street, where Westerners converged to buy souvenirs in Shar-e-Naw and where dozens of merchants, Ayan included, had stalls. They navigated through a Rubik's Cube of cars, trucks, and mule-drawn carts. A traffic light blinked red, but drivers ignored it and the intersection gridlocked, with angry men beeping furiously; women in burqas holding the hands of their children took the opportunity to cross the street, hurriedly weaving in and out among cars; the beeping thickened the air with so much noise that the din and the stifling day felt like a physical thing bearing down on everyone; and the aid worker sank in his seat, closing his eyes until the weight lifted.

At Chicken Street, Firash parked in a lot beneath the open sore of an office building shattered by a suicide bomber, waving away five boys who offered to wash the van's windows. Getting out, the aid worker followed Firash past smoking kabob grills and small restaurants that catered to the fast-food tastes of Westerners by selling hamburgers, chicken burgers, and french fries, and the boys chased after the aid worker with their hands out, but he continued walking, ignoring their pleas until they fell behind and looked for other Westerners to target.

Meandering down an alley, Firash and the aid worker turned a corner into a narrow street that led into a courtyard surrounded by four three-story buildings. Heavy wood doors on the balconies of each floor opened into rooms filled with multicolored carpets, many of which hung from racks. Still more stood in columned stacks reaching so high they blocked the light from bare bulbs suspended from the ceiling. Firash and the aid worker entered Ayan's shop on the second floor of the building facing them. Ayan, a short, thin man with a full, gray beard, sat in a corner on small pile of rugs. A teapot was warming on a hotplate, its heating coil enfeebled with age. Ayan grinned and stood, arms widespread.

Hello, my friend, he said to the aid worker.

They embraced, and then they stepped back and bowed, placing their right hands over their hearts.

It's good to see you again, the aid worker said.

Yes, it has been a long time.

Not too long.

Please sit, Ayan urged and waved a hand to where he had been sitting.

No, thank you. I want to look.

Of course. Just looking, it costs nothing to look. Some green tea for you?

No, thank you.

Whatever you like, it's yours, you know this. For you, don't worry. You are a good customer. You know I'll give you a good price.

The aid worker was already thinking how much he should offer, how high he should go. On his first trip to Kabul, Ayan had sold him a red carpet with a large, quartered octagon displayed in columns and framed within a gold border. When he returned to Seattle on vacation, he asked the owner of a carpet store, Floor Coverings International Rug Gallery on First Avenue, to assess its value. The owner, a slender, elderly man with a thick head of uncombed, graying red hair, carried it into a back room, laid it out on a wood table and peered at it through a magnifying glass. Without looking up, he asked the aid worker where he had bought it and how much he had paid for it.

Afghanistan. Kabul. One hundred fifty. He wanted two hundred, but I talked him down.

Dollars?

Yes.

The store owner blinked and removed his glasses and pinched his eyes.

I could sell this for at least a thousand dollars. More probably. Maybe fifteen hundred.

Fifteen hundred?

Likely. I charge ten percent commission.

I didn't come here to sell it. I just wanted it appraised.

Really? Then why have it appraised? For the insurance?

A thousand?

Fifteen hundred probably.

A week later, he sold it for eighteen hundred dollars and gave the aid worker a check for one thousand six hundred and twenty dollars.

I'll be returning to Afghanistan, the aid worker told him as he put the check in his wallet. I'll be gone nine months before my next vacation.

I'll be here, the owner said.

Ayan poured the aid worker a cup of green tea as he had the previous times he visited, and the aid worker set it down as he always did and ignored the tea to examine carpets. He picked one that Ayan told him it was a fine piece from Herat, one of the best, and then he showed him other Herat carpets. The aid worker sorted through them. A blue carpet with triangular patterns caught his attention. He hefted it and liked its weight. The thicker and heavier a carpet, the better its quality and the less susceptible to crushing, the Seattle dealer had told him. He noticed several other rugs of similar design with green tassels. He picked three. Then he considered carpets from Bamyan and Mazar-i-Sharif. Nothing was marked with a price tag. Ayan tossed out figures as if on a whim, and the aid worker, unable to contain his enthusiasm, set aside twelve carpets, twice as many as he had intended to buy. Ayan produced a dust-covered calculator from beside the hotplate and punched in numbers.

Twenty-five hundred for everything, he told the aid worker.

Too much.

Usually, I sell these for $350, $400 each. But for you I'm giving a special price.

I'll take two more for that price.

Which two?

The aid worker pointed at a red carpet with elongated human and animal figures and a gold carpet of similar design. He and Ayan haggled, interjecting questions about the well-being of each other's families, until they agreed upon a price of $2,800 and shook hands. The aid worker took out his wallet and counted $1,500. He'd have to return to the agency for the difference.

It's a fair price, Ayan said.

I'm not saying it isn't. I just didn't bring that much with me.

We agreed.

We did. I just need to get the rest of what I owe. You have too many good carpets, and I bought more than I anticipated.

No problem, my friend.

No, no problem, thank you.

Take the carpets and come back.

I'd rather come back and get them.

Ayan shook his head.

Does not the holy book say, And if someone is in hardship, then let there be postponement until a time of ease?

I'm not in hardship. I have the money. Just not with me.

My friend, take them and come back.

The aid worker knew Ayan wanted to complete the sale, worried perhaps he would change his mind and not return. No worry there. He wanted the carpets, but traffic would be hell. Might take an hour or more to go back, get his money, return and then go back again. It would be simpler to take them now, so he could pack them tonight. He could come by in the morning on his way to the airport. No problem.

OK, he agreed. I'll pay the rest tomorrow morning.

Ayan wrote, "thirteen hundred owed," in a notebook beside the day's date. The aid worker signed his name.

Tomorrow, the aid worker said.

Yes, tomorrow, inshallah.

Inshallah, the aid worker said.

The next morning, running late and worried he'd miss his flight, the aid worker did not stop at Ayan's shop. At the airport, he told Firash to tell Ayan he'd pay him when he returned in three weeks. He considered giving Firash the money to give Ayan but decided against it. The agency paid Firash just fifty dollars a day. To receive an envelope with $1,300 might risk temptation. If Firash were to disappear, the aid worker would still owe Ayan and be out $2,600. No, Ayan could wait.

When he reached Seattle, he received an email from Firash who said Ayan was very upset and wanted an additional one hundred dollars for the delay. Cursing, the aid worker deleted the message without answering. Greedy bastard. The next day he drove to Floor Coverings International Rug Gallery and delivered the carpets. Within a week, the owner of a Silicon Valley tech startup bought them online and the aid worker collected a check for $15,000 after commission. Fifteen grand. He stumbled outside in a daze. He had not expected that much. On the walk home, he started to run and skip, spinning in circles and shouting into the air, drawing confused and annoyed glances from the people he passed. He shouted, I made $15,000!, pumping his arms as if he was rooting for a favorite sports team. At home, he took the few dollars in his wallet and threw them in the air. Fifteen goddamn grand! His yearly salary was $30,000. Jesus! He couldn't stop laughing.

The following morning, he deposited the check, withholding $1,300 for Ayan. Napping in the afternoon, he stayed up late and took long walks, relishing the cool air, the absence of traffic, and the ability to talk to people without a translator. He raised his arms and felt soft breezes lift his shirt, and he squeezed his fingers, clutching the empty spaces around him.

Before he went to bed, he compulsively counted the money he had put aside for Ayan, stuffing the bills back in an envelope afterward, putting it in a pocket of his duffle bag. They were new and crisp, and he felt their newness each time he counted them, rubbing his thumb and forefinger together until he felt a growing resentment that he owed Ayan anything. He hated that he had made $15,000 minus $1,300. That left him with $13,700. Not bad, but not as good as $15,000. The aid worker stewed. Ayan had already made a profit. No Afghan would offer that much for carpets, and with the fear of violence there weren't that many Westerners left who would give him that kind of money, either. The bastard had scored like a bandit. To pay him an additional $1,300 was nothing less than allowing Ayan to take advantage. He regretted he had not sent Firash in alone, certain he would have gotten a better deal.

The aid worker had been home for ten days when news broke about the Qur'an burnings. His return trip delayed, he deposited the money he had put aside for Ayan. Better than having it around the house, he reasoned. Three weeks later, after his supervisor gave him the all-clear, he rebooked his flight. The day before he was to leave, he packed his bags and drove to the bank to withdraw Ayan's money. Ten people stood ahead of him. He waited, shifting from one foot to the other and checking his phone for messages. He wondered what the holdup was. There were tellers in every window. He tugged at his collar, the shirt he wore feeling a little snug. It was his last day in Seattle. He shouldn't have to waste his time standing in line for Ayan. He checked the time. Five minutes had passed. Felt a lot longer. Ridiculous. He tapped his left foot against the floor. The woman in front of him looked at him curiously. Screw this, he said to her, and left, each step he took echoing on the shined tile floor. He pushed the glass door open to the sidewalk and raised his head to the clear sky, the tension in his body easing when he stopped thinking of Ayan.

I don't think there's any reason for you to speak with Ayan, the aid worker told Firash.

If I see him, I must.

No.

I gave him your message that you'd pay. You haven't paid. He will hold me responsible.

I don't think so.

He doesn't know you're back.

Exactly. Let him keep waiting.

He'll tire of waiting.

The ceiling fan whirred above their heads. The shouts of the gardeners interrupted its clicking sound, and families in the courtyard stood as if they had been called; they formed into loose lines, only to fold in among themselves when they realized that whatever it was that had caused them to rise held no purpose, and they sat again, waving their hands at flies. I don't think your plan will work, Firash said.

You don't know my plan. Listen. I can't hire you back as my driver because then I'd have to answer to my supervisor.

The aid worker leaned toward Firash.

However, you can still earn money.

Firash listened.

You'd be working for me, not the agency.

Firash blinked but did not speak.

I'd like you to buy carpets for me.

The worker watched Firash, who cleared his throat.

Buy carpets, sir?

They see me, prices go up. You alone would get a better deal. Take pictures with your phone, show me what you find, I pick what I like and then you go back and buy them.

How would I buy them?

I'll give you the money. You would earn five percent of everything you buy.

Firash frowned.

OK, ten.

Maybe twenty, sir.

The aid worker smiled. Maybe fifteen if you get great deals. The better the price, the higher the percentage. And you don't speak with Ayan. You don't buy carpets from him. I'm finished with Ayan.

Yes, Firash said, I understand this … but if I see him?

You're Afghan. He won't expect you to have money. What can he do? He can't get nothing from nothing. Forget Ayan. Start today. Come back with some pictures when you can.

I'd rather work for the agency.

You're working for me.

It is not the same.

It's a job.

And if you don't want to pay me, like you don't want to pay Ayan?

This is very different.

Firash crossed his arms and looked off to one side. Dogs barked, and the fading afternoon sun had turned the sky orange. Shifting in his chair, Firash looked at the aid worker. The aid worker stared back at him.

Twenty percent, Firash said.

The aid worker showed no expression. Sweat glossed his forehead. He leaned back and cracked his knuckles and ran numbers through his head.

Very well, he said finally, twenty it is.

Inshallah.

Inshallah.

The aid worker stood and stuck out his hand, and Firash bowed and left without shaking it. He might tell Ayan I'm back, the aid worker thought, watching him go. He probably will. For his security. Whatever. If Ayan came to confront him, the aid worker would renegotiate what he owed, perhaps squeeze another carpet out of Ayan. Or, he might just deny knowing him. Keep a straight face. You have me confused with someone else, sorry. Have Ayan escorted out. He imagined his fury, the curses that would spew from his mouth. Another angry Afghan; get in line. The aid worker would file a report.

He looked outside toward the families in the courtyard. At the next staff meeting, he'd mention the kid with the apprenticeship. Good news everyone will want to hear. They'll clap. They'll feel good. Something ought provide satisfaction—a positive outcome was a positive outcome. And fifteen grand was a tidy sum. A lot tidier than $13,700. He sat and returned to the report he had been reading before Firash interrupted. He thumbed through its pages, flapping his sweat-stained shirt against his chest. Today, tomorrow, next week, at some point, Firash would return, the aid worker was certain, and Ayan too. Each in their own turn, each with their own need. It didn't matter who came first. He'd deal.

A Father's Wish

My mobile phone rang. The voice of my good friend Hafez Mohammad shouted through the receiver asking, no, demanding that I meet him at his house.

It has been a long time since I've seen you, I said.

He was in no mood for sentiment.

Just come to my house, he insisted. I need to speak to you.

Hafez and I have been friends since childhood. My daughter, Asal, married Hafez's son, Raziah, a police officer. After the Americans defeated the Taliban and we were allowed to take photographs again, Hafez bought a small digital camera. Over the years he took many pictures of Raziah. Too many. Raziah as a baby, Raziah playing fútbol, Raziah graduating from the police academy. Enough pictures, I would tell Hafez. I have known your son since he was born. I don't need to see his pictures. Hafez would laugh. He is my only son, he would say. I am too proud of him. I love my three daughters but Raziah will carry my name and my father's name. Do you not see me in his face? he would ask, showing me yet another photo.

Looking at all those pictures of Raziah, praise Allah, I have to admit I felt a little jealous. As Hafez knows, I have only Asal and my wife, Hamdiya. If Hamdiya could have only one child, inshallah, why not a boy? But it was not Allah's will. Sometimes, Hafez would rest a hand on one of my shoulders as if to comfort me as he showed me pictures of Raziah. His touch burned, and I would shrug him off. Other times I avoided him because I did not want to be reminded my close friend had a son and I did not. I would stay home with Hamdiya and Asal, missing a part of me that I would never be able to realize.

Then four weeks ago, Raziah's commander called Hafez while we were in Shar-e-Naw Park watching a quail fight. Your son has been injured, the commander said. He had been on a patrol near Jalalabad when American planes attacked Taliban forces in the Khūdrow mountains. One of the planes struck the police patrol by mistake. Where is he? Hafez asked. I don't know. Where is my son? Hafez insisted. Go to Kharkush Hospital, the commander told him. He spoke loudly and I heard every word. Hafez put his phone in his pocket and stood. I hurried after him.

Raziah was a spoiled boy and although I never liked him, I felt a little bit guilty for that now, seeing the worry on Hafez's face. Still, I could not help my feelings. One afternoon when I asked Asal to run an errand at the bazaar for her mother, Raziah interrupted. She is my wife now, he said. I will tell her where to go and when. He always wore his police uniform. No matter how hot the day, he would have it buttoned to his neck. More than once I told him that when he came to my house he was in no position to tell my daughter what to do while she was under my roof. She was my daughter first, his wife second.

Despite my dislike for Raziah, when Hafez approached me last year about arranging a marriage between him and Asal, I saw an opportunity. Only a few months before, Asal had been suffering horrible pain near her stomach. Down there, Hamdiya told me, when I asked her what was wrong, and she pointed down from her stomach and I asked no more questions. Hamdiya took her to a doctor. Two hours later she called me from Ali Abad Hospital. Our Asal has a big problem, she said, and needs surgery. What is wrong? I asked. A tumor, Hamdiya said.

I hurried through Kabul's busy streets until I reached the hospital. Hamdiya sat on a bench outside. I stood beside her beneath a tree not far from where some men gathered in a circle, swatting at torn plastic bags carried by the wind, and farther away women stood beneath halos of flies trying to calm their children. We stayed in the shade and when the shade shrank to nothing we moved inside to a waiting room, and just as we sat down a secretary called our name. She led us into a small room with a desk and chair. Blue paint curled on the walls. I let Hamdiya sit. In a short time, a doctor walked in. She wore a blue burqa but showed her face. I am Dr. Shukriya Dost, she said. She told us we could see Asal in one hour. The surgery was successful, but she was still groggy from anesthesia. The tumor was not cancerous. However, Dr. Dost said, I have sad, difficult news. She paused and then said, Your daughter will never have children.

Hamdiya bowed her head and her shoulders began shaking. I listened to her cry. Dr. Dost placed a hand on her back and did not look at me. There was nothing she could say to me as a father who would never have grandchildren. I left the room and walked outside. I wanted someone to bump me, to say something insulting so I would have an excuse to beat them. But I saw no one other than the same people who had been outside before and the black clouds of flies above the children, and I stood and did nothing, shivering with anger and helplessness and then I left for home, my hands clenched. Later, Hamdiya said nothing when she returned to the house. She went into our room and closed the door. When she came out to prepare dinner, she told me she had sat with Asal. The doctor said she could come home in the morning. I nodded. I had no questions. What was left to ask? Asal could not have children. What was her purpose now? For that moment, she was as dead to me as if the tumor had killed her.

Hamdiya and I told no one about Asal's misfortune. Our neighbors are superstitious. They would wonder what we had done wrong to have a daughter with such a problem. Hamdiya warned her not to discuss her condition even with her closest friends. I did not speak of it to anyone, even Hafez.

Then last year, he asked me to his house for tea. He said we had been friends for so long it was time our families became one. He asked if I would agree to a marriage between Asal and Raziah. Under any other circumstance I would have been overjoyed. My friendship with Hafez meant more to me than my dislike for Raziah. Of course if I had I told him about Asal, he would never have asked. What father would want a barren woman for a daughter-in-law? No man I know. If Asal remained unmarried, she would spend her life with Hamdiya and me, and when we died she would move in with an uncle and watch his children and be little more than a servant. I would be re-membered as the father of an infertile girl. I knew I should tell Hafez. But what if I didn't? What if I said nothing? I knew Asal would make a devoted wife. She was a good girl. She would care for Raziah, cook and clean and make a good home for him. Why say anything? Raziah would learn soon enough that she could not have children. He could then marry a second wife. He was young with a good job. It would be no problem for him. She could bear him sons and daughters. Our families would be joined and he could still have children and Asal's condition would no longer be our burden.

I agreed to the marriage.

At the hospital in Kharkush, a doctor told Hafez and me that seventeen officers had died in the bombing. He took us into a room and showed us a body that he said was Raziah. We stared at the dead man. He's not my son, Hafez said. Perhaps there were two Raziahs? the doctor suggested. Survivors, he said, were transferred to Sardar Mohammad Dawood Khan Hospital in Kabul.

We returned to Kabul but doctors at that hospital had no record of Raziah and would not let us in unless we could prove Raziah had been admitted. Hafez wrote a message for the administrator explaining what the doctor in Kharkush had told us. A secretary folded it in her hand and hurried down the hall and through a door. We waited. Hafez flipped through photographs of Raziah on his phone, his eyes red and unblinking.

Four hours later, a man walked up the hall with the secretary. She pointed at us. He wore a western suit and tie and the grit on his white Hafezt showed it had not been cleaned in many days. He told us to return in the morning and he would have information for us. Hafez looked at me. His eyes were so vacant I became lost in his stare. I want to be alone, he told me. I am sorry my friend, I said. I will see you tomorrow.

The next morning, I met Hafez at the hospital gate. He had not changed clothes and his drawn face told me he had not slept. He barely said hello. When he took my hand and kissed my cheek, I felt the dead weight of his sorrow.

A security guard told us the hospital was closed to visitors. Hafez erupted like a lion, his dead eyes alive now with fury, and threw himself at the man, punching and kicking him until other guards pulled him off. Two policemen ran up. One of them recognized Hafez because he had attended the academy with Raziah. He told us to go home. His son died in Kharkush, he explained to the guard Hafez had punched. Died? Hafez shouted. Is my son dead? No one has told me anything! Come back tomorrow, the officer told him. Is he dead? Hafez insisted. It's not for me to say, the officer said, come back tomorrow. Hafez turned to me, tears in his eyes. I embraced him, and I felt his body con-vulsing with rage and torment as if at any moment he might explode.

That evening I sat alone while Hamdiya tended to Asal in her room. I cannot imagine how Hafez feels. To lose a son, I can't imagine! A son is an impossible loss. My friends wonder why I never took a second wife who could give me more children and inshallah, a boy, but I am a poor man and have little to offer another man for his daughter. I contented myself with the knowledge that Asal has my long nose and brown eyes and high forehead. I had once thought that she would pass these things on to her children and a small part of me would survive. It is too sad for me that that can't happen. Nothing will be left of me and my father's name.

At the hospital the next morning a different secretary called the administrator. I noticed he still wore the same tired clothes. The light switches in the waiting room did not work, or perhaps the lights were dead. We moved through shadows following the administrator to a room where a young man wrapped in bloody bandages stared at us. He is not my son,

Hafez said. The administrator took him to more rooms where more injured men lay in beds. Raziah was not among them.

We left and took a bus back to Kharkush and asked for the doctor who had told us Raziah had been sent to Kabul. The doctor had gone home, the hospital administrator told us. Hafez showed him a photo of Raziah. We have looked everywhere, Hafez said. He must be here. The administrator passed the picture around and a nurse said, Yes, I went out with the ambulance and I pulled this man from a car. Where is he? Hafez asked. The nurse shook his head. Where is he? Hafez asked again. He was in pieces, the nurse said. Half of his body was burned. We buried him by the road. The nurse drove us to the spot. Hafez stared at the barren, pebble-strewn ground. I remembered when Raziah was a boy. One night, Hafez told him that long ago giants had roamed Afghanistan and played fútbol with boulders. When they got tired they left the boulders where they had rolled to a stop and that was why so many of them cluttered the mountains of Afghanistan. Boys believe anything their fathers tell them about power and strength, and Raziah was delighted by the tale.

Do you want to take him to Kabul? the nurse asked. No, Hafez said in a low voice. He is already buried. Leave him. We prayed over the spot: Oh, Allah, forgive our living and our dead, those who are present among us and those who are absent, our young and our old, our males and our females. Oh Allah, whoever You keep alive, keep him alive in Islam, and whoever You cause to die, cause him to die with faith.

After a long moment of silence, we returned home. We did not talk. When we reached Kabul, Hafez turned to me and said, I have to tell my family. All they know is that Raziah is missing. I followed Hafez to his house. His wife, Azyan, opened the door, his three daughters stood behind her. Hafez said nothing. His family knew by the expression on his face. I bowed my head and clasped his hands. Azyab screamed and the girls too. I could still hear them as I walked home.

For four weeks, I saw nothing of Hafez, but Hamdiya told me disturbing stories that Azyan had passed to her when they would see each other at the bazaar. She said Hafez had drawn all the curtains and spent his days hanging Raziah's photos everywhere in the house: in the front hall, the bedrooms, even the kitchen and bathroom. No matter where Azyan turned, there was Raziah's unrelenting gaze. The daughters, who had adored their brother, now hid in their rooms, and when they ventured out they would hurry through the halls looking neither left or right at Raziah's pictures until they had emerged, as if from a cave. Once, one of them knocked down a photograph when she stumbled and fell, and Hafez bellowed like a wounded animal and chased her from the house.

I think he has lost his mind, Hamdiya told me.

I did not know what to say. Sometimes when I wondered about Hafez I said to myself, Well, now you and I are the same. Neither of us have a son. I felt ashamed thinking this way and struck my head and prayed to Allah for forgiveness. Still, a part of me—a bad part, I know—was pleased. There would be no more talk about sons between us.

I was worried about Asal. Since Raziah's death, she rarely came out of her room. Sometimes I would hear her weeping in the middle of the night. Hamdiya would get up and sit with her. I felt caught between them. In this situation, she understood Asal. As a father, I was helpless to comfort her. When Hafez called me this morning, I thanked Allah for the opportunity to leave the house.

He must have seen me walking up the street because I had not even reached to ring the bell when he opened the door. One look at him and I knew he had not slept for many days. His lined face, drooping mouth. Circles like ponds under his eyes. We embraced, his body slack in my arms. Kicking off my sandals, I stepped past him and stopped, unable to conceal my shock. Just as Hamdiya told me, photograph after photograph of Raziah covered the walls like a giant collage. Even the ceiling held pictures. His eyes followed me no matter where I turned. Hafez pointed at two boxes of framed photographs on the living room floor. Creases, small tears, and water marks blemished some of them.

Help me with these, Hafez said in a flat voice.

He tapped a nail in the wall with a small hammer, picked up a photo of Raziah playing soccer and hung it. He then selected a picture of Raziah in his blue police uniform. Unlike his father's full beard, thin patches of hair dappled his young face.

This is the last room, Hafez said. Give me a picture. Any one.

I did not move.

You have to stop this, I said.

Hafez ignored me. He took another photo. This one showed Raziah and Asal at their wedding. Hafez traced a finger around Asal's face.

One of Hafez's daughters, a black veil across her face, carried a tray with a pot of green tea, two glasses, a bowl of sugar and a plate of raisins. She bowed, set the tray on the floor and left. Hafez gestured for me to sit. He poured the tea. Setting the pot down, he picked up his glass and looked at me.

It's too late for Azyan to have children, he said.

You'll have grandchildren one day, I said.

They won't have my family name.

Yes, I know this, I said. I face the same problem. Still, they will be your grandchildren. That is what I tell myself.

That may be fine for you, but it is not fine for me.

It has never been fine for me, I said. Now you hurt, but for too long I have carried the hurt you now have.

He gave me a contemptible look.

Wishing you had a son and losing one are two very different things my friend, Hafez said.

I said nothing. Knew I should tell him Asal would never have given Raziah children but I was angry. For years he had boasted of Raziah and showed me his pictures in my face. Did he never once think of the pain he had caused me? The humiliation.

Asal should marry again into my family, Hafez said, setting down his cup. Allah tells us when there's a widow, she has three months to sit in a house and mourn. After that, her family has the right to arrange for her to marry again. The Qur'an does not prohibit a man from marrying his brother's widow.

But Raziah had no brothers, I said.

I want Asal as my second wife, Hafez said, sounding a little impatient. I've thought about it a long time. Asal is young. She and I would have a son and I would name him Raziah so the world will never forget my martyred boy.

I stared at Hafez, speechless. My palms got damp and I wiped them on my legs. My heart beat faster. I knew I should tell him Asal would never have given Raziah children, but I did not. I could not imagine his fury. His whole family would turn against us and all of our neighbors too. Asal was my daughter, my only child. All that matters to a father is what is best for their child even if she is a girl.

When she married Raziah she became your daughter, I managed to say. A man does not marry his daughter.

We both know she is not my daughter. Not in that way.

You would not be happy with her. I'm sure Raziah told you she can be difficult.

Raziah said no such thing.

Allah does not tell us if our daughters will have sons, I said finally. You might only have daughters again.

My friend, I am asking for my life, he said.

Your life? We are too old, Hafez, to marry again. Asal is young. You will die and leave her alone.

She will have our children to care for her.

No, I said, my throat tight. She will not.

Hafez looked at me for a long time.

What are you saying? he said.

You cannot marry her.

Hafez did not move. Then he stood and picked up a nail and pounded it into the wall and put up a picture. And then another and another.

You are the death of me, he said in a quiet voice.

He struck each nail harder and harder. Dust drifted to the floor. The pictures rattled in their frames, tilted against the wall. I thought they would fall.

Raziah is dead, I said.

Leave my house! he shouted, his back to me.

I hurried out. In the hall, Raziah's blank gaze followed me to the door. When I stepped outside the bright midday sun froze me in place and I stood motionless, my hands raised to my forehead until my eyes adjusted. Once I could see, I walked away. There was no shade. I moved through the dry heat with the certainty I would never see Hafez again.

Another man may desire Asal when she finishes mourning, and I may allow her a second marriage if he is young. I would ask Allah's forgiveness and not tell him she is sterile. I would love him like a son and grieve with him once he understood her condition. He could marry again. If his second wife bore him sons, inshallah, perhaps he would honor me by giving one of them my name, the name of my father and his father and all the fathers who have come before, but only Allah's mercy is guaranteed in this life.

Having Once Served

He was twenty-five and even though he was a captain, because he had been in a logistics unit in the reserves before being assigned to the 82nd Airborne, he was a REMF—a rear echelon motherfucker—several rungs below those in the enlisted ranks who actually had their knees in the breeze, and he was given shit jobs. His CO dumped visiting, low-level suits from the Afghan government on him to give nickel tours of Kandahar Airfield. He'd mutter *Fucking hajis* under his breath, trying to impress any grunt within hearing distance, or he'd shout *Airborne!* to show he was tight with his brother soldiers. The Afghan suits looked at him in surprise, but no one else paid any goddamn fucking attention. *I gotta carry these guys,* he'd complain when he escorted journalists from one interview with the brass to the next. Again no one gave a rat's ass, though sometimes he did get a sucks-to-be-fucking-you shrug. He showed new reservists where they'd bunk. You ever been shot at? he'd ask. Do you know what it means to be situationally aware? Don't fall behind or stop moving, even if you drop your equipment. You're going to be cold, wet, miserable. You're going to get enemy fire. Can you handle that? They looked at him wide-eyed, kids who had joined the reserves to pay off college. After a while, he knew, they'd stop listening. They'd get bored and restless and say *Fucking hajis* just like him, and not because they hated Afghans but because they hated the time, the pointlessness of doing drills only to escort food convoys to some shithole village they'd never see again. Why that village? Why not another? He never knew and neither would the new guys who, after a while, were no longer new. He rarely went out on a mission. The few times he did, his M4 looped around his shoulder, he'd carry a wag bag to woof in because he got airsick. Despite his queasy stomach, he always found a formation of idling Chinooks inspiring. He'd jog aboard, strap in, and feel himself rising into the air lifted by the two turboshaft engines and lulled by the flap of the rotors. Before they deplaned, he'd shake hands with the other grunts because no one knew whether they would live or die after they landed. They'd run down a ramp hunched over and dive on the ground in the heat. Peering through the sights of his M4, lying flat on his stomach, legs spread behind him, the reservist never saw anything but desert and scrub. With no incoming fire, he'd get up and trudge at least five meters behind the man in front of him, just as the man did behind him, a precaution to prevent insurgents from taking them out as a group. But if the bad guys were out there, they weren't shooting. He walked through grain fields and flocks of sheep grazing on grass sprouting between rocks, and he'd suck water from his CamelBak and watch the young sheepherders and the old men sitting outside square mud huts, and feel nothing but tedium, and perhaps, he thought, the Afghans felt nothing but tedium too. After a long day he'd return to base and hang out with the pilots who had flown the choppers that day. He got to know them but not well. He just hung with them. He didn't say much. He sought nothing more than to exist on the periphery of their lives and be mistaken for a pilot instead of a reservist. They didn't give a shit about a wannabe sitting at their table.

So, it really fucked his mind when two pilots died on a medical mission. They had flown a UH-72A Lakota out of Kandahar on a Sunday night to deliver supplies to a village near Mazar-e Sharif in the north where some children had eye and head injuries from a mine blast. The bird crashed from mechanical failure about an hour after liftoff.

The reservist had just finished chow. As he left to do laundry, the pilots received orders about the mission. Maybe an hour later, a soldier he didn't know came into the laundry room and said, You're not going to believe what happened, and told him.

The reservist wanted to feel grief but he felt only sadness, something short of grief, a dejected feeling that did not filter down into raw, emotional pain. He felt bad for the pilots he saw weeping, clutching each other, their hands dug into each other's shoulders, their faces tearful and bewildered, but nothing deeper. He had hung with them but had never been one of them. He didn't know the dead pilots. He couldn't put faces to their names. For all he knew, they may never have been around when he sat with the other pilots.

Afghanistan was just a name too. He hadn't known where it was, other than on the other side of the world from his home in Palm Bay, Florida. He looked like every other fucking reservist, did the same drills, felt the same nothingness with each passing nothing day, even when he sat with the pilots. The CO called the dead men heroes, but the reservist didn't see anything heroic in the freakish accident that killed them. They could have died that way at home. There's still a lot of fighting going on here, the CO said. There's still a whole lot of dying.

Maybe, the reservist thought, but not from the Taliban.

In his bunk that night, the reservist thought about death. If he died like the pilots, what impression would he leave behind? He was nineteen. Would he be remembered for serving his country or as a fucking reservist who got whacked with a big-ass dose of bad fucking luck? People might even laugh. Poor fucking bastard, they'd say. How long would the memory of his service linger and be appreciated by nineteen-year-olds at home who would marry, have children, careers, and lives much longer than his? To lose someone in an airplane accident in Palm Bay is one thing. To lose someone like that here left him weak and fearful of dying for no good goddamn reason.

He finished his deployment two months later and returned to Florida, no scalps, no kills to his name. Friends asked, How was it? but before he could answer they'd say, I bet you're glad to be home. Then they told him about all he'd missed while he was away. Scuttlebutt about who was fucking whom, and he'd listen without listening and when they finished, he'd drive home aware that they were unaware that he had never answered their question. He'd fall asleep at seven watching a fucking movie on Netflix and wake in the middle of the night and take a walk, arousing dogs chained to posts. He tore off faded, yellow ribbons tied around trees because they pissed him off. He burned the ribbons in a barbecue pit behind his apartment, a cremation ceremony for the pilots who died and all the other dead over there he didn't know and who died stupid deaths and had not been saved by some wishful, sentimental idiot tying yellow ribbons around trees. He didn't understand why civilians behaved the way they did. He didn't understand himself or why he was alive.

He told his friends about the dead pilots. They thought their deaths sucked. But, hey, if it had to happen at least it didn't happen to you, right? and they'd slap the reservist on the back and give him a thumbs up. Then they'd talk about going out for a Whataburger. He knew the dead pilots had nothing on a Whataburger, so he shut up and went with them to chow down. Afterward, they'd all agree to meet later for beers at Pin Ups, a strip joint, but by the time the others were ready to hit it, the reservist was crashed out on his couch, another Netflix movie playing in his darkened apartment. He'd wake up stiff and groggy and realize he had missed out on a night with his friends again. He was falling into a routine, establishing patterns, defining his life.

In the morning, he'd stumble out of bed and watch Fox News and listen to updates about the war. He expected to be taken back, to relive moments at Kandahar, but he didn't experience anything other than a numb impatience with snippets of footage that showed the bare landscape he had once walked. Turning off the TV, he'd jog around the block and more often than not he'd see a guy who had a clubfoot pedaling around on a bike, just like he had seen him every morning before he shipped out. And just like before, the guy would wave and say nothing, and the reservist appreciated that just as he appreciated another guy, a Hungarian immigrant, who had been a boxer back in the day, and now sat outside his trailer home at a table with a large, soiled, stuffed panda, and the Hungarian would raise a hand and the reservist would wave and continue jogging.

Then he'd shower, and go to Izzy's Diner next door to the Molly Mutt Thrift Shop on Palm Bay Road, not five minutes from his apartment. Getting on Dixie Highway, he'd drive along Indian River Beach where he watched kayakers bob on the waves, stroking the water with their paddles, their arms rising and falling, the waves breaking over them, and gulls floating far above them, and no matter how fast he drove, the reservist understood a kind of liberation existed beyond his reach.

He'd reach Izzy's just as it opened at six and sit at a corner table and stare out the window at the few pickups in the otherwise empty parking lot. Retirees sat at the counter. They all knew the gal who worked the early shift and commiserated with her when she complained about her kids or a regular who didn't tip. The reservist showed up enough to be recognized but not so frequently that the waitress asked his name or tried to engage him in conversation beyond, What can I getch ya, hon? Coffee?

Izzy's stood near the airport and periodically a plane would fly low overhead, drowning out all conversation, and the reservist thought of the dead pilots, and the memory of the moment when he'd heard that they'd died—while a dryer tossed his clothes—appeared very clear in his mind until he no longer heard the plane, and then his mind returned to Izzy's and he resumed staring at the parking lot, waiting for his coffee.

One of the regulars, an older guy—Big Man, the waitress called him—liked to talk loud, like a ward boss taking charge. He worked on cars and as a plumber and drove a truck for a carpet company. Whatever job came his way, the reservist often heard him say, was a bump to his Social Security check. He had a bullet-shaped, shaved head and wore shirts with the sleeves cut off, the threads dangling against the faded tats on his arms. He smelled of sweat and grease no matter the time of day. He liked sports, especially football, and always talked about whatever game had watched recently.

One morning, he complained that he had missed a game between the Dolphins and the 49ers. Who won? He wanted to know, but the guys around him gave a collective shrug. Turning around, Big Man noticed the reservist and said, *Hey bud,* and asked the same question. The reservist shook his head.

I don't follow football, he said.

What do you follow? Big Man asked, baseball? The reservist shook his head again.Nothing.

What kind of man doesn't follow sports? Big Man said. You got a little sugar in your walk, son? You prefer ballet? And he laughed and the other guys smirked and then Big Man bitched about the weather and turned back to the counter.

The reservist glared at Big Man's back. He felt an overwhelming anger flush through him. He saw himself shooting Big Man with an M4. He saw Big Man with a beard and a black turban and he saw himself killing him again and again until Big Man rose up and shot him. He saw his body collapse beside the dead pilots, not a mark on them. The reservist, however, was all fucked up, an American serviceman killed, like them, in Afghanistan but not like them. He was not that man. He had not died.

He pushed his chair back and stood. His head cleared but he retained little sense of himself.

Have a good day, hon, the waitress said. She took a dishrag to wipe his table. When he didn't leave, she asked if he wanted anything else.

Yes, I do, he said, staring at the floor without saying anything more.

Clearing a coffee cup and torn sugar packets from another table, she waited while he decided.

Hridi's Dilemma

From behind a counter inside *Tasty*, her brother Anik's bakery shop, Hridi watches an old Westerner repeatedly tug on the glass door until he realizes he needs to push to enter. He has been stopping here every day for a week, and still, he makes the same mistake. Pulls instead of pushes.

As-salamu alaykum, the Westerner greets her with a slight bow of his head as he covers his heart with his right hand.

Wa-alaikum-salaam, she responds, averting her eyes. Muslim women, as her father taught her when she was still a girl, do not look into the eyes of men they don't know.

The Westerner orders coffee. Tucking a stray strand of hair beneath her blue hijab, Hridi takes a paper cup from below the counter and drops it under the spout of a coffee machine.

At first, surprised to see a foreigner, Hridi did not acknowledge the Westerner's greeting when he started coming to the shop. This part of Old Dhaka City is at least an hour's drive from the glitzy, high-class downtown neighborhoods of Gulshan and Banani, where most foreigners stay when they visit Bangladesh. Here on Indira Street, spilled bananas, green grapes, eggplants, and squash from vendors' stalls make the sidewalk sticky as tar. Rickshaws compete with cars on the narrow road and buses scraped to a shine from countless accidents spew black exhaust, maneuvering around men and women darting across the roads at every unanticipated, fleeting break in traffic, their faces covered with surgical masks—protection from the smog-laced air black with soot. Across the street, homeless families gather on blankets in Khamar Baneji Park where grass no longer grows, feral dogs roam, and men squat to piss. The dense traffic, brown air, and crowded sidewalks at times so overwhelm Hridi that inside the shop she feels submerged in an aquarium, short of breath, and unable to come up for air, preserved only by the glass windows separating her from the tumult outside.

As she hands the Westerner his coffee, Hridi wonders, as she has other mornings, what brings him to Indira Street. He offers no hint as he sits at a table, sips his coffee, and looks outside at a boy holding an infant. The boy returns the Westerner's stare and turns up a palm, his eyes pleading. The Westerner shakes his head, a firm, unblinking no. However, despite his refusal to be persuaded by the boy's theatrics and the prop of the infant, the Westerner's shoulders slump resignedly as if the decision not to help burdens him. The boy's face flattens into expressionless resignation and he rises and leaves, hauling the infant to his chest like a sack of rice.

The look on the Westerner's face, assertive, refusing to be taken advantage of, and yet infinitely sad, impresses itself on Hridi as it has on other mornings when he has refused the entreaties of beggars. The Westerner, Hridi has concluded, lives with an exhausting sorrow the source of which she can't fathom but one that has turned his short hair gray and lined his lean face. She assumes he eats only when necessary and sometimes not even then, reducing him to the gaunt old man before her.

What Hridi has seen all her life, impoverished children, strikes the Westerner as something shocking and depleting, and his reaction, unique to her, leaves her discomfited. These past few days, she has carried home the image of his despondent eyes like a secret he has shared only with her.

The Westerner lifts his cup and gestures for one more. Hridi fills a clean cup and hands it to him with a napkin. He gives her 20 *taka* but Hridi shakes her head. The Westerner smiles and nods in thanks. He sits down again and stares into the street.

Hridi noticed how the Westerner's forlorn expression brightened when she refused his money. His smile, she knew, would linger with her on the bus ride home, a welcome relief from the dejection she so often has seen in his eyes.

Smiling herself, Hridi cleans stray coffee grounds from the counter. She enjoys working at the shop. Enjoys standing behind the counter taking orders and being in charge when customers approach her and make requests. No, we have no donuts today. Yes, we have Kalojam. Very fresh. If she disappoints them, they can leave. Hridi decides, not the customer. She likes that.

From a mirror beside the coffee machine, she watches the Westerner drink his coffee. She wonders where he stays. She has read about rich Westerners who retire and travel the world. Is he one of them? He probably had a wife who died. He carries a picture of her in his wallet. He is alone in the world without children, moving from one country to the next.

Her father has told her that when she marries she will live with the family of her husband. He has begun negotiating with the father of a nineteen-year-old boy. Hridi thinks she has met this boy although she can't be positive. Her father mentions his name but because Hridi does not remember him, she easily forgets it. It annoys her father when she asks again and again, Who is he, father? So, she has stopped inquiring. There are other families who would like him to marry their daughters, so Hridi assumes she may not know for some time if the boy's parents will accept her. It is not her decision.

She prefers not to dwell on interrupting her life for a boy whose name she can't remember. Her girlfriends tell her that if the boy has no experience with a woman, nothing will happen on their wedding night. He will be too nervous and only lie awake beside her looking miserable. If he has experience, however, he will take her. And once you are pregnant, Hridi, you'll forget the pain that produced the baby and remember only this new pain of a swelling body and of a child demanding to be released after nine months. Your body will feel torn apart, and your husband may not wait as long as you would like to take you again to have more children. Producing children will become as normal as waking up every morning to feed them.

Hridi has told herself that being a parent would be much the same as working in the shop. She would tell her sons and daughters what they can and cannot have. No different, really, than what she explains to her customers. Hridi's friends agree with this comparison in a noncommittal sort of way that suggests to Hridi that they have decided to let her think what she will.

The bell above the door rings and a woman with graying blond hair enters the shop. She wears a green hijab loosely on her head as if she just put it on. The bright blue T-shirt she wears has an insignia, *Médecins Sans Frontières*. The Westerner stands to greet her, and they embrace and kiss each other on the cheek. Hridi blushes at this public display of affection. They hold hands and the Westerner grins wider than Hridi has seen him smile before. After another long moment spent just holding her hand, the Westerner steps toward the counter and places his empty cup by the register.

Hridi takes it, her fingers brushing his. She thought she understood him. She had taken comfort in his story, the story she had created for him. She enjoyed the idea of caring for him and easing his loneliness and her own, but she sees he has a life she had not imagined. Was this woman his wife? Fiancée? Surely he is too old to be marrying now.

The Westerner considers Hridi with the despairing expression she has seen him wear so often. His face fills with pity, and Hridi has the impression he, like her friends, knows what she does not, but unlike them he does not humor her but instead regards her now with an intimate candor, and she feels a rush of anger, but despite it, or because of it, and although she knows she shouldn't, she stares directly into his mournful eyes and sees her reflection, small and distant, aged and ghostly, yet all too recognizable, lost within his dark, wavering pupils, and she steps back with a shudder and turns away.

The Westerner and the woman step outside. They stand on the sidewalk, shifting to one side to avoid a boy who almost bumps into them as he enters the shop bringing with him the noise and putrid odors of the street.

Do you have milk cake? the boy asks without giving Hridi the courtesy of a greeting. He raises his cell phone, snaps a selfie.

No, she says firmly, a hint of satisfaction in her voice. Try again tomorrow.

Missing Gene

Evening.

Fran's at night school studying for her associate degree. I don't feel like watching TV, so I get out the knife one of the terps gave to me in Kandahar and start throwing it at the wall. He said he got it off the body of a bad guy who blew himself up laying an IED in the road, but I think he stole it off one of our guys because it's a Gerber and it doesn't look like it was in any explosion. The terp could throw it and stick it every time. I'm not that good, but I throw it at the wall anyway. I can do it for hours.

I was a contractor over in Kandahar. Electrician. Worked there for twelve months. When my year was up, I flew home to Kansas City and took up with Fran. A couple of months later, I moved in with her. Mr. Fix It, the soldiers called me. Did some plumbing too. A little out of my league but at two hundred tax free grand a year I was more than willing to say I could do anything. I got used to noise: mortars, sniper fire, return fire, .50 calibers, AKs, generators grinding all night, guys living on top of each other telling dead baby and fag jokes. Awful quiet now that I'm back. Behind Fran's house, I hear buses turn off Prospect and onto 39th Street, drone past, and slice into the night until it's quiet again. The knife helps. I like the steady repetition of tossing it. The precision of it. Like fly fishing. Gene understood. He fought in Korea.

The trick with the knife, I told Gene, is you got to establish a rhythm. You do that and the silence becomes part of the flow and the *plink* noise the knife makes when it enters the wall interrupts the silence, and the small sucking sound it makes when you pull it out, and then the silence again until you throw it over and over.

Right, Gene said.

Next day.

This is the third week I haven't seen Gene at Mike's Place. Out of all the regulars, he's the only one missing.

Melissa isn't here but we all know where she is. A public defender, Melissa has a court case this afternoon. I overheard her tell Lyle yesterday she would be working late. And Lyle? He may have a job painting or installing a countertop or a new floor or fixing someone's shitter. What I'm saying is, Lyle's around. He's a handyman. He'll be in later, as will his buddy Tim.

Bill's here. He's a retired millwright. I like to think that Bill hangs here because it reminds him of all the bars in those little one-horse towns where he used to go to work on grain elevators. And Mike, of course. It's his bar. The floor dips and the stools wobble—all of them—and the top of the pool table's got a big slash in it and someone walked off with the cue ball, but it's a good place—cheap, and it's only a couple of blocks from Fran's.

Then there's Gene. Or was. He drove off is how I look at it. Flew the coop, as they say. Well, that's it. I'm leaving too. Montana is what I'm thinking. I've been considering a move for a while. I mentioned Montana to Gene. He thought it was a good idea.

Wide open, no people, he said.

Right, I said.

I'll tell Fran tonight.

Evening.

What's on at seven?

Golden Girls reruns.

Oh.

You've had beer.

I was at Mike's.

Well, you missed my mother.

Oh … yeah?

Yeah. It's alright. I wasn't expecting her.

Fran's mother does that: drops by without calling. She's divorced and bored. Good thing Fran was here instead of me. Her mother nags me when Fran's not around. She knows I'm not going out on many jobs. I've told her we're okay. I earned a bundle in Afghanistan. She thinks I should have stayed another year and made even more.

I'm going to Montana.

Montana?

Yeah.

When?

I don't know.

Oh.

I play solitaire, spreading the cards across the blanket on our bed. I tell Fran not to move her legs beneath the blanket and disturb the cards but she does anyway.

Why Montana?

It's wide open.

Fran doesn't look up from her book, *The General and the Spy*. A man on the cover wears an open red tunic and some tight ass white pants a real guy'd never wear. His skin's the color of a dirty penny and he has no hair on his chest. A woman's got her hands on his stomach ready to rip into those pants I bet.

Fran folds the corner of a page, closes the book and wipes tears from her eyes.

Nobody cries over those kinds of books, I tell her.

Montana?

I'm thinking about it. Gene's missing.

Who?

A guy I know.

Fran goes, Let's change the channel. Then let's talk.

Go ahead. Change it.

I changed it last time.

What do you want to watch? I ask.

I don't know.

She picks up her book and puts it down again. We stare at the TV, the remote between us.

Next day.

Bill sits beside me at Mike's, buys me a beer. Crass old fucker, Bill. Bald as a post and bug-eyed. He's always hunched over and rocks back and forth and makes these sick jokes about his neck being so long he can lick his balls like a dog. Deaf as Stevie Wonder is blind.

Hey Bill, Tim says.

What you say? Bill says.

Fuck you, Bill, Tim says.

What you say?

Tim laughs. Laughs loud and talks loud like we're all deaf as Bill. He sits at the end of the bar where Gene always used to stand, wipes his hands on his sweatshirt and jeans. Tim works in a plant in the West Bottoms. Makes refrigeration parts. Something like that. Comes in grimed in grease and oil. Starts at five in the morning and works all the time, weekends too. With jobs the way they are, is he going to say no when his boss offers him extra hours? I don't think so. Not with paying out child support to his ex.

With money being so tight, he killed his dog's puppies. At least that's how he explains it. The dog, a brown and white mix between this and that, had a litter of seven. He kept one, put the other six in a pillowcase, and dropped them in Troost Lake. Then he shot the dog. Easier than getting her fixed. I stopped sitting next to Tim when I heard about the puppies.

Every time I think of his drowned puppies, I'm reminded of some Afghan laborers at Kandahar. One afternoon they found a litter of puppies while they were collecting trash. A trash fire was burning and they threw the puppies into the fire. You want to hear some screaming, listen to puppies being barbecued. I hear them now. I ball up my fist and right hook my temple once, twice, three times and wait for what I call *relief* pain to wrap my skull and take their shrieks out of my head. Tim and Bill look at me. I open my fist.

Fucking mosquito, I say and smack the side of my face again.

Big-ass mosquito, Tim says still looking at me.

It's strange seeing him in Gene's spot at the end of the bar. Gene never sat, just stood. No matter how cold, he always wore shorts, a T-shirt, and a windbreaker. Brown shoes and white socks. Legs skinny and pale as a featherless chicken. Wore a cap that had the dates of the Korean War embroidered on it. He told me that Kansas City winters didn't compare to a winter in Korea.

I saw frozen bodies stacked like cord wood covered with ice. Some of them I put there.

It got cold in Afghanistan too, I said.

I remember one time when this truck driver got to Kandahar in December. Brand new. Just off the bus. Green as fuck. He was so wet behind the ears, I had to tell him where the chow hall was. He kept rubbing hands together and I pointed out the PX where he could buy some gloves. He went on his first convoy an hour later. This guy, he got in his rig, took off but realized he'd joined the wrong convoy. He turned back to the base and approached the gate fast because he was out in no-man's-land by himself. You didn't approach the gate fast. You didn't do that. But he was scared. Some Australians shot him five times with a .50 cal. I mean he was obliterated. They had to check his DNA to figure out who he was. Less than two hours after I showed him the chow hall, I saw them put him in a body bag in pieces.

Evening.

Fran tells me what I'm planning is called a *geographic.* Moving to get a new start somewhere else in the mistaken belief you'll leave your bad habits behind is how she puts it. She studied psychology last fall and thinks she can pick my mind apart now.

I mean it. I'm gone, I say.

She goes, when you decide to do it, just go. Don't bother telling me because I'm not going with you. Men have left me before. I survived. I'll survive you. Leave before I come home. Make it easy on us both.

I will, I say. I can do that.

Okay, she goes, okay.

Next day.

Just me in here this afternoon.

What's the latest on Gene? I ask Mike.

Haven't heard a thing, he says.

Mike has owned Mike's for ten years. He was in a band, got married, and had a kid. In other words, time to get a real job. So he bought the bar and named it after himself. He's divorced now, sees the kid every two weeks, plays gigs occasionally, and runs this place. Says if he ever sells it, the buyer will have to keep the name. Years from now nobody will know who the hell Mike was, but his name will be here. A piece of himself nobody will know and can't shake off. That's one way to make an impression.

I first came to Mike's by chance. I used to drink at a bar on the Paseo, but one night it was packed. After Kandahar, I can't handle crowds, so I left. On my way home, I stopped at Mike's. Some lights on but barely anyone in here. I had a few beers and came back the next night. Two nights in a row and Mike figured he had himself a new regular. He bought me a beer and introduced himself. We shook hands. Sealed the deal as they say.

I met Fran here. She was shooting pool by herself. Bent over the table, her ass high and round against her jeans and any man with a nut sack would have known that if she looked that nice from behind she'd be more than tolerable face to face. And if she wasn't, so what with an ass like that. But she was fine all the way around.

She had light brown hair and a determined look. My glance moved down past her chin and rested on a set of perky tits that pressed just hard enough against her T-shirt that my imagination did not have to strain too hard to know would be revealed when she undressed. I asked to shoot pool with her, and we got to chit-chatting. One thing led to another is what I'm saying.

I'm not sure when I noticed Gene. I just did. I remember seeing this old man at the end of the bar and thinking how solitary he looked, how he was off in his own world. He had one of those faces that sort of collapsed when he didn't talk, mouth and chin merging into a flat, frowning pond. When he took off his hat, the light shined off a bald head speckled with age spots. He'd still be standing there when I left a couple of hours later, the same bottle of Bud he had when I first came in, half-empty and parked in front of him. He barely said a word to me in those days. Just nodded if we looked each other's way. But then as I began showing up every night, he started saying hello and I'd say hello back.

Evening.

Fran and I drop our plates onto the crumb-graveled carpet for our beagle to lick. Partially chewed pizza crust, orange grease. Slobbered up in seconds. I reshuffle the cards.

I'm going to sleep, Fran says.

Say what?

Turn the TV off.

I'm still up.

Turn it down then.

It's not loud.

Please.

But it's not.

Shhh.

I shut off the TV, go out to the living room. I sit in the dark fingering my knife. How could Gene, an eighty-year-old man, vanish? I can't get past it. Like a radiator turned off. All that dead air, dead space.

Funny what you learn about a guy after they're gone. For instance, Tim and Lyle said that Gene would come to Mike's at eleven in the morning. He would stay all day and apparently be pretty toasted by the time he left at closing. Really, he never seemed messed up to me. Maybe he kicked in and drank like a horse after I left.

One night, Gene told me he had taken his landlord to court. It wasn't clear to me why. I believed him and whatever the reason, he made it seem like he won the case. After he disappeared, Bill told me Gene lived in his car. There never had been a court case or a landlord. Bill put him up in his place but not for long. Said Gene wandered around the house with nothing on but his skivvies. I couldn't have that, Bill said. Not with my wife in the house and the grandkids coming over. I don't care if he is a vet.

Next day.

Hey Lyle, Mike says.

Mike, Lyle responds, and takes a seat near Tim. He has his hair roped back in a ponytail and wears a Carhartt jacket whose sleeves hang well past his hands. His feet hang off the barstool and tap the air. He reeks of pot.

I was just getting ready to leave, Tim says.

No you're not, Lyle says.

He turns to me.

What's going on? Working?

Absolutely, I tell him. Staying busy.

You were in Afghanistan weren't you? How was that?

Good. It was good.

That's good.

Actually, it was kind of crazy.

Crazy can be good, Lyle says, and he and Tim laugh.

Mike, I'll have another, Bill says.

I notice Melissa come in the back door.

Hi Melissa, Mike says.

Hey Melissa, Lyle says.

Melissa what's up? Tim says.

Hey, Melissa says.

She sits next to Lyle and orders a Bud Light and a shot of Jack. She has on heels, a gray suit, and a white blouse.

Won my case, she says. Got him off.

Since none of us know who she's talking to, we all nod at the same time. Melissa smiles. She starts talking about the first time she came in here, as she always does. I don't know why it bears repeating. I mean, I've got the story memorized. But she likes telling it. Maybe it gives her a sense of seniority. With the exception of Lyle, she has been coming here longer than the rest of us. Like it makes her feel that she belongs is what I'm saying.

It was just before closing, Melissa says. Mike and Lyle were shooting pool. Gene was in his usual spot. She remembers Mike saying he was about to close. Then he let her stay and the four of them had beers and got stoned after Mike locked up.

Gene got stoned? I marvel.

Yeah, Melissa says.

I hadn't heard that part before.

Evening.

Fran tells me that instead of doing a geographic, I should go with her and visit her sister in St. Louis. It would be cheap, she says. No hotel or eating out expenses.

Sounds okay, I say.

Did you order a pizza?

Not yet, I say. I'm tired of pizza.

What do you want?

I don't know. Shit, what's up with all the questions?

Fran goes into the kitchen. I hear her making herself a drink. I try calling Gene. I gave Gene my cell number one night. He called me a few times before he disappeared, but I could never make out what he was saying. He had a sandpaper voice that came at you like radio static. What's that? What's that, Gene? I'd say, and then he'd hang up. I'd call him right back, but he'd never pick up. He doesn't pick up now. I get one of those female-sounding computer-generated voices telling me to leave a message. I'd like to talk to Gene, I say and hang up.

Next day.

Anybody hear anything about Gene? I ask.

Lyle shakes his head. Melissa and Tim look at Lyle and shrug.

Getting to be a while, Lyle says.

Yeah, a while, Mike says.

I shout in Bill's ear and ask him what he knows. Well, he says, speaking like he's got a mouth full of cotton, I spoke to one of his sons in San Antone. Yes, San Antone it was. Gene gave me his number when he stayed with me. An emergency contact, he said. Well, let's hope this isn't an emergency because Gene's son wants nothing to do with him. One of those kind of deals, if you know what I mean. Still a lot of unsettled water under that bridge, I guess. Anyway, I told his son, I just want you to know your father is missing. We haven't seen him for the longest. Maybe he's headed your way. But his boy said again he wanted nothing to do with him. What can you do?

He doesn't expect an answer and I don't give him one because, well, what can you do? Melissa and Lyle go out back to smoke. Mike steps into the kitchen. Bill stares at his glass. I tell him that today for no good reason I was reminded of this private, a young gal. We got mortared and she got all messed up. She lay on the ground, her right arm rip shit to confetti. Some medics put her on a stretcher and got an IV in her, and her shirt rose up exposing her flat stomach and full tits and despite all her screaming I thought she was beautiful. I went over to see if I could help and she looked at me wide-eyed and said, Am I going to die? No, I said. You're fine. You're going to make it.

Do I know if she did? No, I don't. That bothers me.

What you say? Bill says.

Evening.

I call Fran from the union hall on Admiral Boulevard, shouting above the traffic noise of cars backed up overhead in the tangled mess that is I-70, I-35, U.S. 71, and I-29 looping around one another. I only worked a few hours this afternoon, I tell her. I stuck around for something else to come up but nothing did. Can you pick me up?

Okay, she says.

By the time she gets me, I'm pissed off. Pissed I had only four hours of work today, pissed I couldn't get a ride home, pissed I had to wait around until Fran got off her job at Dollar General to get me. I was 360 pissed off is what I'm saying.

I get in the car, ball my hand into a fist, and press my knuckles against Fran's right temple. She tilts her head away and I keep pushing with my fist until I press her head against the window and I feel the vein in her temple pulse against my knuckles.

Stop it, you're hurting me, she says.

Next day.

Mike, I'll have another one, Melissa says.

She's dating this gal Rhonda, a schoolteacher. I don't know how old. Younger, I'd say by the look of her in a photo Melissa passed around. I don't care that she's gay. I mean lesbian. She corrected me one time. Men are gay; women are lesbian. OK. What do I do with that bit of knowledge? Keep my mouth shut is what I'm saying.

Melissa talks about how nice it is to be involved with a woman who doesn't trip when she has to work late. Doesn't ask a thousand questions to make sure that nothing is wrong. It's nice to be with someone who's an adult, Melissa says. She says that a lot. Nice to be involved with an adult. Like she's trying to convince herself that it's nice. Like maybe the confidence of her lover makes Melissa wonder what she's doing.

I'm going home, Tim says. Make some dinner.

What're you going to have? Lyle says.

I don't know.

What you say? Bill says.

Fuck you, Bill, Tim says, and he and Lyle laugh. It's not as funny as the first time he said it. It's starting to get old, but I can't help but smile a little.

Gene and I had dinner together one night. I met him in the parking lot behind the Sun Fresh Market off Southwest Trafficway. I didn't know then he was sleeping in his car. Just ran into him there and he asked me if I was hungry. Come to think of it, I said.

A bunch of clothes were heaped in the back seat of his station wagon. An old rusty job with fake wood paneling peeling off the doors. He had rigged a towel to take the place of a window that would no longer roll up. Laundry day, he said explaining the clothes.

We drove out of the parking lot to Mill Road and followed the curve into Westport and a little joint called Johnson's. Some bums who might have been hippies years ago stood on Broadway wiping down car windows at a red light while the drivers waved them off. Gene and I sat down and a waitress wiped down our table. I ordered a burger. Gene had the meatloaf special.

Johnson's closed not long after that. A big *For Rent* sign hangs above the front door along with the name of some real estate company. I went by it the other day and noticed the table where Gene and I had sat surrounded by other empty tables, made all the emptier by the emptiness of the place.

Evening.

Fran's mother sits with me in the kitchen. Her perfume gives me a headache. I stare at her hair, all puffy and piled up on her head and bleached so blond it's almost white. She twirls the lazy Susan with a finger, touches the corner of her mouth and then goes back to spinning the Lazy Susan her finger skating along on a film of lipstick she rubbed off.

What's it taste like, your lipstick?

Why would you want to know? What kind of question is that for a man to ask?

I don't know it just came to me, I want to say, but don't. One night, I was walking to the shitter and mortars started coming in. We were always being mortared. This is the real deal, baby! someone yelled, and the blasts lifted an eighteen-year-old private into the air tossing him backward like a rag into all this dirt and noise and smoke, and his blood sprayed over my face. I can still taste it.

Where's Fran? her mother says.

School, I say.

Have you thought of going back to school?

No.

Is it your plan for Fran to do all the work while you sit around? Have you thought about being more than an electrician.

No, Mrs. Lee, I haven't.

Well, it shows.

I apply piece of scotch tape to a corner above the cabinets where the wallpaper is pealing.

Fran's mother gets up and walks to the sink. I listen to the linoleum creak beneath her shoes.

When do you plan to clean these? she says of the dishes. Or are you waiting for them to pile up to the ceiling?

I throw the tape down and face her. She steps back, a little aren't-I-clever smirk on her face, and I turn on the hot water and squirt some soap in the sink. I find a sponge and start wiping down a plate. My fingertips turn white I'm squeezing the plate so hard. A littler harder and it would break. I want to feel it break but I ease up, put the plate in the rack. I start cleaning another one.

You two should get married, Fran's mother goes.

I keep washing the plate.

You're living together, she says. Not having a job hasn't stopped you from doing that. Married, you'd at least be official. It would show responsibility. Now wouldn't that be something?

I rinse the plate, set it in the rack. I lean on the sink, arms stiff.

I'm leaving, I say.

You're leaving. Where you going?

Montana.

Montana. What are you going to do in Montana?

Work.

Work? Work here for a change. You think some cowgirl is going to put up with you?

I raise my hand before she says anything more. There's this nasal termite sound to her voice that chisels into my head.

I press my fingers against my eyes. My neck feels hard as a tree trunk.

Fran's mother stands beside me. I ignore her, work on another plate. She runs a finger over the dishes in the rack and shows me a spongy speck of pizza crust glued to her fingertip.

You can't do any better than that? She says.

I smash the plate on the edge of the sink and throw the jagged piece still in my hand against the wall. She steps back, her eyes betraying panic, her finger still poised accusingly, and I grab her finger with a fury that fills me with a terrible heat and force it back until she kneels screaming. A pasty white color washes through her face when the bone breaks, and I feel something break in me and I keep pressing back on her ruined finger, until the bone tears through the skin and into my palm. Her eyes swell like something wide and deep rising out of the ground bubbling tears, and her screams take on a new level.

I let go of her of her hand and jam my knee in her solar plexus and put all my weight on her chest. She gags and spits up whatever she had eaten that morning. I rise up and then drop my knee into her chest, and her neck and face go all purple, and I do it again until I feel ribs cracking under my knee. I sink into her chest and down to her spine like falling through ice. Blood geysers out of her mouth and then her eyes roll back. Her tongue lolls out of her mouth like a slug, and I smell her bowels. I push myself off her and sit at the table. The silence is almost as loud as her screams. I focus on the hum of the refrigerator. White noise. I take up my knife. My hands shake and at first my throws are way off. Then my breathing steadies and I get my rhythm back and throw it once, twice, three times into the baseboard, the refrigerator steadily droning behind me.

Next day.

Rhonda's not answering, Melissa says, looking at her iPhone. Why isn't she answering?

The front door swings open.

Hey, Heidi, Mike says.

Hi, Mike, Heidi says.

She plops down beside Lyle, her mop of curly red hair flouncing on her shoulders. The two of them started dating not too far back. She tends bar here on the weekends. Has two kids. Their daddy dealt drugs and got busted. Lyle sells drugs but hasn't been busted. I think she can do better. I bought books for her five-year-old daughter. I figured she'd appreciate that. Little picture books. But she started seeing Lyle and I quit the book thing. Maybe books weren't what I should have been giving her in the first place. But I was with Fran, so books seemed appropriate. Neutral. Not too over the top is what I'm saying.

I force a smile at Heidi but I don't strike up a conversation. I'm not really here. Yesterday seems far away and today doesn't feel like today. I hear Heidi and Lyle talking, but it's all background noise to Fran's mother dying. That's how I look at it. She died. She was in the wrong place at the wrong time. Something snapped inside me, and she died. It was not me that killed her but something working through me I can't define. That something left me afterward as suddenly as it had come on, and I almost fell asleep in the kitchen throwing my knife. But then the old me came back, and I knew I had to clean up the mess left by that something else.

I carried her body into the garage, put it in the trunk of my car, and covered it with a blanket. Finding a mop, I went back into the kitchen and swabbed the floor. Back in the garage, I looked for a box of five-, ten-, and twenty-pound weights Fran had bought at a yard sale when she got it into her head she was going to exercise. Dust and cobwebs covered the weights and clung to the hair on my arms, and I felt each hair released when I wiped the cobwebs off.

I put some rope and the weights in the trunk and drove to Troost Lake. Clouds sealed the sky so that no stars shone. I followed Troost Avenue to the turnoff into the lake, and the road narrowed and wound around the lake and my car lights skimmed over the oily blackness of the water and the wet stone walk where old men fished during the day. I parked the car under some trees, opened the trunk and trussed up the body with rope. It wasn't too heavy even with the weights I'd wedged beneath the rope. I held it and listened to what I thought was an owl. Shadows rose and dipped above me and then darted away and I could only assume they were bats. I waited for the owl to stop calling. In the vacancy left by its silence, I rolled Fran's mother down a hill and she splashed into the water and was absorbed into its darkness leaving only ripples that spread into nothingness.

Evening.

When I'm with Fran, I think of her mother. I don't need that. I sit alone in the kitchen while Fran sleeps and punch my temples until my head feels like it will explode and thoughts of Mrs. Lee shatter into bits. I think of Gene and what he would say.

The last time I saw him, he was standing in front of a Church's Chicken near Gillham Plaza and 31st Street. It was hot and the wind picked up some napkins, pinning them against Gene's knobby white knees. We said hello and he offered me a ride, but I told him I had my car. I'm getting some coffee, I said.

When I went back outside, he was still there. I looked at him and he gave me a knowing wink like we were both in on something no one else would understand. I don't know what that might have been. But I'm thinking now he might have done some awful things in Korea besides killing gooks and letting their bodies freeze, and I think he saw in me the ability to do some awful things too, and then Fran's mother died, and he was proven right. I'm just saying. I don't know. Gene didn't say and I never saw him again.

Next day.

OK Mike, I'm outta here, Tim says. After one more.

I'll do one more too Mike, Lyle says.

What you say?

Fuck you, Bill.

Lyle and Tim stand and walk outside to smoke. Melissa follows them tapping a number into her iPhone. Heidi looks at me and smiles. She asks Mike for a cigarette. Watch my purse, she says. Then she goes outside too. Mike puts two bottles of beer on the bar for Tim and Lyle. I wave him off when he looks at me. I feel all hemmed in. The beer congests me. It's difficult to breathe.

I'll pay up, Mike, I say.

Evening.

In bed Fran rolls over with her back to me, her head on my right arm. I grit my teeth. Her touch sends shock waves through me, and I get all jittery. I edge away from her. She says she has called her mother a few times but no one answers. It's not like her, she says, so Fran is going to go by the house in the morning.

That settles it. I'm out of here. When Fran leaves for work I'll be right behind her but headed in another direction. It'll still be dark. I'll take 39th to Broadway and hang a right on Broadway by the Walgreens and drive into downtown. A few blocks east, I'll see the glow from the Power & Light District keeping the sky open like an illumination mortar, and I'll cross the Broadway Bridge and get on I-29 north until I reach I-90 and then it's a direct shot west to Montana and wherever.

I feel my arm falling asleep beneath the weight of Fran's head. I curl it to get some circulation and realize I could choke her, no problem. I drop my arm and slide it out from under her head and punch my temples with both fists until the pain overwhelms my thoughts.

I kick off my blankets; get my legs out from under the sheets. I long for a breeze. I imagine Fran's mother at the bottom of Troost Lake. I think of Tim's puppies, and then I think of Kandahar and of other things I've seen. My head throbs. I shut my eyes against the room closing in on me, get up and sit in the kitchen. I find my knife, hands shaking. I start tossing it but can't establish a rhythm.

I drop the knife, think of Gene and of dead Koreans calling to him. I imagine he is sitting in his car miles away parked beneath a streetlight unable to sleep. Moths flutter against the windows. Flies crawl on the windshield. Beetles scuttle across the hood. I tell him that when I was a boy, my friends and I would drop grasshoppers into empty trash barrels and then we'd scream into the barrels and listen to the screech of our voices ping-pong against the sides like shrapnel, crumbling antennae, wings, legs. We'd pluck the grasshoppers out barely alive and bury them. I see them now their jaws working furiously, filling with dirt. Hear the crunch-scrape of seeking mouths sucking air.

A Day Doesn't Go By When I Don't Have Regrets

Marge has lacquered on the eye makeup thick as asphalt and her false lashes are long enough to catch an updraft. The wrinkles in her face could carry rivers and her arms have the lean, leathery look of someone who used them at one time for more than serving drinks. I don't know her age but she's somewhere north of fifty.

She shakes my empty Budweiser bottle and gives me a fresh one, popping off the cap and looking inside it at the picture of playing card. I win a free beer if I guess what it is. Next to me at the bar, this guy we all call Jimbo, watches.

Ace of spades.

King of diamonds.

Shit!

I give her three dollars.

Bad luck, Jimbo says.

Another Budweiser? Marge asks him, in that scratchy voice of hers, leaning so far over the bar that we get a good shot of her freckled cleavage. She takes his empty bottle and gives him a fresh one.

Put it on my tab.

I got this one.

On my tab, Marge, Jimbo shouts, slamming the bar. I don't want your help.

Jimbo got laid off last week. He managed this little pizza joint but the owner shut it down. Wasn't doing enough business, I suppose. I don't ask. I don't need his problems any more than he needs mine.

Raise your voice again and you're done, Marge says. I got this one.

I'm in The Hitching Post, a bar down the street from where I live in Willow Hill Heights Apartments. I've got a one bedroom and a little kitchen with a microwave. The beige carpet's the kind that gets dirty just by looking at it.

The other night, I'd just popped open a beer when I heard someone knock on my door. I go see who it is and there's this gal, no more than twenty-five, in a gray sweatshirt and jeans.

I live above you, she goes, and I locked myself out. Would you mind calling the front office?

Sure. Come in.

I got my phone and called the after-hours number. Some guy answered and I explained the situation and he said he'd be right over. I set the phone down, picked up my beer and faced her.

You drink, she said.

If I'd been deaf I still would've heard the scolding tone in her voice. I don't know what's gone on in this gal's life that she'd say a thing like that but I didn't need it.

Someone'll be here in a minute, I told her. Why don't you wait outside your apartment?

She left without a word, not even a thank you. I sat down. I smelled her, smelled her perfume. Like a field of flowers. I was pissed off but I liked that smell, the way it filled the apartment, and the way she looked. I closed my eyes, still smelling her and then nodded off. When I woke up, the smell was gone and my beer was warm. I couldn't do anything about her, but I could get another a beer and I did.

Marge bums a smoke from me. I give her my lighter and hear a motorcycle pull into the parking lot. A rangy looking dude walks in, windblown and sunburned but not from some Miami Beach vacation, faded tats up and down his arms, long gray hair limp around his shoulders. He squints until his eyes adjust to the light. Fiftyish. Sagging in the middle like the rest of us, arms large but fleshy. Maybe he worked construction back in the day. He leans over, starts coughing,

Don't die on me, Marge says.

He straightens up, jerks a bandana from his hip pocket, clears his throat, and spits into it. He folds the bandana and shoves it back in his pocket, wiping his hands on his pants. I see a faded tat on his right forearm: *Always a Marine.*

Give me a Miller draft.

Marge pours him a beer.

Your bike's in my space, Jimbo says.

The biker turns to him. His breath rattles in his throat.

You have a problem with where I parked?

No, Jimbo says. I could give a shit where you park.

Jimbo stares at the mirror behind the bar and watches the biker sit at a table.

Harleys are crap bikes, Jimbo says. Leak oil and the handlebar bushings ain't worth a crap. Barely any room to get a torque wrench on the drain plugs. Like a fashion statement to own one of them. That's all it is. To impress a girlfriend. A hooker's cheaper.

He laughs. I hear the biker push his chair back. He gets up and stands next to Jimbo. Jimbo stands. They stare hard at each other and then the biker doubles over and coughs once, twice, three times. He raises his head and wipes his mouth with the back of a hand. Without a word he walks out and starts coughing again. We hear the rumble of the Harley's engine as he turns out of the parking and onto the road.

He should trade his bike for an oxygen tank, Jimbo says.

You're through, Marge says.

Jimbo smirks, sits, and picks up his beer.

Finish and go, she says.

About five minutes later, two motorcycles turn into the parking lot. The biker with the barking cough is back and goes directly to the dartboard followed by a second, younger guy with biceps the size of footballs. He struts through the bar, showboating his body. He stops at the pool table, runs his hands over the billiard balls and keeps walking until he stands beside the first biker and tells Marge to give them both beers. Miller draft.

Six bones, Marge tells him.

He takes the beers without paying.

You brought your bitch, Jimbo says.

The older biker stiffens. He coughs and takes a deep breath. Without a word, the second biker moves to the pool table, picks up two balls and approaches Jimbo. Jimbo slides off his stool. The second biker keeps moving toward him, his hands curling around the pool balls. Jimbo smiles, cocks his arms and crouches.

Jimbo, Marge says.

He ignores her.

I've never had to call the police and don't want to now.

Jimbo and Muscleman circle each other.

I'm calling. You hear me? Marge shouts, I'm calling!

She grabs her cell phone, knocking over a Jack Daniels bottle in the process, and Jimbo half turns at the noise, and then realizing he has taken his eyes off Muscleman, ducks and steps back but he doesn't duck low enough or step back far enough and Muscleman nails him on the left side of his head, blood spurting from his ear, and he collapses. He tries to stand but his knees give out. He shakes his head and pulls himself up by a barstool. Blood gushes down the side of his face and neck. Muscleman lets him stand and they start circling each other again. Marge screams at a dispatcher, and the first biker watches and Jimbo leans on one leg like he's having trouble keeping his balance and I look at a stool next to me and think, *Throw it*, but I don't move, heart racing, knowing I could pick up the stool, looking at my hands, seeing them grab it, and crack it over Muscleman's head, but I don't move, and he hammers a fist into Jimbo's face, and I hear the stomach-turning crunch of his nose breaking.

Jimbo gasps and collapses on the floor. He shoves himself backward with his heels, saliva dripping out of a corner of his mouth, blood spouting from his nose, eyes wide but unfocused. Muscleman stands above him and raises a foot above his crotch. I look at the stool and try to will myself to pick it up. Marge hurls her phone, hitting Muscleman in his right eye. He drops the pool balls, covers his face, and stumbles backward, the shrill sound of a police siren somewhere far off coming toward us.

Cops're coming! Marge screams. Get out! Now!

The first biker walks to the door, starts coughing, and reaches out to the wall for balance. Muscleman stands beside him, holding a hand over his eye. Still coughing, the first biker gives him his wallet. The second biker takes some money, pockets the bills, and hands the wallet back. He kicks open the door and goes outside. The first biker stands with his hands on his hips, head back, taking deep breaths before he follows him out. I hear them roar off, the fading noise of their engines mixing with the rising wail of the police siren.

Marge helps Jimbo to a stool. She scoops ice into a bar rag and presses it against his nose until he can hold it himself. Blood covers his shirt and forms streams down his chin. She packs another rag with ice for his ear.

Get out of here, she tells me. I'm shutting down once the cops get here.

I go outside and turn around and look through the window and see Marge holding the ice-filled rag on Jimbo's face. I should've picked up that fucking stool. I just wanted to drink and get a glow going and not think but I should've done that much. A day doesn't go by when I don't have regrets. I run my hands through my hair and walk toward the lights of Willow Hill. Maybe I'll see that gal. The one who locked herself out. Maybe she'll come to my door again. I'd take her in my arms and hold her like this was the one moment we'd ever have, because it would be.

The Cleavers

The Cleavers left their Chicago home at eight in the dry heat of a Saturday morning to visit friends in Denver over spring break. Sixteen-year-old Wally Cleaver had just passed his driving test the day before and asked his father if he could drive partway. His father said he'd think about it. Wally knew what that meant: He wouldn't be driving. He helped his father put their suitcases into the trunk of the car, got into the back seat, put his Airpods in his ears, and began listening to iTunes.

This is a family outing, his mother told him. Turn off your phone, honey, and let's be a family.

Wally sighed loudly to make his displeasure known.

Oh, you poor, put-upon thing, his mother said.

They stopped at a Denny's for breakfast. Sunlight shone through the windows. A waitress closed the blinds and a dim gray light consumed their table. A television with the volume turned off hung above the counter. It showed a crowd of Black women and men marching down a street waving signs: *Justice for George Floyd*; *No Justice, No Peace*; and *Cops Kill*. Wally stared at the television. His mother tapped him on the shoulder.

Elbows off the table, she said.

Wally's father thumbed through a menu and set it aside.

I know what I want, he said. June?

Yes, I know, Wally's mother said.

Me too, Wally said.

The waitress who had closed the blinds took their order. Wally's father asked for a ham and cheese omelet. His mother ordered two fried eggs with wheat toast, no butter, and Wally said he wanted pancakes. The waitress picked up their menus and refilled their water glasses. Wally's father glanced at the television. A reporter stood in front of a burning storefront.

I heard someone took a video of the police after they arrested George Floyd, Wally's father said. That person should be charged with something. These people wouldn't be tearing up the streets if whoever did that hadn't taken pictures and put them all over the Internet.

I think it was a girl—a high school student, Wally said.

I don't care who it was. She should be charged.

Let's talk about something pleasant, Wally's mother said.

After breakfast, the Cleavers drove for three hours until they reached LeClaire, Iowa, where they visited the Buffalo Bill Museum. They stayed for about thirty minutes—Wally rolling his eyes and sighing to display his boredom—before his father said they should leave if they expected to make any time.

They stopped for the night at a Holiday Inn just outside of Omaha. Wally and his father carried their bags to the front desk. His father asked the desk clerk for two connecting rooms. Behind the counter, computer monitors showed the hotel parking lot. Wally saw their car and a couple walking past it.

When they got to their room, Wally's mother began sorting through her suitcase. Wally opened a door to the room where he would sleep. The bed looked perfect, without a wrinkle. He put his suitcase by it and closed the door. He told his parents he wanted to use the pool.

Okay, his father said, but we'll probably get something to eat in an hour.

Did either of you bring toothpaste, Wally's mother asked. I thought I had packed it.

Ward, did you put it in your bag?

No, Wally's father said. I saw a Walgreens on the way in. We can get it when we go out for dinner.

I'll go, Wally said. C'mon dad. Let me drive the car.

His father frowned.

I thought you wanted to use the pool?

I'd rather drive.

I don't know.

It'll take two seconds.

We're going out for dinner. There's no rush.

Please!

You know where to go?

Yeah, Wally said. It's like two blocks away.

I think it's all right, Ward, his mother said. I'd like to clean my teeth.

His father gave Wally the keys.

Don't be gone long. Five minutes.

Wally bolted from the room and down the hall. In the lobby, he noticed his reflection in a large convex mirror in one corner of the ceiling. His face ballooned and shrank. The receptionist watched him and he noticed her continuing to watch him as he walked to the parking lot. The setting sun flared a bright orange. He saw the security cameras perched in corners beneath the roof and adopted what he considered to be a serious look in case the receptionist was still watching him. Digging into his hip pocket, he approached their car and took out the keys. He got in and put his hands on the steering wheel. He felt good. He felt older. He pulled the seatbelt across his chest and started the engine. He felt it kick on and hum. He drove to the highway. He saw the Walgreens about two blocks ahead on the left-hand side. When he got closer he turned on his blinker and entered the parking lot. He saw an empty space beneath a tree between two cars. He turned. An acorn dropped on the roof of his car. He looked up, startled, and hit the rear of the car on the far side of the parking space. He braked hard and lurched forward. He backed up, braked to a jolting stop again. Staring out the windshield, he saw that he had broken the lens on a side marker light. He didn't move. His heart hammered against his chest and he backed up a little more, almost hitting a car behind him. The driver honked and Wally stopped and looked in the rearview mirror. The driver beeped again and drove around him, flipping him off. Wally heard himself breathing. He turned on his four-way flashers. He got out and looked at the front of his car. He didn't see anything, not a scratch. He walked to the other car and ran a hand over the broken light. It was no bigger than his palm. Splinters of yellow plastic crunched under his feet. He saw no other damage.

Glancing around, he noticed an old man on a concrete bench by the Walgreens door staring in his direction. He saw no one else. He wondered if the old man had seen him hit the car. The old man took out his cell phone and dialed a number. He pressed the phone against his right ear and looked out into the parking lot. Wally couldn't tell if he was looking at him or past him at something else. He turned away and then turned back. The old man continued staring into the lot. His pale skin looked damp in the glow of the lights from the store, and Wally remembered when he was a small boy he would imagine ghosts hovering in his bedroom at night and then yank his blankets over his head to sleep. He wanted to run, to rush back to the hotel and his parents, but the comfort he sought would be doomed, he knew, by the fury of his father.

After a long moment he went back to his car and found a piece of paper and a pen in the glove compartment. He wrote a note to the owner of the car and explained what had happened. He said he was very sorry. He signed his name, wrote his cell phone number, and slipped the note under a windshield wiper. He glanced at the old man one last time and left.

When he returned to the hotel, he parked in the same spot and hurried to his parents' room. He saw the worried look on his face in the hall mirrors. He was afraid to tell them what he had done, especially his father, but at the same time he thought that telling them might somehow fix it. He pounded on the door. His father opened it.

Good God, he said, is there a fire?

Wally gave him the car keys and pushed past him to a corner of the room. His mother stood in front of the bathroom mirror combing her hair. The TV was on. Men and women ran across the screen from a storefront carrying boxes. A reporter spoke into a microphone: *Looters have taken over the streets despite calls for peaceful protest.*

I think I hit a car, Wally said.

What? his father said.

His mother put her comb on the sink and walked out of the bathroom and turned the volume down on the TV. She stood beside Wally's father.

What honey? she asked.

I was pulling into a parking space next to a car and I hit it. I broke a little light on the side. That's all. About the size of my hand. Our car's fine.

What are you talking about? his mother said.

You hit a car? his father said.

Wally didn't answer.

You hit a car? his father repeated.

It wasn't bad.

What isn't bad? his father continued.

Our car's fine. I just broke a little light on their car.

The rear light?

It was on the side. I left a note with my cell number.

You shouldn't have done that, his father said. Whoever owns that car is going to claim damages for every little scratch they can get away with.

I just hit this little yellow light on the side.

It doesn't matter, his father said, his voice rising.

You don't know what people will do, his mother said. They might claim you did a lot more.

I told you to be careful but you don't listen, his father snapped. You think you know everything and now you've hit a car!

Wally stepped back against the wall. He wanted to shrink into the floor. His parents looked at each other and then at him. He had written the note because of the old man. He never would have left it had he not seen him. He wanted to explain but he knew better than to talk now.

I never should have let him go, June, his father said. Wally, come with me.

Where're you going? June asked

To get that blasted note.

Ward, they're probably gone.

Maybe. We'll find out.

Wally followed his father out of the room to the parking lot. He looked up but couldn't see stars. The night had turned pitch black and a damp breezed pressed against him. He waited by the passenger door while his father examined the front of the car. His father got behind the wheel without a word.

Get in, he said.

It started to rain, coming in at a slant, slapping the car. They drove to Walgreens. Streetlights cast a pale glow over the parking lot.

Do you see the car? his father asked above the noise of the windshield wipers.

Wally pointed.

It's that Ford.

OK.

Wally got out, hunched against the rain. A woman hurried into Walgreens and another woman ran in behind her. Wally looked for the old man but didn't see him. He ran to the car and saw that it wasn't the one he had hit. It looked just like it, but it wasn't the one. He ran back to his father. His father rolled his window down. Rain streaked his face.

Not the car, Wally said, wiping his face. They must've left.

His father shook his head.

Get in.

Wally ran to the passenger side and opened the door.

Never again, Wally, never again. You don't drive until you know what you're doing.

Dad!

Don't 'Dad' me!

They returned to the hotel without talking and hurried inside.

You're wet, Wally's mother said when they entered the room.

It's pouring, Wally's father said in an annoyed voice that Wally knew had nothing to do with the weather.

Wally's phone rang. He tugged it out of a pocket and looked at the screen. He didn't recognize the number.

Hello?

This is Judith Matts, a woman said. I found a note on my car with this number. Is this Wally Cleaver?

Wally's eyes widened. Shit, he thought. He pressed the phone against his chest.

It's the owner of the car, he whispered to his father.

Dammit, his father said.

He glared at Wally and stuck out a hand. Wally gave him the phone.

Hello, he said. This is Ward Cleaver. … That was my son who answered. … Yes, Wally. I'm his father. He left the note. … Well, he just got his driver's license. We've been driving all day to Denver and he wanted to drive to Walgreens. … Yes, well, if you have a teenager you know. … I guess he needs more practice.

He forced a laugh.

What's that? … Yes, for spring break, a vacation. … Well, that's very kind of you to say. We, my wife and I, we try. We certainly taught him to own up to his mistakes, but you never know if your children listen.

He laughed again.

I'm glad your husband knows about cars. I'm all thumbs.

Another forced laugh.

Well, thank you again, Mrs. Matts, but are you sure? … You're being very kind. Thank you. Good night.

He hung up, put the phone on the dresser. He stared at it for a moment and then turned to Wally.

Well, that was the owner of the car, he said.

Wally almost said, I told you, but stopped himself.

You broke a marker light, his father continued. Her husband will buy a new one and put it on. It's only about twenty or thirty dollars.

Really? Wally's mother said. Well, that's fortunate. How nice of her.

She sounded very nice, Wally's father said.

Thoughtful?

She was.

You won't run into too many people like that.

No, you sure won't, Wally's father said. We were lucky. Someone else would have hit us up for every dent. Let this be a lesson, Wally. Driving is a privilege. You have to be responsible.

I know, Wally said.

We'll see if you do. You won't be driving again until you've convinced me.

Wally rolled his eyes. His father reached for a laminated card on top of the television with a list of area restaurants.

Let's try for a less eventful rest-of-the-night, he said.

Shut off the TV, Ward. We don't need to watch any more of that nonsense.

He took the remote, pressed a red button, and the TV snapped off.

We still need toothpaste.

I know, June. Where should we go for dinner?

Wally wasn't hungry. He took a shirt and a pair of pants out of his suitcase to change out of his wet clothes. He wondered how long it would be before his father let him drive again. Not long, he hoped. If the owner of the car wasn't pissed off, then why should he be? Maybe he would tell his father about the old man. Stupid old man. Maybe then he would understand.

Love Engagement

Noor and his wife, Damsa, moved to Paris when the Russians invaded Afghanistan in 1979. Twenty-two years later, after the collapse of the Taliban, they returned to Kabul and rented a house with a large backyard in District Ten on Taimani Street. Withered red, yellow, and white roses grew beside a bare concrete wall and geckos perched between the thorns, immobile, alert, leaping at the slightest disturbance into the branches of a poplar. Fallen leaves curled on the faded tiles of the cracked terrace. One afternoon, while he was watering the roses, Noor met a neighbor, Abdul Ahmadi, and invited him for tea.

Right off, Abdul noticed Damsa in the kitchen without a burqa. She looked him up and down without a hint of self-consciousness. Another woman stood beside her. She was wearing a burqa and turned away when Abdul glanced at her. Damsa carried a tray with tea and a plate of raisins and cashews, sat with Abdul and Noor, and lit a cigarette. Abdul was dumbfounded and turned to Noor. Noor shrugged.

It is no problem for a woman to smoke and sit with a man in Paris, he said.

Don't apologize for me, Damsa snapped.

I was not apologizing for you.

Yes, you were!

Turning to Abdul, she scolded, You are stuck in the old ways.

Abdul's face reddened with anger but he remained quiet. He closed his eyes as if the darkness would remove Damsa from his sight. When he opened them again, he ignored her and asked Noor about the other woman. Was she his second wife?

No, Damsa answered and laughed.

I spoke to Noor, Abdul said.

Yes, and now I am speaking to you, Damsa said. She is my friend from long ago. We were in school together.

We are not in France, Abdul said, trying to control his temper.

Yes, but you are in our home, Damsa replied.

Please, Noor said.

No, don't "please" me, she snapped.

When neither Noor nor Abdul spoke, Damsa continued: The woman's name is Arezo, the daughter of a friend. She is still not used to the idea that the Taliban are gone and she can now show her face to men. Slowly, slowly, Damsa said, she has been encouraging Arezo to relax and trust in the new Afghanistan.

Abdul understood her hesitation. He still had a long beard and wore a salwar kameez. His friends told him to shave but his mind did not switch off and on like a lightbulb. One day, the vice police had been measuring his beard, the next day his friends were waiting for barbers to shave theirs off. It was all very sudden, and as unbelievable as Damsa's behavior.

Excusing himself, Abdul returned home. He lived alone. During Talib time, when his father arranged for him to marry the daughter of a close friend, Abdul fled to Pakistan. The idea of marriage scared him, especially to a girl he did not even know. He had rarely spoken to any girl and never without an older person present. He had vague memories of playing tag with female cousins in the back of his house when he was a boy but after he turned ten or eleven his father told him to play only with boys.

Abdul refused to return from Pakistan until his father relented and promised not to force him into marriage, but his father did not speak to him again. He moved around him like a detached shadow behaving as if Abdul did not exist.

A tailor who owned a small shop in Shar-e-Naw hired Abdul as his assistant. When he died, Abdul took over. Then al-Qaeda attacked the United States, and the Americans came. In the days and months that followed, Abdul would sit behind the counter of his shop beside a sewing machine and stare at the busy sidewalk traffic, incredulous. Young men strode by in blue jeans and button up shirts with bright, flowered patterns, much of their pale chests exposed. Girls wore jeans too, and high-heeled shoes, and the wind from cars lifted their saris and they held the billowing cloth with both hands and laughed, their uncovered faces turned toward the clear sky, sunlight playing across their flushed cheeks. Abdul struggled to absorb all the changes that had occurred in such a short time.

One day a year after they had met, Noor called Abdul and told him Damsa had died. She had awakened that morning, stepped into their garden, lit a cigarette, and dropped dead of a heart attack. He found her slumped against a wall, a vine reaching above her head. Abdul hurried to his house. When Noor opened the door, Abdul embraced him.

Well, now I can watch American wrestling shows on TV without Damsa telling me it's entertainment for boys, not men, Noor said. I can play panjpar[1] with my friends and she won't tell me I'm wasting my time.

Two months later, Noor stopped by Abdul's shop with some news: his nephew, the son of his older sister, had become engaged. But it was not a typical engagement. He and the girl had decided to marry on their own. Their parents had not been involved.

My nephew calls it a love engagement, Noor said.

Their fathers do not object? Abdul asked.

No. Now that the Americans are here, I think it is okay.

A short time later, Arezo walked into Abdul's shop and asked if he could mend a pair of sandals. She gave no indication that she recognized him. She still wore a burqa but she had pulled the hood from her face. Her hair fell to her shoulders. She

---

[1] A card game popular in Afghanistan

would not look at Abdul directly, but he noticed a smile play across her face when he spoke.

That night, as he got ready for bed, Abdul thought about Arezo. He wondered what it would be like walking beside her in public as young men and women now did. Just thinking about it kept him awake. When he finally fell asleep, he dreamed of them on a sidewalk together, their fingers almost touching. Then he leaned into her face and pressed his mouth against hers. As their lips touched, he awoke with a jolt.

Night after night Abdul had this dream. He always woke up after he kissed her. Eventually he would fall back to sleep and dream of Arezo again until the dawn call to prayer stirred him awake. Then one night the dreams stopped. He awoke feeling her absence, his head empty of even the slightest impression of her. The next morning, Noor called. His voice broke. He sounded very upset. He asked if he could come over. Yes, of course, Abdul said. When Noor let him in, Abdul was shocked by his friend's sunken eyes, his unkempt hair and disheveled clothes. His lower lip was cut and swollen.

What's wrong? Abdul asked.

Noor did not answer. Abdul made tea and they sat on the floor of his living room. After a long moment, Noor sighed and began talking. Two days ago, he had spoken to his nephew. What is a love engagement? he had asked him. It is the most beautiful thing, his nephew replied. Why do you ask? Noor told him he had fallen in love with Arezo. Sometimes, accompanied by her father, she would stop by his house with food. Damsa would want to know you are taking care of yourself, she would tell him. Noor could not stop staring at her. He wanted to speak to her father about marriage. No, no, his nephew said. That is the old way. You must ask her yourself.

With his help, Noor composed a letter. He told Arezo he did nothing but think of her all day. When he watered the roses, when he walked to the bazaar, when he had tea. *I want you to be my wife*, he wrote. His nephew shook his head.

Be humble. Ask her if she would accept you as her husband.

Noor did as he suggested and signed his name. His nephew delivered the letter. The next day, Noor woke up and found a note from Arezo's father outside his front door.

Noor Mohammad, the letter began, *Arezo loved your wife Damsa as a sister and continues to respect you as her husband. You are like a brother to her. She cannot feel anything more for you without betraying Damsa. In the future do not talk to Arezo again. I, as her father, Haji Aziz Sakhi, insist upon this.*

Noor walked to his sister's house and beat his nephew, slapping him in the face until the boy's father threw him out. Noor stormed off to Arezo's house and pounded on the door. No one answered. He paced on the sidewalk until nightfall. Then he went home but his frustration was so great he was unable to sleep. This morning, he returned before the sun had fully risen and stood impatiently across the street. As a dry, lazy heat began spreading across the city, he saw Arezo walk outside with an empty sack and turn toward the downtown bazaar. Noor followed her. When she went down an alley, he called to her. She stopped and looked at him. The hood of her burqa was raised and he saw her face, the uncertain smile creasing her mouth. He grabbed her and kissed her. She stiffened in his arms, tried to shake loose from his grip and bit his mouth. He stumbled back and she ran, the burqa inflating like a balloon as if it might lift her into the sky.

When he finished talking, Noor stared at his tea. After a moment, he looked up at Abdul, stood, and let himself out without speaking. Abdul followed him to the door. As he watched Noor enter his house, Abdul thought of Arezo. He hoped Noor had not scared her from his dreams. He would never hurt her.

The Company I Keep

Sitting at an empty table in the Leon Café, I look up at the twirling ceiling fan and slide over to another table to avoid the dust drifting from its blades. I remove a folded copy of *El Heraldo* from beneath my right arm and order a café negro.

I read most of the paper this morning. I'll reread a few stories now, probably again skip the ones I passed over earlier. The paper is my prop: I'd rather have the *Heraldo* open to the few things that interest me than have nothing in my hands and be seen sitting by myself staring at one of three TVs, like those two older men by the open door who I suspect spend most of their day here mesmerized not by the TV but by their inability to think of anything better to do. I am like them, I know, but I don't want to be seen as like them. If I can't call it pride, I can say that I have lines I won't cross.

People in a booth behind me talk in loud voices and I listen to their laughter and wonder what's so funny, and I'm tempted to turn around and give them a look because for no good reason they annoy me. But I don't. They would look at me and I'd look at them and then I'd back off. Everything ventured, nothing gained. I read my paper and listen to the tinny noise of 1970s disco music playing from an overhead speaker.

La Botella.

You're right, a voice tells me. The voice belongs to another part of me that has no physical shape, at least none I can envision. It is me, but not me is how I'd explain it if asked. Which I won't be. I don't talk to it by muttering to myself. We converse in my head. It serves as a kind of guardian-angel-alter-ego sounding board. It responds to my thoughts and actions, providing comfort and assurance—a presence that never leaves me except when, much to my surprise, I find myself talking to someone.

A waitress refills my coffee cup and puts it on a napkin. I study the front page of the *Heraldo* and notice a story I'd not read earlier about a gang shooting. Three people dead. The news doesn't surprise me. This is Guatemala City. It's common enough to see masked police officers on the streets, their fingers on the triggers of their weapons. I navigate around them with little concern about getting caught in a crossfire. I don't have a family. If I lose my life, I'll leave no one behind. I only worry about dying slowly. What would be the point of an agonizing death when I have no one who would hold my hand, no one to weep words of love before I lose consciousness, no one to leave a lingering kiss, no one to write my obituary?

I turn to the sports page just to do it, and the waitress sits beside me.

What's she doing?

I have no idea.

The waitress props her elbows on the table and rests her chin in her hands. She stares at a TV but I can tell that, like me, she isn't paying attention. She's pretty, blond hair falls down her back, and she has a ring.

Wedding ring, I bet.

Yes, no doubt she's married.

I guess the woman is a good thirty years younger than I. Why did she sit at my table when there're plenty of empty ones? Who knows; who cares? Just one of those things. I got my spot. I sit at this table every time I come in. Other people tend to sit near the center of the café, where sunlight streaming through the open door settles like an onshore beacon pointing the way to a shelf of plastic-wrapped sandwiches. I go back to my paper. But the woman disturbs me. Of all the places she could choose to sit, she sat with me. Her perfume fills my head. I glance at her until her presence, like the unsteady fan above my head, no longer throws me off and after a few more seconds, I no longer notice her, no longer allow my imagination to meander toward fantastical expectations. Then for no good reason I can think of, she speaks to me.

Do you come here often?

I put the paper aside. She looks directly at me, turns away for a bit, then faces me again, and waits.

Yes and no. Sometimes. I guess I do, come to think of it. Yes.

I'm sorry. I'm on break. Do you want to be alone?

I shrug. This is a surprise. I don't want to be rude.

You're fine.

We look at each other without speaking. That was that. I turn back to my paper. She resumes looking at the TV. I should have told her I do mind. I already miss her.

Some nights, a friend might call me and suggest we see a movie. I've lived alone so long now that the very notion of doing something in the evening exhausts me. But then the melancholy passes, replaced by a surge of energy and I say, Yes, let's see a movie! with the enthusiasm of a child too long cooped up. The idea of going out and breaking my solo routine has me rushing about my apartment as if I were late for an appointment. I am unable to focus, unable to sit down until I dash out to meet my friend.

Afterward, when I return home, I can't sleep. Possibilities of other things I might do, should do, and of other people I might call fill my mind, but as I eventually settle between sleep and wakefulness, I know I will return to my routine—days and weeks without interruption—a routine that by its very nature allows me the certainty of certainty. My good feelings about the evening turning into a simmering resentment of the interlude that disrupted my evening and opened my eyes to what had been missing from my life, until enough days have passed that I can view my outing as an aberration. I might even ask myself if I'd left my apartment at all or only imagined it.

The waitress brings back memories of Mariana. A once-dormant volcano of feeling rising up from a great depth. Mariana. Engaged and then we weren't. When we attempted to reconcile, we sat silently in a counselor's office, beside each other but apart. It felt like I was watching a movie, viewing our life together on the screen of my memory, transfixed like a witness to a car wreck, marveling at the velocity of our unraveling. The years we'd spent together vanished just like that, as if we'd never existed as a couple. Even after we broke up, I litigated in my mind all the ways I believed she'd wronged me, until I had successfully prosecuted my point of view. I became obsessed with my arguments, muttering and repeating them daily until enough time had passed that I thought Mariana no longer mattered. My loss became a kind of companion, replacing her and accompanying me through the years like a dutiful spouse.

We wanted kids, the waitress says.

Sorry? I say. What's that?

We wanted kids, or my husband did, and I did too, of course, and he wanted them to go to a private school away from the gangs, and Guatemala City has good private schools.

I see.

I said, 'Well, okay,' and got pregnant and I'm so glad I did. I mean it's amazing. He's a wonderful little boy.

How old?

Two.

A handful, no? Yes?

My husband is very happy. And so am I of course.

Congratulations.

She doesn't respond. The silence drifts between us again until I can almost convince myself she's not sitting beside me, that we'd never exchanged a word, our chance encounter a figment of my imagination. Then she speaks again.

And I get to stay at home. I had a job but now I have to stay at home. Fernando doesn't want his son taken to daycare. Strangers taking care of his kid? He said, no way. So, I stopped working and, well, I stay at home. I think he's right. About day care, I mean.

What did you do?

Sales. You?

Maintenance.

Oh, she says.

Like a janitor.

Yes. I don't call it that.

Of course not. Maintenance. It's more professional.

You have to know what you're doing. It's more than pushing a broom.

Of course.

She doesn't believe me. At one time, I enjoyed my work. Maybe because I saw the results so fast. Mop the floor, and it's clean and shiny in a matter of minutes. I liked that. Liked the pride of rubbing my floors with a cotton ball to show my patrón how spotless I kept them. But it didn't take long for me to see mine was a occupation that enjoyed little respect. You need to do something else, Mariana would tell me, and my friends too. You can't just mop floors the rest of your life. After Mariana and I ended our engagement, I applied the word "just" to about everything I did. I'm just going to work. I'm just getting the mail. I'm just going to the store. The number of insignificant tasks that had once given me pleasure left me amazed by their blandness, their shallowness. I adopted an attitude of indifference to what I had once enjoyed doing until I felt as indifferent about my work as everyone else. I woke up each morning feeling my life ease into a kind of inertia, absent of all ambition to do things only because they had to be done.

It's a job, I say.

I go back to my paper.

Do you have children?

Yes, I say.

She raises her eyebrows and leans in and places a hand on my arm.

Well? she demands. What? Boys? Girls? Names?

Girl. Camila.

Camila. I like that. Do you like being a parent? I mean did you have any doubts?

I feel a tiny zepher from the ceiling fan touch the spot where she has clasped my arm. I like the warm, light pressure of it.

I like the idea of her hand remaining on my arm. I imagine gripping her fingers. I imagine walking out with her.

No, I had no doubts at all, I say. I was grateful.

It was not me but Mariana who had a daughter. She married someone else, and they had a girl they named Camila. A mutual friend told me the news. She should've married me and had children. Camila was my daughter. Or at least should've been.

And your son? I ask. His name?

Fernando. Like his father.

Of course. A strong name.

My husband thinks so. He wants another baby. And so do I, of course. How old is Camila?

I do the math. Mariana and I were twenty-eight at the time of our engagement. Give or take a couple of years, we probably would've started having kids at thirty or so. I'm sixty now. Thirty.

Does she have kids?

Not yet.

I think I would've been a fine father, a fine husband. No better and no worse than most men. I'll never know, so I've no reason to think otherwise.

My mother is watching him.

Your mother?

Yes. Little Fernando. She's watching him today.

Oh, I see. Well, that's nice. A bit of a break for you.

She'll have him for two days. I think it's important he has a chance to bond with her.

And you have a chance to be alone with your husband.

Fernando works a lot. I don't know how much we'll see each other. She offers a tight smile. All these years later, I can recall each argument, each disagreement I had with Mariana almost word for word, except now I understand that they weren't quarrels so much as declarations. Each of us would approach our differences by expecting the other to concede. Neither of us would. We pummeled each other with our anger until we were left gasping and so exhausted that words failed us. She'd storm out the door, but the next morning she'd return and we'd go to bed and hold one another without passion but rather with the comfort of two people who, despite our differences, knew each other too well to let go. I try to remember when we did let go but I can't. Not a specific moment. She left many times. One day the shouting stopped because she stopped coming back.

Excuse me, the waitress says.

She stands and walks behind the counter to the cash register.

That was unexpected.

Yes, it was.

And now here we are again.

Yes.

Long shadows stretch across the pale walls. The two old men who had been watching fútbol have left. Slumped in his chair, the Tarot card reader sleeps, his cards stacked crookedly on the table. The waitress comes from around the counter and moves toward me. She smiles. My heart fills with possibilities. She gives me a receipt.

I'm getting off now. If you want another coffee, you can start a new tab with the next girl.

The Wait

The two men lean against the side of their pickup and consider the distant figure ahead. He stands in the middle of the road and appears to be wearing a turban and a salwaar kameez. More important than his clothing, the men wonder if what the man holds in his hands is a gun or a heavy stick. If he's a shepherd, it may be a stick to prod sheep, but they see no farm animals. Neither of them has binoculars.

It's a stick, one of the men, an American aid worker, says. Too thin to be an AK.

The other man, the American's Afghan driver, shrugs noncommittally. Annoyed, the American folds his arms across his chest. He expected affirmation. He likes to throw out names, abbreviations. AK, short for AK-47. Makes him feel knowledgeable and therefore superior. Like he's been around, and he expects others to view his "expertise" with deference. He squints, imagines this gives him an aged and even more experienced look; but the silence of the Afghan, who has survived the Soviet invasion, the civil wars that followed, the Taliban, and now the Americans, makes him feel small.

The Afghan and the American have stopped on this stretch of dusty mountain road off Highway 1 between Kabul and Ghazni because their vehicle overheated. Rock cliffs jut overhead, and dust-covered scrub twist out from between boulders. Buzzards circle in the empty sky and somewhere far off dogs bark and then stop and start again. In a valley below, mud huts stand scattered on bare ground. Another mile or two, the American thinks, and they would have been headed downhill and all would have been well. But once the engine began to overheat, the Afghan, without seeking his permission, pulled over. After they'd rolled to a stop, the Afghan got out, opened the hood and unscrewed the radiator cap with a towel. He jerked back to avoid burning his face as water geysered above his head, then looked upward and closed his eyes against a warm, descending mist before leaning against the pickup still holding the radiator cap. That's when he noticed the man in the road watching them. The Afghan said nothing but pointed, drawing the American's attention to the lone figure.

You know the expression, farmer by day, Taliban by night, the American says. What do you think? It's getting late.

The Afghan doesn't respond. It had been the American's idea to drive from Kabul to Ghazni to visit an NGO that specialized in irrigation projects. As the Afghan waited by the car, the American followed the NGO's director to a field where rows of wheat withered under the sun, strangled in cracked earth, dampened by stooped, barefoot men futilely tossing water from plastic buckets. The irrigation system for the field had broken down, the director explained. He wasn't sure what happened. He'd put in a request for repairs to his home office and was waiting for a response.

I return home to Portland in a week, the director said.

Not your problem.

Not my problem.

In Kabul at his own NGO, We Are the World, the American saw himself as a despot ruling a deteriorating empire, propped up by the fiscal department of the agency's Des Moines head-quarters. Someone he'd never met financed education projects in the belief that more schools at some point would enhance the lives of children in Kabul province to such an extent that eventually the agency would no longer be needed. The American, however, knows that the Afghans who come to him for food, water, and a small monthly allowance to support their families while their children are in school instead of working in the fields beside their parents don't look at him as a temporary provider. They've grown accustomed to living off his largesse, while they wait week after week for sappers to clear the land-mines in the desolate fields so the hundreds of pounds of seed locked securely in a shed can be put to use.

Wiping sweat from his forehead, the American recalls a trip he took to Jalalabad to tour education projects similar to his. Before he got back to Kabul, he stopped at an American military base to apprise its commanders of his work. He had just been escorted through the gate when militants began shelling. A soldier wrapped his arms around him and hustled him to a concrete bunker crowded with other soldiers. The shells went wide and the soldiers laughed at the militants' inefficiency, but later the American believed he had experienced a defin-ing moment. At least he hoped so. He wanted to experience something—he didn't know what exactly—that would result in distinguishing him from everyone he knew. He wanted to be defined by something far removed from their understanding.

For days after the mortar attack, the American wondered if he'd experience post-traumatic stress disorder. He waited for a sign. He lay awake at night, waiting. In the morning, he examined his dreams for something frightening and haunting. After a few weeks, he acknowledged he felt nothing out of the ordinary, concluding that the experience had been little more than an interruption to his routine. Back in Kabul, he resumed sitting behind his desk, no different from hundreds of other people who sit behind desks, whether here or in Iowa.

Look, the American says, pointing.

The Afghan turns his head and both men watch the man in the road raise a hand to the side of his head. Was he talking into a cell phone? Calling someone? Who?

Is there another road? the American asks. Can we just take a different route and avoid him?

The American steps away from the car and sits on a boulder in the shade at the base of an austere hill. He doesn't know his driver well. He's seen him in the compound, hanging around with other nationals. Always unfailingly polite, but a man who spoke little. On their way to Ghazni, the American asked about his family, even though he'd never met any families of the national staff and really didn't care about them. Projects were his responsibility, not people. He gave families food, water, a cash allowance. He paid his staff, and there his responsibility ended.

The American found the Afghan's silence disturbing. He knew what people wanted from him in his office, but outside of it he found the locals enigmatic. He wondered about the Afghan's loyalties. He knew this man had lost his family in fighting between U.S. forces and the Taliban, but he did not seem angry or bitter. He expressed his grief in a resigned fatalism: If they take my life, they can take nothing more.

The engine is still hot, the American says, touching the radiator with a light tap. We can't sit here all day.

The Afghan stares at the ground.

Do something, the American tells him.

I will talk to this man, the Afghan says.

He turns and starts walking up the road, his sandaled feet scuffing the loose stones in his path. Watching him, the American feels both fear and a kind of giddy liberation. He sees himself seated behind his desk and feels an indescribable loneliness within his exultation.

He observes the Afghan approach the man. Both shimmer in enveloping heat waves, as if they had entered another dimension. The American closes his eyes. He sits half swooning in the stifling air until he hears, or imagines, a sharp crack and lurches with surprise. The fear and thrill that jerks through him almost instantly becomes subsumed into the vacancy of his isolation. He doesn't know what to feel. What had he heard, if anything? He waits without moving, without opening his eyes.

The Guest

Viraj was sitting in a room behind the motel reception counter, eating a bowl of bhaat with his fingers when the desk bell chimed. He set the bowl down and opened the door. A man in a heavy green coat stood at the counter. His pale blue jeans hung off his waist and he tugged them up. He had a wide, bearded face and smiled easily, but Viraj thought his eyes looked tired. A small, leashed brown dog stood beside him and sniffed the floor. The man whistled a high, sharp note, and the dog looked at him, ears perked, and sat.

May I help you? Viraj asked.

Do you have a room for the night?

Yes, Viraj said.

Do you allow pets?

Yes.

Okay.

I'll need to see your ID and credit card, Viraj said. The man reached into a pocket and withdrew a worn leather wallet held together by duct tape. Opening the wallet, he slid his driver's license and a Visa card under a plexiglass sneeze guard that Viraj installed at the start of the coronavirus pandemic. Is your dog a pet, or do you have him for emotional support?

What do you mean?

If it's for emotional support, I won't charge you a deposit.

I was in Afghanistan, the man said.

I see, Viraj said after a moment. Army?

No, I was a contractor. But sometimes there wasn't a difference.

Something in the tone of the man's voice made Viraj uneasy, or perhaps he just felt bad for him. He didn't know.

I'm sorry, he said.

He examined the driver's license. *Lubic, John Donald. Colorado.* He entered the credit card number into a computer.

Where are you from? the man asked.

Viraj glanced at him but didn't answer. Was he one of those America First people? Around town he had begun seeing American Owned signs in the windows of other motels. Some guests had come into his motel only to leave when they saw him behind the counter. He didn't feel anger as much as contempt. How ignorant some of these Americans are! he thought. He was just an infant when his father, frustrated with the low salary he earned as a history teacher in Hyderabad, India, brought Viraj and his mother here to McAllen, Texas, near the Mexico border. They moved in with his father's older brother, Madhav, who operated a Motel 6. With his contacts, he helped Viraj's father become a manager at the Grand Star, a motel just two blocks away. The family made a home of two rooms on the first floor where they still lived. Viraj's father always wore a dhoti and his mother wrapped herself in a sari, and they continued to speak Hindi to each other and to Viraj but he would answer them in English. After school, Viraj helped his mother clean rooms. He collected bedding and damp towels, and carried them to a laundry room, sometimes tripping on blankets trailing on the ground. His father worked the front desk. In those days, Viraj thought of the Grand Star as a warren of mysterious rooms within which anything was possible.

Are you from India? the man asked.

Yes, I am, Viraj said.

He pushed the driver's license and credit card under the sneeze guard. The man put them in his wallet.

How long have you lived here?

Since I was very small.

When he was a senior in high school, Viraj's father suffered a stroke. Viraj began filling in for him and managing the motel with his mother. As the months passed, the hopes for his father's full recovery faded. Now the family patriarch spent his days in a wheelchair staring out at the parking lot behind the motel, and Viraj's mother had to help him eat. He could speak only a few words. Viraj thought his parents would move back in with Uncle Madhav so he could continue with school. However, Madhav told him this was not possible. It is your job as a son to care for them, not mine, he said. Viraj considered attending college at night but too many guests arrived in the evenings for him to take time off. He considered other options but the routine of managing the day-to-day operations of the motel soon became as much a part of his life as breathing. The plans he had made for school assumed the vagueness of dreams he had difficulty remembering. His mother told him that when he had a family he could fulfill his ambitions through his children, as she and his father had hoped to do with him. After Viraj turned eighteen, Uncle Madhav introduced him to Meera, the daughter of an Indian friend. They married and Viraj brought his new wife to the motel where they lived in a room next to his parents. She helped his mother clean after guests had checked out. Viraj and Meera tried to have children but she was unable to conceive. He told her it was God's will and she agreed but he knew she felt ashamed. She told him he was wasting his time with her. He took her to a doctor who prescribed antidepressants. She began spending more time away from the motel—where she didn't say, and Viraj didn't ask. Her unhappiness was another trial. He didn't know what to say without burdening himself further so he said nothing. When she didn't come back one night, he wondered if she was at peace and if so, how she had found it.

I stopped in India on a layover and spent about twenty-four hours in New Delhi, the man said. Not enough time at all to see it.

In New Delhi, no, it would not be, Viraj said.

Do you go back and visit?

No. I am the manager here now and work all the time. He printed a receipt for the room and asked the man to review and sign it and to write the make, model, and license plate number of his car in a box next to his signature. He looked out the glass front doors at the heavy, gray sky and saw his mother pulling weeds from a pot that had once held geraniums. Uncle Madhay had scolded him for not replacing the dead flowers. Remove the pots, he told him, or plant something. What would your father think? Viraj agreed but did nothing. He doubted his father would care at this point so what did it matter? Viraj checked-in guests. Let his mother worry about the pots. Across the street, cars pulled into the Waffle House. Next door, people streamed in and out of a Shell convenience store. A woman and a boy walked from sunlight into shade. On slow days like today, Viraj read books about ancient India that belonged to his father. His mother would check on him and he would feel her beside him peering over his shoulder as he read. He heard his father's labored breathing in the other room. I am fine, mother, he would tell her. After she left, he continued to read until his eyes grew tired. Putting the book down, he stared into space. Sometimes, he would go through his father's closet, change into a dhoti and then return to his chair. He imagined being a physician in the time of the Gupta dynasty, when advances in medicine helped create India's golden age. In another life, Viraj thought, he might have worked with the celebrated fifth-century physician and surgeon Sushruta. In another life he might have been him. Instead, he had this life. You're in room 201, around to the back, Viraj told the man.

The man nodded, leaned down and patted the dog's head. Then he straightened up and waited while Viraj put a plastic card key in an envelope.

Thank you, he said.

He tugged on the leash and the dog stood.

Did you know that from the Middle Ages to around 1750 some of eastern Afghanistan was recognized as being a part of India? Viraj asked.

No, I didn't.

It was, Viraj said. There was an Afghan who died in 1576 on behalf of an Indian king fighting the Mughal Empire. His name was Hakim Khan Sur.

I didn't know that either, the man said.

He turned to leave. The dog walked beside him, its nails clicking on the white tile floor. Viraj watched them get into a dented Ford Explorer checkered with mud, and drive toward the rear of the motel. He looked out the door for a long moment. Then he took a pen and wrote Hakim Khan Sur on a Post-it. He put the pen down and walked around to the man's room. The dog barked when he knocked, and the man opened the door without removing the chain lock. Viraj noticed a green duffle bag on the floor and a bottle of water and a vial of pills on the night table. The dog sat bolt upright beside the man and growled. Viraj stepped back. He offered the man the Post-it.

I wrote down the name of the Afghan who diedfighting the Mughals, he said. Hakim Khan Sur.

The man looked at it and Viraj had the impression he didn't remember their conversation.

Hakim Khan Sur, he repeated. In case you want to Google him. You can tell me when you check out what you have learned.

Thank you.

I live here with my mother and father, Viraj said. I like to read history books about India.

I appreciate your trouble, the man said.

He folded the Post-it.

Google him. You will see I come from a great country.

The man stared at Viraj.

He was a very important person.

The man nodded. Viraj walked away. He had not gone far when the man shouted, I can't help you. Viraj paused but didn't reply or look back. He felt the man staring at him. He had been to Afghanistan. Viraj knew about Hakim Khan Sur. He thought that was interesting. He had assumed the guest would think so too, and would see they had something in common. Now, he felt foolish. He knew he would not see him in the morning. Viraj returned to his station behind the counter. He wondered if he should read or just go to bed. He knew all there was to know about the golden age of ancient India. He often had dreams of that time as if he had lived in the fifth century, and he would remember them the next morning. He didn't know if that was a good thing. Maybe he read too much. Maybe this evening he would just sit with his mother and father and clear his mind, accept the silence as his own, captive to the slow pace of a quiet night.

Fledgling

Flo points out the window.

There. What's that?

I'm in the kitchen; she's in the living room. I lean back in my chair and look through the doorway that connects the two rooms, past Flo, and out the window. It's one of those hazy San Francisco days when I feel like I'm looking at everything through frosted glass.

Fuck if I know, I tell Flo.

Nice language, Hank.

Language, shmanguage. Be offended. She's been drinking. I don't know how much, but I smell it on her breath. Not stumble drunk drinking, she never does that, but drinking. Stops off somewhere after work. Maybe with coworkers or by herself. I don't know. The point is she's a little buzzed and maybe not seeing so straight. I can't tell what the hell she's looking at. It moves a little. Maybe a chipmunk. Or a mole in the grass. Not a mole. That would be too much like a mouse. Flo would lose it. I don't know what it is. Too far away to tell. Do I care what's out there? Now that's the question that needs to be asked. Why would I care?

I go back to reading one last job posting on Craigslist: We are looking to expand our Brickell Avenue cleaning business. We are looking for a part time/full time worker who can drive. You will clean 2-4 homes per day. Hours are 8:30am-4pm, Monday through Friday and some Saturdays and possible evenings.

We can give you 10-20 hours a week, minimum wage. Then I shut the computer. I used to work at Target. Now I don't. Enough said.

Flo has a daughter from a guy she divorced five years ago. Her name's Cathy. She's fourteen. She wanders into the kitchen listening to music on her phone, opens the fridge for a Coke. Cathy's on the Mission Community Center's girls soccer team, The Tigers. She's wearing her soccer uniform. Blue jersey, white shorts, blue and white socks. She has a seven o'clock game tonight and every Wednesday for the next eight weeks. I'd rather not go. I don't care about soccer. But since I'm living with Flo in her house and Cathy's her kid, I don't have a choice, do I? My one trump card is she knows I know she's a drinker. I don't hold that against her, but it pisses her off. Piss her off enough and she won't want me around and I may get out of it.

I want to see what it is, Flo says of the thing outside. She speaks slowly and carefully like she doesn't want to slur her words around Cathy.

What? Cathy says.

I'm about to explain that her mom saw something in the yard, but Cathy skips off to her room jamming to whatever music she's listening to without waiting for an answer.

Flo walks out the front door and crosses the yard to the spot where the newspaper lands every morning just off the drive-way. Neither of them really reads the paper. I don't understand why they get it. I watch Flo, see our neighbor Jeff parking his pickup across the street. He's a Marine. He deploys to Iraq in the next week or two, his second time. He's got on tan shorts and a green polo shirt that clings to him so tight he looks like he'll bust out of it any second. He tosses a duffel from the pickup, unzips it, and begins rifling through it. He takes out some rope and a harness. I don't get it. Jeff's going to Iraq, and tonight I'm attending a girls soccer game. How's that happen?

About a month ago, a little more maybe, I was out with two guys I had worked with at Target, Patrick and Alan. We were in the Comeback Club. They picked it. The drinks are cheap. Hookers hustle the streets, and they like to watch them do their thing. They don't know I'm a recovering alcoholic, that I used to sleep on these streets. After I got into recovery, I worked at detox not far from here. It was a good job. I got hired right after I graduated from a forty-five day program, but after a while I needed another kind of job. It was just too weird putting guys I used to drink with on the street into detox. They'd give me shit like I'd forgotten where I'd come from. Hey, man, I'd tell them, I stopped, that's all. I'm the same guy. But they wouldn't hear it. Sometimes after work I played pinochle with them in the drop-in, but they still gave me crap. Oh, you think you're better than us, Hank, Mr. Sobriety. They were always trying to get me to drink with them. I resented that. I mean, c'mon. Why bring me down to your level? Then I'd get crap again about how I thought I was high and mighty. I had to remind myself that when I was drinking I was no different, but all the same it got on my nerves. Six months ago, I applied at Walmart and Target. Target called and I quit Fresh Start.

Patrick and Alan don't know I'm an alcoholic. You tell people you're in recovery and they get all squirrely, like they got to be real careful around you. Man, I'm not a piece of china. Drink in front of me, do whatever, I don't care. I got the problem, not you. Or maybe they do, and that's the real problem. That's what's going on with Flo. I should talk to her but it will just turn into a shouting match. I don't want problems. I don't need the stress. I've got stress. I don't need more. Instead, I do what she does: I go out. I can't live in a cave. I got to have some friends. So when Patrick ordered a round of beers, I said I'd pass. Got an upset stomach. I asked for a Coke. I'll have your beer too, Patrick said, and laughed. I hope it's not gas. I don't need you farting. He laughed again. He didn't give a shit. That's how I like it.

As we waited for our drinks, rain started coming down hard, real hard, enough water for Noah to do a test run of the ark. I could just hear it through the thick windows of the bar, kind of faint but I heard its steady drumming. A bus shelter stood empty across the street. Nothing moved except soaking wet hookers. Hustling suits from the financial district, I bet, getting their freak on, cars lined up two to three deep.

That night was the twentieth anniversary of 9/11. Patrick was in the Army in the Gulf War. Said he still dreams of burning oil wells. But that was before 9/11, he said. No one was calling him a hero.

So what do you think, I said. Did 9/11 change your life?

Patrick and Alan didn't say anything at first. I let them think about it. I listened to an old man playing a video game behind him. The brother was rocking. I heard the pling, pling, pling of his scores like something rushing up on me.

Traffic was bad the night of 9/11 and some neighborhoods had gas lines, Patrick said.

Yeah, but that was that night, I said. How has your life changed since then?

Look at airport security," Alan said. You hear on the radio that it's a bitch to fly now.

Yeah, I said, but if you don't fly, how's your life changed?

Alan shrugged, threw up his hands like what do you want from me? He was coming off a weeks-long fantasy about a redhead and was in a shitty mood. He installs countertops. She was one of his customers in Walnut Creek. Alan said she had an ass that wouldn't quit. Said when she spoke his name, she had enough sugar in her voice to melt his gums. Alan did a lot of discount work for her but finally realized that beyond dreaming he never would come close to that ass.

What about fighting terrorism? Alan said. That's all 9/11, dude.

You're not getting it, I said. I'm not fighting terrorists. I don't know anyone in the Middle East or wherever. Do you, Patrick?

No, not really.

What about you? Alan said to me. How's your life changed?

A lot in some ways and not in others, I said.

What's that mean? Patrick said.

I don't know, man. I expected more. Like a change as big as those buildings coming down.

And then, wouldn't you know it, a week later something more did happen. I got laid off.

It's a baby bird, Flo shouts at me.

She walks into the garage, weaving a little, and comes out wearing a pair of gardening gloves. Bending over, she scoops up the bird and holds it out in her hands for me to see. It looks like a speck of gray fluff. I get up and open the living room window and lean out. It's a baby bird, alright, a fledgling. That's what it's actually called, a fledgling. I know. My mother called them that. It means almost old enough to fly.

Flo bends down and lets the bird go on the lawn. Its head bobs and it opens its beak like it wants to scream. I watch it leap, flapping its small wings until it settles between two exposed tree roots. Turning toward the sky, I see only haze; no sign of its mother circling, the way birds are supposed to do, I guess, when a fledgling falls from the nest.

I look back at Flo. She's staring at Jeff. He's taking a chain saw from the back of his truck. He's handy that way. Cutting wood for his fireplace, maintaining the yard, fixing shit. Flo has a drawer full of tools. Screwdrivers and hammers and pliers and whatnot. She patches holes in the walls, puts up wallpaper, paints. She even mows the lawn. I clean and mop the bathrooms, vacuum the house. That's what I do. My contribution, so to speak.

Flo smooths her blouse and skirt, shimmies a little to get rid of any remaining wrinkles. She's a loan processor at Wells Fargo Bank and dresses up for work. She brushes her hair back from her face, and calls to Jeff, asks him to come over for a second. He sets the saw down and walks toward her.

It's called a fledgling, I say, watching Jeff approach. Must have fallen out of its nest.

Jeff moves like his chest is shoving away invisible objects, like Moses has nothing on him when it comes to parting waters. His legs eat up the street. Snap of a finger and like that he's standing beside Flo. She smiles and takes a deep breath and her chest rises. She breathes Jeff in. She points at the bird.

What should we do? Flo asks him.

Jeff considers it for a moment staring at the ground. I wonder if he knows she's a little buzzed.

Leave it alone, he says. It's wild. Its mother will find it, or she won't.

We can feed it, I say.

I wouldn't bother, Jeff says. It's too little for bird seed.

Flo looks at him and nods and says, I agree with Jeff.

I'm thinking she's thinking Jeff knows about birds because he's good around the yard. Because he knows how to use power tools. Because he's going to Iraq.

Okay, but here's the thing, when I was growing up, birds would slam into the living room window all the time. I don't know if they did that at Jeff's house when he was a kid, but they sure did it at ours. If they didn't break their necks and drop dead, me and my mom would put a wire cage over them to protect them from stray cats until their brains stopped rattling and they could fly again. If they were little like this one, we'd soak bread in warm milk and dribble it into their mouths until a park ranger or someone who knew about wild animals would drive over and take the bird to a nature sanctuary. It's not all about Jeff is what I'm thinking. I know some things too.

You'll have to tell Cathy not to touch it, I tell Flo. It's not a toy.

I think she's old enough to know it's not a toy, she snaps.

I look at Jeff, but he doesn't offer me any support. He stays out of it. I don't have children, that's part of the problem. The idea that a guy like me, someone with no kids, could criticize or imply criticism of Flo's daughter, a daughter she has raised alone since her divorce, is something Flo can't tolerate, especially when she's had a few.

Jeff probably could get away with it because he has a kid. A boy. Flo says his ex-wife complains that he's too tough on him. That even though the boy turned eighteen last month, Jeff still expects him home before midnight on the weekends. I'd go further. I'd say, You're not only eighteen, you're out of the frickin' house. But he's Jeff's kid, not mine. And Cathy is Flo's kid, not mine, either.

She could be your stepdaughter if we married, Flo used to say whenever I left myself open for her to take a shot. Then she stopped. She got the message.

I don't want to marry Flo. I didn't move in with her to get married. I just thought it was time to do more than work and sit at home alone watching TV and go out with Patrick and Alan. I didn't know what to do with myself. When I was working in detox, everyone knew me. I was Hank from Fresh Start. I'm not that now. I'm not even working. I go by the detox sometimes and say hello to Katie but I always seem to catch her when she's busy. Good to see you, Hank, she says. Maybe another time.

I met Flo three months ago on my way to work at Target. She was standing at my bus stop. Some change had spilled from her purse and I helped her pick it up. She thanked me. I saw her there again the next day and the day after that. We went from, Good morning to What's your name?

I'm Flo.

I'm Hank.

We shook hands and chit-chatted about the weather and work. She told me she lived in Balboa Park. We sized each other up and liked what we saw. We exchanged phone numbers and started going out. I didn't tell her I was in recovery. Maybe she'd think I was weak. Some people do. Not everyone believes alcoholism is a disease. I figured I wouldn't score points telling her. I said I had damaged my liver from a bout of hepatitis and couldn't drink. Rigorous honesty out the window, but she didn't ask questions and I got in her pants. After a few more weeks, I moved in with her. Really, it was that simple. I thought, This'll be different.

I got to get going, Jeff says. I have to take care of a dead tree in my yard and a whole bunch of other chores before I go.

He doesn't say where he's going, doesn't say: Before I deploy again to Iraq. He knows me and Flo and everyone else knows. Our street has gotten very patriotic. Small flags limp from the spray of water sprinklers line the edges of yards, and it seems that everyone but me wears a yellow wristband and thanks Jeff for his service. Jeff barely notices. He treats all the fuss as his due. He's a fucking Marine. He considers people walking their dogs past his house like a military review.

Flo smiles, raises a hand, and wiggles her fingers goodbye. Jeff nods, and without another word goes back to his house with that walk of his. Flo watches him pick up the chain saw. I flinch at the blast of noise it makes. Jeff raises the saw above his head and begins taking off a thick branch from a leafless tree in his front yard. I watch the branch dip and break with a sharp crack and bounce off the ground. Jeff shuts off the saw, walks around the fallen branch in a kind of crouch as if he expects it to jump up and throw down on him. Then he starts the saw again. I turn back to the bird.

Here's what I know: Adult birds regurgitate partially digested food into the mouths of their chicks. That's how they eat. That's how they grow. That's why my mother softened the bread in milk. I don't know where she learned that but that's what she did. Jeff has a point, an adult bird might find the fledge. I get that. But I have a point too. The thing is, I know people listen to Jeff. He is who he is, and I'm who I am.

Maybe I should not have moved it, Flo says of the bird.

You didn't move it very much, I tell her. We can fix it.

I put a hand on her shoulder. I feel the thin material of her blouse and her skin and bone beneath it. I imagine the two of us as a statue you might see in a park by a fountain surrounded by trees. We'd be part of some well-tended, really green land-scape where nothing is out of place. Two people carved from stone with permanent smiles on our faces staring down at a tiny bird that is looking up at us waiting for me and Flo to put it back in its nest.

How do you "fix" a bird? Flo snaps. You don't fix birds.

I meant save it.

My hand slips from her shoulder. She gets bitchy when she's high. I go into the garage and find a hamster cage that had belonged to Cathy before she lost interest in hamsters. I take out the bottom tray and walk back to the bird and set the cage over it. It shifts its weight and lifts its wings but otherwise doesn't move.

You're scaring it, Flo says.

I'm protecting it, I say.

Flo looks at her watch.

Cathy's soccer game starts soon, she says.

I don't know who would schedule games for Wednesday nights, I say. People are tired after work. They don't want to watch a girls soccer game at seven o'clock at night. They've had a long enough day already. They have to get up the next day and work.

What are you complaining about? You're not even working, Flo says.

Doesn't mean I'm not looking, I say. Looking is a job in itself.

See if you can get it to pay as well.

She's got a point. I'm not looking that hard. I don't have that get-up-and-go, job-hunting spark. I quit drinking, got off the streets, worked at Fresh Start, got hired at Target, and then got laid off. That's enough striving for one lifetime. I'm spent. I'm no Marine like Jeff, I admit that, but I'm no pussy. I've slept in doorways and under trees. That's not going to war, but it's something to survive that. I need to take some sort of vocational classes at night is what I'm thinking. Something to give me some want-to. They offer them at Fresh Start. That's new since I left. The director made a big thing of it when Target hired me. How I was an example that Fresh Start didn't have to be the end of the road but a springboard to better things. "We hire you out of halfway houses, provide you with a work history. Where you go from there is up to you. Who knows what will happen to Hank, how far he'll go."

This is what happened, I'd tell him now. Right here.

Target gave me the boot three weeks ago. You're in good company, I was told. We're letting a lot of great people go we hate to lose. You're in good company. That was supposed to make me feel better I suppose, but what I'm feeling now is taking some getting used to. No more talking about the mer-chandise. "Merch" everyone called it. The shorthand conveyed our knowledge of the job. Merch. When will I ever say that again? To tell the truth, I don't think I ever will. I wish I knew how I feel about all this. I'm feeling but I'm not sure what. I can't bring myself to toss my Target name tag. Why not? I don't have an answer for that. I need time to myself is all.

Before I got laid off, I would sometimes call in sick so I could be alone in Flo's house while she was at work and Cathy was in school. I'd walk around the living room, study, dining room, and two bedrooms. Run my bare feet over the smooth hardwood floors, my hands over the faded furniture, the pictures on the walls. I liked the lived-in feel of the house, the sense of place. The fullness of it, the way it breathes. I walked upstairs to me and Flo's bedroom, set my phone on the toilet across from the shower and clicked on Pornhub. I scrolled down to "blond blowjob," clicked twice and got in the shower. I left the shower curtain open. The bathroom steamed and I soaped up and watched this blonde deepthroating this guy who had shaved his pubes. I stroked myself thinking of her going down on me with her tongue and that mouth and not saying a word until my shit was hard as a log and my legs were shaking and just when I thought I'd burst, I came like a stallion.

I can't remember the last time Flo and I screwed with any conviction. We rocked it a lot at first. She liked to drink. Before I moved in, when we went out, she'd have a beer, no big deal. But living with her, I noticed she'd come home from work more often than not smelling of booze. She wasn't wrecked, but some nights it was obvious she'd had more than a few. Wrapping her arms around me, she'd press her mouth against mine and I'd taste what she'd been drinking, felt it on my tongue and down my throat. Sometimes, I enjoyed it like a contact high, and I knew where that could lead. One night, I pushed her away and told her not to kiss me when she'd been drinking.

I don't drink, she said.

You drink.

You say it like I have a problem.

No, I didn't mean it that way.

What's wrong with you?

Nothing. Nothing is wrong with me. I just don't want you to kiss me drunk.

I'm not drunk.

Then whatever it is you are, don't kiss me.

I won't kiss you. I won't touch you.

Fine, I said.

Now that I'm thinking about it, I guess it's sort of my fault things went south between us. I should have kept my mouth shut. Or told her I was in recovery. It was easier to say, Don't kiss me. In bed that night we laid together like mummies. Then she apologized and said she wouldn't drink if it upset me, and I apologized too, and we fucked but it wasn't like before. I knew she'd drink again. I should leave her but I don't want to deal with finding a place until I have a job so I'm coasting. There's always something.

After I finished jerking off, I slouched under the shower and breathed deeply until my breathing slowed and I felt totally empty and desired nothing but to stand under the water. The blond understood. She was still polishing the guy's knob when I shut off the water. She didn't look up to ask if I felt better. She didn't look at me at all but just concentrated on what she was doing. Up and down with her head, one, two, one, two. I reached for a towel and turned off the phone. It made a zip sound and then went blank, and she was gone, bye-bye, just like that.

I stood there and didn't move. The bathroom faucet dripped. I listened to the slow plunk … plunk … plunk of the water and realized I could live alone in Flo's house but not feel alone because it felt so lived-in. But then by late afternoon Flo and Cathy would come home and that would be the end of that.

Leaving Flo outside, I go into the kitchen and take a piece of white bread from the loaf on top of the refrigerator and drop it on the counter. Flo comes in behind me and runs upstairs to change.

You ready? she shouts to Cathy.

I warm a bowl of milk in the microwave and dribble it on my wrist. It's good, not too hot. I break the bread into small pieces and drop it in the milk. Squeezing the bread with my fingers, I test its softness. Spongy but not falling apart. Just right.

Taking the bowl in both hands, I walk back outside through the garage. I stop to get the gloves Flo wore when she picked up the bird and notice Jeff stacking the wood he's cut beside his garage. Jeff wipes an arm against his face smearing dirt across his forehead. He starts the saw again and approaches the tree. I put on the gloves.

What I'll do is: I'll grip the bird in such a way that its head peeks out between my thumb and forefinger. I'll hold bits of the bread a little way above its beak with my other hand and squeeze the bread and let the milk drip out until the bird opens its beak. Then I'll drop the bread in its mouth. I think fledglings eat every half hour. Something like that. I'll stay up all night, if I have to, feeding it until its mother returns. If that means I miss Cathy's game, I miss the game. I need to see this thing through with the fledgling.

The fledgling is lying on its side. A thin gray film glazes its eyes. Staring down at it, I hear Jeff cutting into another branch. I kneel beside the hamster cage and put the bowl of milk on the ground.

Is that the bird? Mom told me she found a bird. What happened to it?

I look at Cathy standing above me. Her hair is pulled back in a ponytail and she holds a soccer ball under her right arm.

Cathy, let's go! Flo yells from the house. We'll be late.

I'm ready already! Cathy screams. I'm outside with Hank.

She turns back to me.

It died, I say. It was alive but it died while I was in the kitchen. I don't know why.

Oh … Cathy says and her voice trails off.

I was going to feed it, I try to explain. Bread. I soaked it in warm milk.

How'd you know to do that?

I just did.

Huh? Cathy says.

Let's go, Flo says from the garage. She's got on a faded green T-shirt that doesn't fully cover her stomach, some shorts, and a worn Marlins baseball cap with her hair pulled out the ponytail hole. Her stomach is a little flabby but she's not fat. A few sit-ups would do the trick. In this getup she looks younger than she is. I stand. I think she must be desperate.

The fledgling died, I tell her.

The what?

The baby bird.

What happened?

I don't know. Shock maybe.

Did you move it?

No. You did earlier.

Well, I didn't kill it. It didn't just die.

Yes, it did, I say.

I told you, you were scaring it, Flo says.

She shakes her head and gets in the car.

Do you think you should drive? I ask.

She stops and turns.

What's that supposed to mean?

Just asking.

What?

I walk up to her.

You've had a few. I can drive.

She stares at me, the anger in her eyes flaring. I think she might slap me. Instead, she steps around me and shouts to Cathy.

Let's get to your game!

Flo gets in her car without another word. Cathy half walks, half skips into the garage and climbs in the back seat. I hear a loud snap and look at Jeff standing in the tree with his saw as a huge branch beneath him falls to the ground. He's rigged himself up with the ropes and a harness he took from his duffle bag. He stands in the tree without his shirt looking out over the street.

Flo backs the car past me out of the driveway.

What about Hank? I hear Cathy ask.

I look at the bird, at black ants crawling over it. What went wrong? I knew what I was doing. What did I miss? There'll be other fledglings, I'm sure. But I don't think I should wait for the next one to fall.

Flo drives away. Cathy looks out the back window at me. Maybe I'll leave with Jeff. Not to Iraq, but just leave. Ask Jeff for a ride when he goes to the airport. He could drop me off someplace on Highway 101. It wouldn't matter where. On the way out, I'd tell him what I know about fledglings. Jeff would interrupt and start talking about Iraq and I would cut him off. Not now, I'd tell him, I'm talking.

Jeff would back off. He'd shut the fuck up. Then after a while I would say, You got any questions?

In a hesitant kind of voice like that of a little kid, Jeff would ask me why the fledgling died. I don't know how I'd answer. But since Jeff isn't leaving right away, I got time to think about it. If I'm lucky, I might figure it out.

Pleasantries

Wasi couldn't sleep. He looked at the wall clock: four in the morning. He rubbed his stiff neck, wincing at a dull, persistent headache. He sat up in the dark, kicked off his blankets, stretched, and looked out the window to guess what the coming day would be like, sunny or cloudy, but he saw only stars, which he thought predicted a cloudless day. He listened to the rising chorus of birdsong as he felt the back of his head. The gauze bandage had come off in his sleep, and he touched a bare patch of warm skin and the tight line of ten stitches with the tips of his fingers. He was conscious of the wound, its need for protection. His naked scalp beneath the gauze, its exposure now with the gauze off. Healing will take time, the doctor had told him.

He walked into the bathroom, chips of paint from the water-stained ceiling sticking to his bare feet. He opened a drawer in the fractured vanity, pulled out a square piece of gauze, covered the stitches, and taped it as the nurse had done. Then he took two ibuprofen. Mindful of the doctor's warning not to get the stitches wet, he washed his face and body with a washcloth instead of showering. He held a plastic baggie against the gauze with one hand to keep the wound dry while he shampooed and rinsed his hair. Glancing out the bathroom window, he noticed the stars had dimmed. Light frayed the farthest reaches of sky.

Coming into the kitchen, he adjusted the cracked blinds above the sink. He heated water for green tea and put two slices of bread in the toaster. By the time he finished eating, the sun had risen, revealing a clear blue sky—just as he had thought—and he put on sunglasses and walked out of his apartment, pausing to put a mask over his nose and mouth. Shirts and pants hung over railings above him and he heard the voices of people from Syria and Iraq, who like him were refugees placed in the apartment complex by Interfaith Ministries of San Diego.

He opened a gate to the sidewalk and waited for a garbage truck to pass. It stopped and picked up a black trash bin with a mechanical arm, dumped its contents into the hopper behind the cab, and set it down. The noise bothered him. Wasi pressed a hand against his bandage to make sure it was secure and hurried across the street. A small dog yapped at him from behind a fence and its owner screamed at it, but the dog ignored her and the noise vibrated up Wasi's spine until he thought he might burst. He clenched and opened his fists. The humid air weighed on him and fallen palm leaves, gray and dry on the sidewalk, broke underfoot and that noise, too, bothered him.

He walked a few blocks into a neighborhood of single-story, ranch-style homes and noticed an elderly man sitting in his kitchen by an open window. The man waved. Wasi hesitated, and then waved back. In Kabul, he had done his best to avoid his neighbors. They would often stop and ask him what sort of work did he that took him from his home for weeks, sometimes months, at a time. Construction, he would answer. A company out of Dubai. It has a big project in Ghazni. He presumed some of his neighbors didn't believe him, perhaps because they would overhear him speaking English when he received calls from the Americans at Bagram Air Base, and mention their suspicions to the Taliban. How else did the insurgents suspect him of being an interpreter? The pipe bomb he found outside his house one morning had malfunctioned, sparing him. He knew he had been lucky, but he also was certain he had been found out.

I see you every morning, the old man shouted.

I walk before I go to work, Wasi said. I drive for Lyft. It's good to walk because I'll be sitting most of the day.

I'm stuck in the house because of COVID.

Are you sick?

No. Just social distancing.

Wasi removed his sunglasses and mask to show his face and not be rude.

I used to have a lot of business at the airport but now it is too slow, he said.

COVID, the old man said.

Yes, Wasi said, COVID.

He knelt to tighten the laces on his left shoe. The old man watched him.

What happened to your head?

Wasi looked up and then returned his attention to his shoe.

I'm sorry but I noticed the bandage.

Accident, Wasi said, standing up.

I see. Something fell on you.

Yes, Wasi said. Something fell on me.

Where are you from?

Why?

The old man shrugged and smiled.

Yours is not a Southern California accent.

Does it matter?

Not at all. I'm sorry if I upset you.

Afghanistan. I was an interpreter for U.S. forces but I had to leave. The Taliban found out about me and it became too dangerous for me.

I am sorry.

I miss my country. In Afghanistan, the Americans paid me seven hundred dollars a month. I thought that was so much money but here it is nothing. Where are you from?

Touché, the old man said and laughed. I'm from here. I've lived in San Diego all my life. I'm retired now. My grandparents were Japanese. They emigrated from Japan to Hawaii, where my mother and father were born. When they married, my parents moved here. My grandparents spoke about Japan all the time.

The old man pushed up from his chair and stood.

Do you mind if I walk with you? I can't stay in the house all day, every day. My wife wants me to, but I can't just hate sitting here around.

Wasi shrugged. He preferred to be alone but he did not want to be impolite. He waited and put on his sunglasses and mask again. He recalled Kabul's winters, when he would cover his nose and mouth with his hands to warm his face. He would stand still, watch his breath spread like gray smoke from between his fingers.

After a moment, the old man walked out the front door. He paused on the porch and removed a mask from his pocket. Wasi pressed his bandage. He again felt the bump of stitches beneath the gauze and the warmth of the wound. The old man approached him, stopping a few feet away.

I'm Mark Sato, he said. I'd shake your hand but we aren't supposed to with the pandemic.

No problem, thank you. Wasi covered his heart with his right hand and bowed. Good morning. I am Wasi Turtughi.

Good morning, Mark said.

He put on his sunglasses and mask.

No one can see our faces, he said. We could be anybody.

Wasi started walking and Mark fell in behind him. Wasi listened to his steps, the steady pace of his shoes striking the pavement, and when he couldn't take it anymore he stopped and told Mark he would prefer to follow him.

I think you walk faster than me.

I don't think so.

Please, Wasi said, waving him forward.

From time to time, Wasi and Mark got off the sidewalk to keep their distance from other pedestrians. They said hello, raised their hands, and some of those they met did the same while others hurried past or crossed to the other side. At the end of the street, Mark paused to decide which direction to take. I always go left, Wasi said. They began walking up a hill. A canyon of dry brush stood off to one side. Wasi leaned into the hill and stared into dry, rocky streambeds choked with weeds. Someone had used chalk to write, *We Miss Seeing Our Neighbors* and *Smile This Will Be Over Soon*, on the sidewalk. He stopped walking when Mark sat on a guardrail to catch his breath.

Do you always do this hill? Mark asked him. It's steep.

Every day, Wasi said. It reminds me of Kabul. Just a little. The mountains outside the city and the fields beneath them where we'd fly kites and play fútbol.

Voices rose from the canyon. Three young men sauntered down one of the streambeds. They fanned out in a clearing and began throwing a Frisbee. They did not wear masks. They cursed without concern about who might hear them, mocking one another when one of them missed a catch. Wasi stiffened and felt his heart race. His breath got short and he couldn't move. Then he stood and told Mark he had to leave. Without waiting for an answer, he began walking back the way they had come.

What is it? Mark asked, hurrying after him.

Wasi didn't answer. He pulled his mask down to his chin and wiped his face and sucked in air as if he had been holding his breath. He kept walking, finally stopping by a tree. A wrinkled, faded flyer with a picture of a lost cat hung nailed to the rough bark. *Black and gray tabby. Whiskers. Call 619-874-2468 if you see her. Reward.* Mark wheezed behind him. Leaning forward with his hands on his knees, he sucked in air.

What is it? he gasped.

I recognized those men, Wasi said, their voices.

What about them?

I was walking last week, this walk, Wasi said. No one was around so I took off my mask. I'd gone up and then down the hill. I followed a nice little side street. Then I heard people running behind me. I thought they were joggers. I moved over expecting them to go by and I started putting on my mask. They started shouting, You fucking Arab! and that's all I remember. I woke up in the hospital. A doctor told me I had been hit in the back of my head with something very hard, maybe a pipe or a bottle. I had a concussion.

Mark stared at his feet. He wanted to say, I'm sorry, an automatic response he knew would mean nothing. But he was sorry, sorry and grateful that these same men had never assaulted him on those rare days when he left the house. They might have. Many people blamed China for the pandemic. They considered—more like accused—every Asian person of being Chinese. They were someone to hate. Mark knew they wouldn't care that he was born in San Diego. He would be Chinese to them because they would need him to be.

I'm sorry, he said finally, unable to think of anything better to say.

Afghans are not Arabs, Wasi said.

I'm sorry, Mark said again. Do you want to call the police?

No. I spoke to the police in the hospital. They said it would be difficult, too difficult to catch them without a witness because I did not see their faces.

I'm sorry.

I want to go home.

They began walking. It was hard for Mark to believe that such horrible people played Frisbee. Nothing was what it seemed. Poor Wasi. Mark felt bad for him while at the same time he could not escape a sense of relief that so far he had been spared.

When they reached his house, Mark stuck his arm out to shake Wasi's hand and then stopped.

Sorry, he said. I always forget.

In Afghanistan, if we want something to happen, we say, Inshallah. It means, If God wills. Inshallah, these strange times will pass.

He covered his heart with his right hand, bowed, and said goodbye.

Mark watched him leave. Tomorrow, he would probably see Wasi again taking his daily walk. He would wave and say, Good morning, but he would keep his distance and not ask to join him. He did not want to catch Wasi's bad luck. There would be no harm in saying hello, however, no harm in being pleasant.

Becoming Them

L T bought a cup of coffee at a Starbucks on 28th and B streets, hefted his backpack and walked to a bench in a vacant lot where a crazy homeless lady spent her nights. He set his pack down and gave her the coffee. It was early morning, still dark. The farthest reaches of the sky slowly brightened and frayed and he stared at a spreading line of pink light and wondered what had happened to Crazy Lady. Why was she the way she was? He knew what had happened to him. You and me, we're not that different, he told her. She cursed him in a low, throaty voice and cupped her coffee in both hands, and talked to herself but he was unable to make out her words. He watched feral cats prowl through the burned and ruined foundation of whatever had stood here, a house or storefront, he didn't know. He remembered this building he and six Marines ran into in Fallujah chasing insurgents. One of the bad guys rolled a grenade down the stairs and the LT's guys turned around and tried to get out the door but they got all bottlenecked, shoving each other and shit and couldn't move, and LT ran into a bathroom, dropped down in a tub. Boom! He heard the grenade go off. Boom! and a fucking cat bolted out from beneath the tub. LT made it but not those other guys. PFC Pilsniak was on fire, leaping and dancing like a marionette, and he ran outside and collapsed and LT stood frozen in place while a fucking haji ran up to Pilsniak with a blanket and put out the flames, and LT saw a dust-covered cat on the street licking itself, was it the one under the fucking tub? and he shot it, so much for your nine fucking lives, and then shot the haji, too, because he could. That night, he wondered if he'd run out on his guys when he broke for the bathroom. They were all trying to get out, not thinking, and he heard their cries again, Pilsniak, Patterson, Waller, Kelman, Crain, and Perez, and their cries became his cries and it was them and not him who dove into the tub. What would they say if they were here now? Would they think they had abandoned him? LT rubbed his forehead. So many sleepless nights and zombie days. In Iraq, at night if he wasn't on duty, he'd stow his Kevlar vest and helmet in the pack and he'd restock his supply of tampons used to shove into bullet wounds and stop bleeding. Packets of dried beef and powdered soup, too, so he wouldn't go hungry if he ever got separated from his squad. When he first got back to the States, he would walk around carrying his pack because it felt odd to leave the house without it and he would stop at Starbucks as he had done most mornings before his deployment. Crazy Lady would be on the bench and just getting up, muttering to herself when he showed up. He would watch her inspect a tarp-covered shopping cart as if she was worried someone might have pilfered from it while she slept. He'd take a table and drink his coffee and see her cross the street to the coffee shop and wait in line, counting coins in her hand. If she stood under an air vent, the funk of her body and layers of unwashed clothes turned toxic and people hurried out covering their noses. She paid for her coffee and returned to the bench and sat talking to herself as cats skulked through the tall grass. LT remembered this one patrol when he was in a vic behind a Stryker in Baghdad and a movie theater blew up. The blast like hot breath pressing against the windows and then withdrawing in an undertow of heat sweeping the vic to the side of the street. LT shouted, What the fuck! and he and the four guys with him scrambled out and positioned themselves behind the hood, crouching, cursing. Fucking hajis running everywhere, holding their heads, staggering, bleeding, and he flashed on dumb movies he'd seen, Night of the Living Dead, shit like that, all the blood slivering down their faces, and he swallowed and tried to clear the ringing in his ears and the screaming that pierced the ringing. He heard sirens from way off and stared through drifting smoke and dust and saw collapsed vendor stalls and the blackened walls of a bank and broken glass and overturned cars. A blue bus burned, the paint dripping off in waves. A man on the ground, his legs curled beneath him, was missing half his chest and LT watched him bleed out. He saw cats, cats every fucking where fanning away from a man with his head on fire, and LT thought of a jack o' lantern, and the man lurched and stumbled and the fire coursed down his chest to his knees and he fell convulsing. A firetruck and truckloads of soldiers with the new Iraqi army careened onto the street. They waved battered rifles and shouted at one another and ran one way and then the other and the man burned until he didn't. The next day LT and his guys ran into another shitstorm when some fucking haji set off an IED in Hillah, about ninety-five klicks outside Baghdad. By time LT and his squad arrived, police were clearing body parts. Cats gnawed on limbs blown to rooftops and LT listened to women wailing and wondered How the fuck did someone's leg land on a roof? He and his guys went house to house butting in doors, looking for bad guys, shouting at old men and shoving them out of the way, getting women and kids in another room and telling them to shut the fuck up with all that crying. Understand somebody kicks in your door, hits your mother and father, it doesn't matter how justified you feel, they will hate us until the day we die, LT told his guys. Don't hold back. Get intel. They'll hate us no matter what so whatever it takes, get what you can out of them.

PFC Bosch got ambushed when he got back on the street. He heard a shot, then heard another one and LT saw him drop. Branches broke and dirt popped up and he saw Bosch run and throw himself on the ground. A sniper had his position. Bosch! LT yelled. I can't move LT, he shouted. He knows your position, LT said. You gotta move! Bosch crawled on his elbows toward a tree, bullets whizzing by. LT raised his weapon and tried to pop the sniper, missed. Bosch squirmed, took one in the temple. LT and the rest of his guys opened up, rip-shitting every building in sight. When they stopped and the noise faded, Bosch was still dead and who knew what happened to the sniper. They retrieved Bosch's body. A fucking cat sniffed blood on the ground and LT shot it and then he unloaded on a charred truck. He knelt, stared at the ground. A pop to the skull. He saw the surprised look on Bosch's face, mouth open, speechless. Crazy Lady belched and put her coffee down. LT watched her sort through her cart. She moved a pair of unmatched shoes, some T-shirts, pants. Discard she found in the lot, he presumed, the remains of others. He noticed her eyeballing him with quick sidelong glances and her lips moved but he couldn't hear what she was saying if anything. Covering his face with his hands, he dug his fingers into his eyes until they hurt and then he glanced up and everything looked blurred and he saw small constellations of moving lights, flickering flames. LT had liked the Iraqi culture, tea, smoking hookah. The people were all right. He trusted them until he was given a reason not to. He'd go into a village seeking intel and they might offer him information and then shoot at him when he left or poison his food and give him the shits for days. One day, LT would give a kid a Snickers bar, the next day a bad guy might pay the kid to dig a hole and another kid to put an IED in it, and a third kid to connect it. If you're some poor farm kid, and someone tells you, Here's two hundred dollars. Eat your Snickers bar and go dig a hole in the side of the road, guess what? You fucking dig. LT saw the scorched bodies of boys and girls who blew themselves up, candy wrappers snagged on rocks beside them. He thinks about them now, thinks about the other side of the coin: killing somebody for digging a hole by the side of the road. It makes no sense in the big picture now that he's back. But that's the thing, you want to go home alive. Killing someone digging a hole might mean that. They dug, you killed. He was consumed by memories of the last moments of those he'd seen die. He imitated their screams until they were his screams. He'd writhe on the floor of his bedroom as they had in the dirt. Crazy Lady stood still muttering, still fussing with her cart. LT listened to her and thought she might be talking in tongues. He heard his guys and hajis, saw them running and falling, their dead faces to the sun. Painful cries rose in his throat. He wanted it to stop. He opened his pack and removed a bottle filled with gasoline. Crazy Lady watched him and he walked away from her to the center of the lot and stood among broken cinder blocks. The cats started and crouched, their bodies taut, ready to flee. He sloshed gasoline in his hair and poured it on his face and he opened his shirt and smeared it across his chest, and he took a lighter from his pocket. Snapping it open, he held it above his head and a thin flame reached out and Crazy Lady began shaking her cart like a totem, and he tilted the flame toward his hair and screamed in voices not his own as the cats began running.

An Arrangement

I escaped to America after my fiancé, Farhid, died. He was an officer in the Afghan National Army in Bagarm when he was killed by a roadside bomb. His friend Abdul called and told me the news. He and Farhid had attended school together and had joined the army at the same time. Abdul used to visit us, but I hadn't seen him in years. When I got off the phone, I felt like still air on a clear day. Nothing stirred. No sound and no one around me. An emptiness engulfed me that was not altogether unpleasant. I was adrift but not grieving. I had never wanted to marry him; it was my father's wish that I do so. Farhid was my cousin.

His father, my Uncle Gülay, was my father's brother. Gülay died in a car accident before I was born, and my father took Farhid and his mother into our family. I saw Farhid as an older brother—someone I played hide and seek with as a child—and not as a husband, but my father said he wanted to have grandchildren, especially a grandson. He also thought our marriage would honor Gülay, and he made it clear I didn't have a choice. I don't like Farhid, I told my father, not in that way. Oh, you are a big shame, he scolded me. I didn't ask for your opinion. I decide. I ran to my room. My mother followed and sat beside me as I wept into my pillow. Your father has decided as my father decided for me when I was your age, she said. It will be fine. Your family wouldn't make a bad decision.

Farhid is a good boy. Open your heart and you will see him as your father sees him and learn to love him.

After Farhid died, I mourned the boy I knew but not the man I hadn't wanted for a husband. I remembered when he stood with me on the second floor of our home in Jalalabad when the Taliban left Afghanistan after the Americans invaded. We watched them drive away, their faces grim, angry. After that, my father allowed me to leave the house without a burqa. Farhid and I would walk to the downtown bazaar, and he'd hold my left hand as he guided us through the crowds. He liked to make puppets, and some mornings I'd wake up and find him crouched at the foot of my bed with socks on his hands imitating sheep and goats. Get up, baaa! Get up, Samira, baaa, he'd say and I'd duck under the sheets giggling as he pinched my toes. These memories made me sad. Farhid—my cousin, my brother—was gone, but I felt a certain lightness too because now I'd never have to marry him. I lay in bed and stared at the ceiling and saw hill-shaped shadows rise out of the dark and spread across the ceiling and loom over me and I knew it was the spirit of Uncle Gülay, enraged that Farhid's death had denied him the honor of our marriage.

My father hung a photograph of Farhid in his army uniform in the entrance of our house. I hadn't seen this picture before. He looked older than I remembered. He had a sharp chin, a firm mouth, and a stern look that gave the impression of someone gazing into their future. He wasn't the boy with the puppets. Perhaps I could have loved him, I thought, and for the first time I felt despair but it was a distant kind of grief toward someone I had never really known.

After his funeral, my life resumed as if he had never died. I woke up early and attended classes at Jalalabad State University from seven to one. After school, I took a computer course and studied English so that one day I could get a good job with a Western NGO. One of my favorite memories: accessing the internet for the first time and establishing a Yahoo email account.

Those leisurely days didn't last. Eight weeks after Farhid's funeral, I began receiving death threats from Taliban supporters. Some of them sent text messages: *We know your fiancé fought against the army of Allah. He is dead and you'll be next.* Some mornings, my father would find notes tacked to our front door: *Whore! You have betrayed Islam by becoming engaged to an infidel. We will eliminate you and all infidels who betray Allah.* Whoever wrote these notes, I believe, set off bombs near our house, too many to count, and sticky bombs on cars belonging to our neighbors. It became normal to hear an explosion and the panicked screams that followed. I became afraid to leave the house and stopped attending school.

My father was a physician. One day he went out with the Afghan National Army to treat sick soldiers when a bomb exploded and shrapnel tore into his left arm and both legs. A neighbor heard the news but didn't want to alarm my family. He asked for some clothes to take to the hospital treating my father. Why do you need his clothes? my mother asked; but instead of answering her, he rushed off without explanation. Then my cousin Reshaf called from Kabul and asked my mother about the bombing. He had read about it on the internet. It killed ten government soldiers, he said. My mother tried to reach my father but he didn't answer his phone. Finally, someone from the hospital called and said he had been injured. We rushed to the hospital and wandered halls where injured soldiers lay on gurneys and stared at us with dazed, hollow eyes. My father lay in a bed in a small room with peeling green paint that overlooked a courtyard. Families sat under trees. Roaming dogs snapped at men who chased them away. A white sheet covered my father up to his chin. His blood-stained legs were raised in slings, and his injured arm was wrapped in gauze soaked by iodine. Dozens of cuts ruined his face. He tried to speak but his voice caught in his throat and I looked away as tears rolled down his face.

He recovered but he couldn't walk without help and often used a wheelchair. Nerve damage in his left hand prevented him from using medical instruments. He spent his days in his small clinic sitting at his desk and offering advice to colleagues. He watched them work, and when he grew bored he scrolled through his computer until he grew tired and rested his chin on his chest and slept.

The threats against my life continued. That summer my father began making inquiries, and through a friend in the Ministry of Interior he secured a visa for me to emigrate to the United States that was given to families who had either fought or worked with Western forces. Her husband was an Afghan soldier, my father told his friend. She can't stay here. That night while I was in my room preparing to go to bed he called for me. I followed his voice out to our garden where he stood in the light of a full moon. Cats yowled and the distant barking of dogs rose above the noise of car horns and of voices in the shopping centers of Shar-e-Naw. My parents' bedroom window opened onto the garden and I could hear my mother crying. Without looking at me, my father said I'd fly to the United States in the morning. Arrangements had been made through an NGO to take me to Houston, Texas, where an American aid organization would help me. You will leave us to start a new life, inshallah, my father said.

I ran from the garden to my mother's room but she had shut the door and wouldn't let me in. There is nothing I can do for you, she called out to me. I slid to the floor and wept. In my bed that night, I wondered where Texas was in the United States. I thought of Farhid and the resolute look on his face in the photograph above our front door. I decided to have that same kind of determination, and I embraced his image, ignored my fear, and withheld my tears until something inside me retreated to a far corner.

My father and mother took me to Kabul International Airport. I held my mother for a long time, our wet faces touching. A plane carried me to Qatar and then to Washington, D.C. That evening, I flew to El Paso and stayed in a tent in a U.S. Army camp. I had never seen so many Afghans in one place. The suffocating summer heat, I thought, was worse than Jalalabad. Sand and dust swirled endlessly. There wasn't a single second I didn't hear babies crying, heavy trucks driving past, and announcements over loudspeakers. One morning a soldier took me to a room in a square, concrete building where a man sat alone at a table. He said he was from the Department of Homeland Security. He asked me about Farhid. I told him how we used to play as children. I know nothing about his life as a soldier, I said. But he was your fiancé, the man insisted. My father arranged our marriage, I explained. He asked about my parents and if they had ever traveled outside of Afghanistan. No, I told him, they hadn't. He thanked me and the soldier returned me to my tent.

I lost my appetite and would sit on the floor of my tent and spend hours rocking back and forth as I had as a child when I was scared. A nurse told me I suffered from panic attacks, and she gave me medication that put me to sleep. I had dreams of bomb blasts. In one dream, I told my father, Let's go away from here. You're in America, he said, don't worry. Another time, I dreamed my father was in great pain. When I called them, my mother said, Your father's legs were hurting him. That's why you had the dream.

Two months later I flew to Houston, where I was met by a man named Yasin from the Texas Institute for Refugee Services. Welcome to Houston, he said, and then he led me out of the airport and into a parking lot. The hot, humid air wrapped around me so tightly that my arms felt stuck to my body. My clothes clung to me like wet paper.

Yasin told me he was my caseworker. What is that? I asked. It means you are my responsibility, he said. He had dark hair and brown eyes and he wore a white shirt with a thin tie and a gray suit. He said he was from the Afghan city of Herat and had worked for an American NGO until he came under threat from the Taliban. He got a U.S. visa like mine and had flown to Houston three years ago. I told him about Farhid. I'm sorry for you, he said. When I think of Afghanistan and everyone I left behind, I shake with fear. His sad look touched me.

He led me to his car, a hybrid, he told me proudly. Turning a knob, he switched on the air conditioning and a chill ran through me as the cold air struck my sweat-dampened clothes. He gave me a bottle of water and told me I could remove my hijab; in America, he explained, women don't have to cover their heads. I told him I felt more comfortable keeping it on. I wore your shoes once, as the Americans like to say, he said, but don't be scared. After a while the U.S. won't feel so strange and you will take off your hijab. He smiled and showed all of his teeth.

We drove to a Social Security office where I signed up for refugee benefits and Medicaid. He said these programs would provide a little bit of money to pay for housing, food, and health care. He took me to a small apartment in a five-story building owned by the institute. A swing hung motionless in an empty playground and large black birds hopped on the ground, and the noise they made flapping their heavy wings reminded me of Jalalabad merchants when they snapped carpets in the air to shake off dust. We took an elevator to a second-floor apartment. It had a sofa and a table with two chairs. A small bed with sheets and a blanket took up most of the bedroom. Blue towels hung from a rack in the bathroom. This will be your new home, Yasin said. I looked out the living room window and saw nothing but the doors of apartments across the way. Through my kitchen window I noticed people sitting on steps leading to the floors above me. Shadows converged over them and I became depressed, and I thought of Farhid's spirit rising toward paradise—a dark journey toward light—and I decided this was my dark journey and eventually, inshallah, I'd find light and happiness in this my new home.

In the following days, Yasin took me to a job preparation class. The instructor was impressed I knew so much English and I explained I had studied it in Jalalabad. That is a good start, but you don't know everything, he said. He told me that when I met someone, I should shake their hand and look them in their eyes and say, How do you do? Nice to meet you. I told him in Afghanistan this wouldn't be possible; a woman would never shake a man's hand or look at them unless they were their husband or family. You aren't in Afghanistan, he reminded me. After class, Yasin would always walk ahead of me and when we came to a door he would stop and open it for me. I told him he didn't have to do this, but he insisted. He was very kind. Slow, slowly, in the evenings in my apartment, I began to think that I might like America. I thought I could love Yasin.

After four weeks, Yasin told me he could no longer see me. Catholic Charities worked with refugees for only one month. He was very matter-of-fact. He told me to stop at a flower shop near his office. It was owned by a friend of his, Shivay. He had spoken to him and Shivay had agreed to hire me. You are fully oriented to the city, he told me, and now you will have a job. You're set. Go and live your life. He smiled his toothy grin and stuck out his hand to shake mine. I don't understand, I said. What don't you understand? he asked. That stillness I felt when Abdul called me about Farhid returned, but this time it was Yasin's absence I began to feel and I didn't want him to go. He looked at me without understanding. I resisted the tears I felt brimming in my eyes and took his hand. Thank you, I said, looking at him. It was nice to meet you.

The next morning, I met Shivay. He told me he was born in Houston but his parents are Afghan. They came to the United States after the Russian invasion. I tried to speak to him in Dari as I sometimes had with Yasin, but he shook his head. My parents always spoke English around me, he said. They wanted me to be an American. That is what you should want to be too, Samira. He provided me with a table and a calculator to ring up sales. I inhaled the fragrance of red roses that filled buckets on the shelves by the door as I waited for customers, prompting memories of my childhood in Jalalabad. In those days, Farhid and I helped vendors put roses in pails of water outside their stalls on narrow streets hazy with dust. Orange trees bloomed in the summer and after the fruit had set, Farhid climbed them and dropped oranges down to me. The Kabul River passed behind the bazaar and we dangled our bare feet in its clear water. The frigid winter weather made us shake with cold and we stayed inside under blankets, eager for the comforts of spring. The sun blistered the sky in summer making the days impossibly hot, but no matter the heat we'd be back in the bazaars helping the vendors with their roses, deep red and cool in their buckets.

The flower shop took up a corner lot in a quiet neighborhood near a park where people gathered in the afternoon. I'd see men walk up to women and hug them and after a brief conversation they'd walk away. In Afghanistan, a woman would never hug a man outside of her family. Who were these men, I asked myself? The women wore slim dresses that revealed too much of their bodies, and I wondered how they felt, almost naked in public pressing their bodies against a man, some of whom didn't wear shirts, and I saw the men's bare chests and my heart beat fast and I blushed when I caught Shivay watching me. He laughed. Here, there are many men and women who aren't Muslim, he said. In America, it isn't shameful to look.

One morning Shivay surprised me with a cup of green tea. My parents always drink green tea, he said. They say it's an Afghan custom. Is it? I told him it was and from then on he made green tea for me every morning.

At midday, Shivay would buy us lunch and after work he'd walk me to the nearby bus stop, and he'd wait with me until the bus arrived. I told him he didn't have to do this but he insisted. You are a pretty girl and shouldn't go out alone at night. When the bus arrived, I'd get on and watch him walk away. I felt warm all over. I thought I could love this man.

Two months later, however, Shivay told me he no longer needed me. He had hired me as a favor to Yasin, he said. That night when he walked me to the bus, he suggested I apply at a nearby Wal-Mart. He promised to give me a good recommendation and then he handed me a half empty box of green tea. I don't drink it, he said.

Wal-Mart didn't have any job openings. I applied at other stores, but no one called me. I called Yasin. He said he'd try to help me, but I was no longer his client. I stayed in my apartment and when I grew bored I drew henna tattoos on my hands and feet, and at night I took the pills that helped me sleep. Then one afternoon, my father called. He said Farhid's friend Abdul had received a U.S. visa and would be arriving in Houston soon. He has visited your mother and me many times since Farhid died so that we'd know he honors Farhid's memory, my father told me. He is a nice boy. I have spoken to his family, and we are in agreement that he'd make a good husband for you in Texas.

I didn't know what to say. After a moment, I hurried outside and took the elevator down to the playground and sat in a swing, gripping my phone in my left hand, and rocked back and forth, thrusting my legs out to gain momentum and stared at the sky through the spare trees. Motionless clouds blocked the sun. Lean shadows cut across the sidewalk. I rose higher and higher, lulled by the rhythmic creaking of the swing. Hello, Samira, are you there? I heard my father shout. No other sound but his voice disturbed the resigned stillness until I was ready to emerge from its quiet consolation. I ceased pumping my legs, let my toes drag against the ground. I slowed to a stop. Yes, Father, I'm here, I said into my phone. I asked him to text me a photograph of Abdul. Seconds later, a young man with a smooth face stared out at me from my phone. He had a distant, moody look that conveyed a seriousness of purpose, of someone who believed he was performing his duty. As would I. Over time, I was sure I could love this man.

Solo Act

She holds a yellow feather.

Do you know anything about birds? she asks.

He shakes his head, no, and moves over to make room for her on a bench in the bus shelter at the corner of 10 A Avenida and 24 Calle. Fog rolls in and weights this lethargic morning in Guatemala City. He closes his jacket against the lingering mist and waits.

The woman brushes a lank strand of gray hair from her face and cups the feather in her hand. She wants to talk, he thinks. Why else would she have asked him about a feather? He hopes the bus arrives soon. The silence and his conviction she wants to speak make him uneasy. He's used to his own company. Well, what do you think we should do this afternoon? he'll ask himself. The sound of his voice breaks the solitude of his apartment and the ears of his dog perk up and then relax. Like an undertow, the silence that follows the unanswered question pulls everything with it until all that is left is his hope that something in the ether—spirits, energy, he has heard various notions—was listening.

Well, the woman says.

He stares at his feet. Out of the corner of his left eye, he can see her looking straight ahead but she might as well be looking at him because of the way he feels her next to him and her desire to talk. He does not mean to be rude but he doesn't know how to respond. He has grown so used to living alone that what social skills he had have all but disappeared. His wife, Martina, was the chatty one.

He doesn't know what to think. A woman alone sitting in a bus shelter a little after seven on a Saturday morning? Well, he just doesn't know. He's going downtown to Sophos, a bookstore. He started three books recently but none of them held his interest. This morning, he decided to buy another one. Sophos won't open until nine. He'll stop for a cup of coffee nearby. He couldn't sleep. Lying in bed and staring at the ceiling seemed less appealing than just getting up and doing something.

He's heard that reading helps keep the mind active and wards off senility. That and exercise, so he makes a point to read each day and take his dog out. His neighbors dub him *el paseador de perros* because they see him three or four times a day with his dog in Zone 10, strolling near the National Equestrian Association of Guatemala. The moniker makes him feel terribly self-conscious. His neighbors must think he has nothing better to do. He's retired, yes, but the idea that people presume he has time on his hands bothers him deeply. He doesn't think of himself as retired any more than he does a widower. How would he describe himself? He can't say. He gets up in the morning. He sees the day through. He occupies his time until he sleeps. Is that not what we all do in one fashion or another? he wonders. He wishes people would leave him alone and mind their own lives without jumping to conclusions about his.

Well, the woman says again.

He had almost forgotten her. He forces a smile to be polite. She lives in a small apartment, he presumes, possibly on 13 Calle, near a shopping mall. Maybe she has a roommate or lives with a friend. She's not wearing a ring so he supposes she's not married, although who knows these days, right? She probably made tea this morning and ate fried plantains, cream, and tortillas. He had fruit. He doesn't drink tea, never has, but he wakes up early, unable to break years of routine when from this very corner he caught the eight o'clock bus to his office at Azteca Bank. Sometimes, he walks his dog past the bank and peers through the windows but he recognizes no one there now.

However, his dog is old, has arthritis, and more often than not he takes it for much shorter walks than would be required to reach the bank. He gives the dog all sorts of pills to loosen his joints and ease the pain, about as many pills as he now takes for blood pressure, cholesterol, and God knows what else. The dog was already old when he picked him up at a shelter in Antigua after Martina died. He'd wanted a puppy. A woman behind the front desk told him to complete a questionnaire. Among other things, it asked his age. He wrote his birthdate and the woman looked at it and frowned. She explained that dogs can live up to fifteen years. Judging by your birthdate, you'll be eighty in fifteen years, she said. Was he intending to make plans if—she became flustered at this point—something should happen? Who would take the dog then?

You think I might die? he asked.

Her faced turned red. She opened her mouth but sounded like someone choking. She didn't know what to say and he enjoyed her discomfort. He didn't think of his age as a sign of impending doom any more than he did his retirement. He gave the woman the name of his niece. She'll take the dog, he said, and then added, if I die before it does, just to see her squirm, but she didn't. She had resigned herself to the candor such a discussion required and looked at him without flinching so that faced with his own mortality in the blunt, steadiness of her gaze, he turned away and wondered, what if I do die?

Perhaps an older dog would be preferable, he said sheepishly.

The woman suggested a seven-year-old black lab.

Martina would have handled the situation differently. She would have said, Here is the name of my niece. You can confirm with her that she will take the dog if I pass away before it does. Pass away. Such a ridiculous expression, he thinks. People don't just float off somewhere like dissembling strands of smoke. They die. Yet, when Martina died, he could not say that she'd died. He could not fathom applying that word to her. If he mentioned her death at all, he said she was gone. Like, she'd gone shopping and would be back in an hour. He avoided friends, the sorrowful, commiserating looks they gave him, and he stopped answering the phone and eventually they stopped calling and dropping by. He found the solitary, empty quiet of his now-still apartment comforting in that its silence became a kind of companion that also left him alone. He rationalized the absence of people in his life as a long-sought effort to have some time to himself.

After he brought the dog home, he gave it a bed of blankets and a water bowl. He sat across from it in his living room and waited to see what would happen, anticipating how this addition to his life would change things. He watched the dog as it stared back at him until he grew bored. After an hour he took it out. Then he resumed his position in the living room and waited until the next time the dog needed to relieve itself. He didn't name it to maintain an appropriate, almost formal, distance between them. The dog would always be dependent on him but he did not want to be dependent on it. Now, *Sin Nombre*, as he has come to think of the dog, is fifteen and still here. So is he.

Do you know the bike trail through Plaza Mayor de la Constitucion? the woman asks.

He doesn't. He hears himself answer, No, his voice sounding hoarse and far away. He has not spoken to anyone this morning. With Sin Nombre, he does not need to speak. He just shows the dog its leash and it responds. After their walk, he washed some clothes. Martina always complained that he didn't separate whites from colors. She never stayed angry with him for long. They'd always laugh at the absurdity of something he'd ruined in the wash. He still throws everything together. This morning, his right hand shook when he poured the soap. He doesn't know what to think of that.

It was so wet out when I started walking this morning to the park, the woman says.

She goes on about how fog had settled just above the coconut trees and how water hung off the leaves and splashed her face. Turning a corner, she saw a young man kneeling in the grass. He asked her if she had seen any hooded grosbeaks. She hadn't. She knew they were some kind of bird but not much more than that. He said he collected their yellow feathers. He took off his glasses and breathed on the lenses, rubbing them against the sleeve of his jacket. Putting them back on he said, "There," as if he had accomplished something significant. He rubbed his nose and smiled and at that moment she fell in love with him.

That's just ridiculous, isn't it? the woman said.

She started walking again, going no more than a few feet when she saw a yellow feather in a puddle. She picked it up. Water ran down her hand and into her sleeve. She smelled orchids, avocado, and pine and she turned around but the man she had just seen searching for feathers had moved on and she saw only the spot where he had knelt in the grass.

You really don't know anything about birds? she asks, showing him the feather again.

He shakes his head.

She drops the feather. It spins in a circle, landing on the wet, sticky pavement just as a bus turns a corner. The woman stands. He stands too. It's not his bus, but it feels good to get up. He stretches and feels joints crack between his shoulders. He should have something. to do this morning, he thinks, some task that needs to be completed other than buying a book.

The bus stops and its doors open. The woman steps in and he thinks of following her and sitting beside her but then a tired feeling he gets when he considers making an effort that would expose the vacancies in his life overwhelms him and he decides no, just buy a book. Even if he joined her, what then? Follow her off the bus to wherever she was going? Then what? Spend the day with her? But the day would end and he'd never see her again just as he won't see her again now by staying put. Or would he? Would he ask for her phone number? Would she ask for his? He watches her walk down the aisle and take a seat. The bus pulls away. She looks out the window at him or through him, he can't decide, and maybe, just maybe, she looks disappointed. Maybe not. Maybe he sees disappointment in the reflection of his own face in the window of her seat. He waves his hands, chasing away these thoughts as if they were flies. He must not have slept well last night.

Going to buy a book today, right? he tells himself.

He watches the bus leave. He notices a group of young people across the street reading a map and waiting for the light to change. They talk excitedly. One of them points to the bus shelter and back at the map and they all nod in agreement. The light turns green and they step off the curb and walk toward him. Sliding to a corner of the bench, he waits for them to approach, appreciating the few seconds he has left to himself.

Last One

Every weekday morning, Lance Dial got out of bed at fifteen minutes before six, as if he still had a train to catch for work. He showered, shaved, and dressed—blue Brooks Brothers shirt, cream-colored slacks, brown oxfords—and headed downstairs, his knees cracking so loudly he wondered why the noise didn't wake his wife, Jo, still buried beneath the comforter. He paused and stretched in the silence and then resumed his steps, the silence following him. At the bottom of the stairs, he looked through the living room's French doors at the backyard and the pink terrace, damp with dew and uneven from years of chipmunks burrowing beneath the square tiles. In the dim morning light, he considered the rotted wood fence that separated his yard from a patch of forest. Just above the treetops, he could see the roofs of condominiums on the other side of the woods. The condos had not been there when he bought his property a half-century before, and they were filled with people he did not know and who did not wave when he drove past them and raised a hand in greeting. Someone had left an unsigned note in his mailbox the other day calling his shabby fence a blight on the neighborhood. He admitted it had seen better days, but it still seemed functional. Boards had fallen off and it listed after a rain, but it had been a dry year and the fence had held. Dial saw no need to do anything about it now. He threw the note away.

As he stared outside, Dial noticed the fence shudder and weave slightly. Crows nearby quickly scattered into a gray sky streaked with the red of the autumn sunrise. He looked closer, tracking the fence's movement, until he saw a dark, thrashing shape.

Jesus, Dial said.

A deer had impaled itself on one of the posts. It reared back and opened its mouth and stayed like that for some time before it lowered its head, tongue lolling out one side of its mouth like a slug. Blood dripped from it.

Jesus, he said again.

He looked away. He had suffered a heart attack six months earlier. Ever since, he worried that any surprise or shock, any unexpected jolt would be the equivalent of a power surge and overwhelm his heart. He pressed a hand against his chest and sat down. He looked at the deer. Its head now hung low, then it turned its eyes toward the house. Dial looked away, pressed his hand harder against his chest.

Dial's symptoms back in the spring were so mild that he initially suspected nothing. He assumed his asthma was acting up because of the heat and humidity. However, the ache in his chest that morning persisted and by lunchtime, when his left arm began to go numb, Dial called his doctor's office. He spoke to a receptionist and explained his symptoms. She told him to stay on the line until an ambulance arrived.

You may be having a heart attack, she said.

What nonsense, he thought, but he didn't argue. The mere fact he got this information from someone he could not see and didn't know, and whose voice was not particularly warm, irritated him. The anonymity of it made him feel lost. He placed a hand on his chest.

Why are you doing this to me? he asked himself as if his body had, in cahoots with the receptionist, plotted against him.

Jo rode with him to the hospital. She held his hand. He breathed through a mask the paramedic had put over his mouth and nose. Machines wheezed and whistled. He listened to the siren, imagined cars pulling over to let them through. He took deep breaths, felt his lungs expand against a great burden.

An electrocardiogram showed he had suffered a minor heart attack. A coronary artery was partially blocked, a doctor explained. He would receive a blood thinner intravenously. He would not require surgery, but he would have to remain in the hospital at least three days.

Dial's 42-year-old son and only child, Lance Jr., walked into the room as the doctor was speaking. Lance quietly took a seat in a chair at the foot of the bed, his spine straight, and said nothing. "Don't slouch when you sit" had been drilled into him as a child.

Any questions? the doctor asked.

Dial shook his head no.

Thank you, Jo said.

The doctor left. Dial stared at the ceiling. He looked at his son and waited for him to speak.

How you feeling, Dad?

Oh, I'm fine. Just a little scare.

He forced a laugh. His son forced a laugh.

A little scare? Really? Jo said.

Lance glanced at his watch. When he felt he had stayed long enough to fulfill family etiquette for situations such as this, he stood. I should go, he said.

Dial looked out the living room window again. The deer was struggling, shaking its head as if in disbelief. Dial could not imagine why it had not cleared the fence. Perhaps one of its legs became ensnared in a vine when it jumped. Something. When was the last time he had seen a deer? Years ago. Before he built the fence, deer would wander through his backyard throughout the year. Then a neighbor sold an adjacent lot to a developer, and Dial fenced one side of his property. Then another neighbor sold to another developer, and he added to the fence. He eventually enclosed his backyard as more properties around him sold and condominiums mushroomed. He added trees to absorb the sound of backhoes and nail guns and the maddingly persistent backup alarms, and to provide a screen against the intrusive sight of "those monstrosities," as he called the condos. He felt hemmed in, trapped in a space he had devised to keep the rest of the world out.

Dial noticed the deer, a buck, raise its head, ears pricked forward. The way it looked made Dial think of a weathervane. He saw the top of the post sticking above the deer's left shoulder. Blood oozed from the wound. Dogs barked somewhere on the road behind the fence. They sounded close but he could not see them through the brush. The deer kicked, its rear hooves breaking bark off a tree. Blood sprayed out of its mouth, and it stopped moving and hung its head again. The fence sagged under the deer's weight. Dial watched the animal submit. He could no longer hear the dogs barking.

Dial's younger brother, Alan, had died the previous year at sixty-eight. Alan appeared fit weeks before he was admitted to a hospital. Still ramrod straight, his hair gray but thick. He walked two miles a day, exercised regularly at a YMCA, rarely ate meat, and played golf. On Saturday afternoons, he would stop by, lean back in a kitchen chair and effortlessly kick his feet up on the table in the breakfast nook in such a natural and casual fashion, while talking about golf, that it always took an envious Dial a moment to say, Alan, get your goddamn feet off the table.

Then poof, Alan became ill. A little stomach upset, nothing more. Then it was nothing more than the flu. Then it was pneumonia, and it did not have to become anything more.

Every day, Dial drove to the hospital to see his brother. More often than not, Alan was asleep when he arrived. He looked thin, pale, and wrinkled in his blue gown, as if age had finally caught up with him. Machines clicked and beeped, and nurses in uniforms as white as the walls walked in and out of Alan's room. They pushed carts with computers atop them, flipped switches, took readings, and left, their sneakers squeaking against the shined floors.

Dial couldn't take it. He would hurry out of Alan's room chased by feelings of despair that followed him to the parking lot like a posse of woes.

Dial walked into the kitchen and dialed the police. A dispatcher told him an officer or a park ranger would take care of the deer. She didn't know when.

Do I know you? he asked.

Before he'd retired, he would stop at a coffee shop on his way to work. He became acquainted with several police officers who gathered there. He had not been to the coffee shop for he didn't know how long. What would he say if people there asked him what he was doing? He'd make up something, followed by the betrayal of a nervous laugh.

I don't know, the dispatcher said. You didn't tell me your name.

Lance Dial.

I don't know you, sir.

I see. You're dispatch. Some of your officers know me, though.

I'll let them know you called, sir.

Thank you. One officer, I can't remember his name but I spoke to him all the time.

We'll get someone out to your house when we can.

Thank you.

The dispatcher hung up.

Dial reached for a loaf of raisin bread atop the refrigerator and put two slices in the toaster. He tried not to think of the deer. He had called the police. What more could be done? He opened two faded curtains above the sink and stared out at the driveway. Two teenage boys bicycled past, disappearing behind some trees. He closed the curtains and looked at the wall clock above the oven. Three o'clock. The batteries must have died. The toaster clicked and his bread popped up. He smelled the cinnamon and opened a cabinet for a plate. He imagined the clock ticking, the hands moving in silent jerks. When would the police get here? How long had the deer been suffering? He lost his appetite thinking about it. The police should have been here by now. He didn't like waiting.

He had founded a chain of office equipment and carpet stores that he sold at a sizable profit when he retired. Whatever he needed had always been a phone call or fax away. He had been in charge. People responded to him. He never waited.

Jo had urged him to volunteer somewhere after he retired, but he refused. Elderly volunteers advertised to the world they had nothing better to do than mince around community centers serving lunch to people of the same age. Doing something for the sake of doing something was how Dial saw it. They seemed proud, almost boastful that they filled their days working without compensation or goals. Their smug self-satisfaction repelled him. He knew he had too much time on his hands, but he had earned it. It was valuable. He had no idea what to do with it, but he had no intention of giving it away.

One night, he overheard his wife on her phone complaining to a friend that he would never just sit with her after dinner and talk. Instead, he rushed through his meals and was off to the kitchen to clean up while she stayed at the table, ready for a conversation about the day ahead or the day just past.

He understood his behavior annoyed her but he could not help himself. He enjoyed washing dishes. The motion of swabbing them with a soapy sponge and toweling them dry relaxed him. It was part of a routine that had been with him since he was a child and told by his parents to clear the table. Once he retired, it was one of the few routines left to him.

His wife often spoke about taking a trip. Let's go to Miami, she would say. They had been there before. Summer vacations had been a natural part of their lives when Dial worked and their son was growing up. Now, the mere consideration of planning a trip against the pressure of all this vacant time wearied him into inaction.

Hello, this is Lance Dial again. I think I spoke to you earlier.

I don't know about that, sir. Why are you calling the Northfield Police Department?

Well, a deer's impaled on my fence. I called earlier and someone was supposed to come out and put it down. I see the report here, sir. An officer has been notified.

When will they get here?

I don't know, sir

I mean it shouldn't take this long.

They'll get there when they can, sir.

I don't understand.

What don't you understand, sir?

Dial got off his phone and considered calling his son. Lance owned a handgun. At least he said he did. He mentioned it one evening while the two of them were watching the TV news. The newscaster had talked about a concealed carry proposition on the ballot. Lance supported it. Then he mentioned he had a handgun. Kept it on his night table. If anyone broke into his house, he'd get what was coming to him. Lance often spoke like this when he got worked up, as if he was still somebody and had not lost his supervisory job at the Princeton, Indiana, Toyota plant. His voice would rise until he shouted his opinions as if he were speaking to a room full of people. Well, Dial thought, if he had a gun and wasn't just talking like a tough guy, he could come over and shoot the deer and be done with it.

Dial didn't remember if he had seen his son since he stopped by the hospital. Lance had been unemployed for a year. He gave all sorts of reasons why he had not found work: he was over fifty and overqualified, not enough job openings at other auto plants, lousy economy, minorities were getting all the jobs. Dial, however, suspected he was not looking for work but was content for the time being to live off his 401(k) and severance package. He lived with his girlfriend. She sold kitchenware at a high-end department store while Lance stayed home and cleaned the house, gardened, and walked their dog. He liked to cook and took great pride in the salads he made from the vegetables he grew in his garden. He drank a lot too, leading Dial to believe his son was not as content as he let on. But he said nothing. He didn't know what to say.

When Lance did visit his parents, Dial and Jo would speak around his "circumstances," as they called his unemployment. They discussed the weather. How odd that it was so warm. Lance would dispute a prediction of rain as if he had something prove. Prove what? That he knew as much as a meteorologist? What was the point? Dial didn't know. It didn't make sense. After a while, Lance would settle down, and they would speak about something else. Dial endured the visit, his discomfort almost suffocating until Lance left.

Why aren't you looking for work? Dial wanted to ask. Just put the question out there. Skip all this other nonsense. He wondered how awkward the silence between them would be. Would they fill the void again with mindless talk about Lance's dog, his vegetable garden, his God knows what? The weather again? How many times can two people discuss the weather? Many times, Dial knew, many times if the goal was to avoid saying what was really on his mind, and he would avoid it because he didn't know how Lance might answer: Dad, I just don't know what to do. Is that what he might say? Or Dad, I've just given up looking.

Dial had never had a conversation like that with Lance. He felt he shouldn't have to. He had never needed such a conversation with his father. Lance was a grown man. He doesn't need me to talk to him, Dial thought, he needs to get back to work. He was a Dial. Not just a Dial but in all probability the last Dial. There would be no more Dials unless Lance and his girlfriend had children, an unlikely event since they weren't married and she was no younger than Lance.

"When I go, you'll be the last one," Dial told Lance after Alan died.

As far as Dial was concerned, he had done his part. He had been a husband, father, and provider. He had bought a house, put food on the table, and held a good job for forty-odd years. He celebrated holidays and birthdays and took his family on vacations. He had visited his parents at least once a week until they died. He put Lance through school, attended his recitals, and watched him play baseball and football. Dial had spent a lifetime doing his part. Since birth, he had been dutiful. Dutiful to his parents, dutiful to Jo, dutiful to Lance. He had conducted himself properly and fulfilled all his obligations. He raised his son the same way.

If my father asked me to jump, I didn't ask why, I asked how far, Dial liked to say.

Dial's values were the values of his parents and their parents and their parents before them. He never questioned them any more than his parents had. If he had not married Jo, Dial would have married someone else. He would have had a different family, but a family nonetheless with the same responsibility to Dial values.

 He caught his reflection in the windows overlooking the driveway. He stared at himself, comforted by the shape of his nose, the curve of his mouth, and the slope of his high forehead, like so many Dials before him.

Lance had disregarded his family's values. He had instead chosen to live in a manner his father could not understand and did not want to. Dial had done all he could. As a father, he felt obligated to love his son, but he did not approve.

Dial would call the police one final time and if they gave him more of their runaround, he'd tell Lance to come over and shoot the deer. Lance could do that much if nothing more.

Dial walked into the living room. He watched the deer jerk and kick, thrashing its head back and forth. Vines entangled its antlers. The two boys Dial had seen earlier on their bikes had followed the road to the back side of his property and now stood behind the deer throwing stones and sticks at it.

Hey! Dial shouted knocking on the glass.

Hey! Stop! Goddamn you, stop!

His heart pounded. He should go outside and stop them, he told himself, but he didn't. He didn't know what to expect. Children no longer had manners. The things he overheard them say, the language they used, would have been unthinkable when he was a boy. He imagined them laughing at him. Perhaps they would hold their ground. Fuck you, old man! Dial had heard worse. Then what would he do? What would they do? He didn't know. He continued knocking on the glass.

Hey! he shouted, hey!

One of the boys slipped and fell and the deer kicked its rear legs and a hoof grazed the boy's shoulder. The boy raised his head and screamed. The other boy pulled him away. They ran out of the woods. Dial watched them go, steaming the glass with his breath.

This is Lance Dial calling again.

What can I do for you, sir.

I'm calling about the deer.

The deer?

A deer that impaled itself on my fence. It needs to be put down. An officer was supposed to come out here. I've been calling all morning. I just chased off two boys throwing rocks at it.

I have the report here, sir. Someone will come out there.

Yes, I've been told that before. But when?

I don't know, sir. It's not a priority call.

Well, who would know?

I don't know, sir.

He pressed the power button on his phone. He looked through his contacts for his son's number. Lots of old business connections. He strained to hear if his wife was getting up. She would know the number. He thought he heard something and moved to the foot of the stairs.

"Jo?" he shouted.

Nothing.

He walked up the stairs and peered in their room. She lay as still as when he had gotten up. He saw the back of her head, wisps of gray hair. He stepped closer, saw the small rise and fall of her shoulders, the heavy tone of her breathing against her pillow.

Jo? He said. Jo?

A weighty sadness settled over him. He didn't like this change in Jo. When they first married, he and Jo awakened early every weekday morning. She made breakfast while he showered and dressed for work. After he retired, he saw no reason to change the routine.

Lately, however, she had taken to remaining in bed until midmorning. She had become so terribly slow. A slowness of batteries weakening, lights dimming, motors unspooling.

His older sister, Edith, had died in a restaurant of what Dial settled on calling "the slows." Her heart, the doctors said, had simply wound down like a clock until it stopped. The last tick occurred just seconds after the entree of broiled salmon, green beans, and coleslaw had been served. Edith's head drooped as if it were being lowered by invisible hands until it settled a little to one side of the coleslaw, snaring a bean with an earring. If she had to die in a restaurant, Dial thought, why couldn't her heart have stopped seconds earlier so that she could have expired on a clean tablecloth instead of coming to harbor in a mound of cold slaw?

Jo never tired of talking about how Edith died, and it pained him to listen to her. He felt so helpless thinking that while he was watching the news and Jo crocheted, only miles away Edith had her face in a dinner plate, dying. There were moments he almost told Jo to stop talking about Edith and the way she had died, but her fascination with the manner of Edith's death in a way kept her sister alive for him. Jo resurrected her with each retelling.

He wondered if Jo's obsession with Edith's death stemmed from the worry that she too might die of the slows. Jo had always enjoyed going out to restaurants, but after Edith died, she stopped nagging him to take her out. He concluded that in anticipation of her own death, Jo had decided to cordon off all paths that might lead to an undignified end.

Hello, Lance, this is Dad. Your father.

I know who you are, Dad. What's up?

I need you to come over.

Why?

A deer. A deer's stuck to the fence. It looks like it jumped and fell on it. One of the posts is sticking through it.

Christ. Did you call the police?

I called the police but you know how they are. They're not in any hurry. But I thought, I thought, well, you said you had a gun. You could come over.

And shoot it? I don't know, Dad. I don't know if I can just shoot it. Just wait for the police. They'll come.

Well, I don't know why you won't just come over.

Because you don't just go shooting a deer in the middle of the neighborhood.

What do you have a gun for?

Not to shoot deer.

You don't know how to use it.

I know how to use it, Dad.

You don't even have one, do you?

I do.

I don't think so.

Lance said nothing.

Hello?

I'm here, Dad.

You're sitting around not doing anything.

I'm not exactly sitting around not doing anything.

What are you doing?

Lance didn't speak. Dial waited and then hung up.

The doorbell rang. Dial hurried to answer it. Finally, the police. The officer wore a perfectly pressed blue uniform and dark sunglasses. Dial saw his reflection in the lenses refracted like a kaleidoscope of faces.

Are you Lance Dial, sir? the officer asked.

Yes. Yes, I am.

Where's the deer?

Dial walked the officer around to the back of the house and pointed. The deer lay across the fence, drooped over it like a wet sock. Its legs kicked feebly. The officer took a deep breath.

Damn. Jesus, that's sad, he said. OK. I have a rifle in my vehicle. I'll call the park service to take it off your property after I'm done here. You can go back in the house. You don't have to watch.

Dial nodded. He watched the officer return to his car. His assertive stride offered Dial a kind of certainty that had been missing from his morning, a sense of purpose that buoyed him, and he turned with confidence to go back in the house when he noticed the deer was watching him. The expression in its eyes asked a question Dial could not answer. After a moment, it released a long breath and its head drooped.

"It's dead," Dial thought.

He walked across the lawn, felt the grass fold beneath his feet. He heard no sounds, of insects or birds or cars on the street. He glanced at the sky. Sunlight blinkered off the roofs of the condos. He stopped before the deer, hands at his sides. The brown fur patchy in spots. A musky odor. He touched its neck, felt the heat of its body through his hand, a rippling of muscle, and then the deer jerked its head, lurched, and floundered violently.

Dial stumbled backward. The deer kicked and kicked and heaved forward. The fencepost snapped, and the deer jolted toward Dial, head lowered, and caught him in the chest, goring and trampling him before it stumbled and collapsed on its side. Dial lay crumpled. He raised a shaking hand to his broken chest. Shadows and lights flickered and darted behind his closed eyes. He heard the officer shout. Lance? Dial thought. Maybe he had come over after all. He could not understand what he was saying. Then he heard nothing. He waited for Lance to speak again. He waited and waited.

Between them, silence had always replaced words, a silence punctuated now by the slowing beat of Dial's heart and the passage of seconds into fewer seconds until the length of something cold ran through him. He allowed himself to sink into a vast, empty space, and his final breath mingled with that of the deer's, a cloud between them that briefly hung there before it vanished.

About Brad

Last night after dinner, a nurse at San Francisco General Hospital called while I was in the kitchen. The phone rang just as I poured a glass of sherry. I'm Nancy Wellen, the nurse said when I answered. I'm sure you don't remember me, Mrs. Billington, but Brad and I were in biology class together our junior year in high school.

She told me that my son, Brad, had been admitted the previous day for alcohol-induced seizures. My throat tightened and the only thing I could manage to say was, Oh my God. He's alright, she said. He was released to Out of the Rain, a program that helps the homeless in the Tenderloin. I had never heard of it. Or maybe I had seen it mentioned in one of those brochures that arrives around Christmas when charitable programs in San Francisco ask for money. I don't know. We live across the Bay in Walnut Creek and I don't go into the city very much, and I certainly don't go in the Tenderloin. Brad, Nancy continued, had been asking for change outside a convenience store when he experienced the seizure. She didn't know who had called the ambulance, presumably the store owner. When she recognized Brad, she Googled our last name and found our number. I'm so sorry, she said. She urged me to call the social worker at Out of the Rain. Ask for Katie, she said. I know her. Tell her I said to call.

Thank you for calling, I said. I began shaking. A seizure! I started to cry. We hadn't heard from him in months. He had not just been out of sight, he'd slipped just below the surface of my consciousness, to a place where anxiety can bide its time. Friends had stopped asking about him, making it a point not to mention his name around us, as people do when they think it is better to say nothing. He became like someone you see out of the corner of your eye, but when you turn they're not there. Thank you, I said again in hoarse whisper as I tried to stop crying. I hung up and put my sunglasses on so my husband, Chuck, wouldn't see my puffy eyes. I picked up my glass. Who was that? Chuck asked from the living room. He muted the TV and spun around in his chair facing me. We'd been watching a National Geographic special about scientists in Congo studying mountain gorillas. When we were a family we used to watch these sorts of programs all the time. I wouldn't let Brad watch TV on school days unless something like this was on. The scientists were young men and looked very professional in their khaki clothes, hauling their specialized gear. They spoke in low, serious tones, and they moved through dense, waist-high grass. Leafy tree branches drooped to the ground, and I felt the heat in the scientist's perspiring faces and sweat-drenched shirts. Shrill, eerie animal calls split the silence. Then Nancy called.

Robocall, I told Chuck.

What are you doing wearing your sunglasses?

I looked at him, at the confused expression on his face and I imagined how ridiculous I must look and I started laughing and crying at the same time. I don't know. My son, our son. I'd reported his absence to the police. They took down his information but I never heard from them again. After Chuck put him out, Brad moved in with Larry, a friend. Nice boy. They'd been friends since middle school. Larry helped him get a job at a garage. I thought he looked like a common laborer in his T-shirt and jeans but he seemed happy. Then one night Larry called us to say Brad was sleeping in his car in the apartment parking lot. He had lost his job. After work he'd been staying up late drinking and watching movies and then showing up late to work the next day. His boss had had enough and fired him. He stopped paying rent and Larry asked him to leave. He was still drinking, Larry said. Chuck and I drove to Larry's apartment but security had chased Brad off by the time we arrived, and Larry said he had no idea where he'd gone. I remember looking at the empty parking space where Larry had last seen him. I thought of the day we had dropped him off at college. He was so nervous. Almost scared. When he called us those first few weeks away, he sounded as forlorn as an abandoned puppy. It's that voice I heard when I thought of him in his car at night, and I almost fell apart.

That was three months ago. He's a grown man, I told myself. If this is how he wants to live his life, what can I say? I don't understand, Chuck kept saying, I don't understand.

Chuck will no longer speak Brad's name. If someone mentions him, Chuck gets all worked up. He's no son of mine! Not the way he's behaving. Now, Chuck, I'd say, please. Don't "now Chuck" me! I wouldn't say another word and after a while, still furious, he'd get quiet and hurt all at once, and I wanted to hold his hand and him to hold mine, but we didn't. That isn't us.

Robocall? Chuck said.

I went into the bathroom and took off my sunglasses. I turned on the water, wet the tips of my fingers and wiped my eyes.

When Brad started drinking in his room, beers stacked in this little fridge we bought for him in college, I told my friend Joanie, Well, he's a grown man. I certainly didn't raise him to be like that. Joanie agreed, or maybe she knew not to disagree and just listen. Once she suggested Alcoholics Anonymous but I told her no. He's depressed, not an alcoholic. He needs to get out. And I told him that. Don't be discouraged, honey. Just keep on trying. Really, it scared me. Honey, look for a job. I am, he'd say without so much as budging from his chair. I don't know. I'm his mother but I didn't want to hound him. Because I didn't know what else to say. I never anticipated this. Who would? But it terrified me, it did. He has to do something, Chuck would say. Talk to him, I'd say. Talk to him? What do you want me to say that you haven't? I don't know, I said.

Chuck was never one to spend a lot of time with Brad. He would come home from the office, make a drink and watch the news. Brad would sometimes ask him to throw a football. Still wearing his tie, Chuck would follow him outside. He'd take breaks between throws to sip his drink and when he finished he would come inside and fix another one and read the Wall Street Journal. Brad would throw the ball in the air, catch it, and run between two elms and throw up his arms as if he had scored a touchdown. He'd look through the living room window at us and pick up the ball and do it again.

Maybe he'll listen to you, Chuck.

He sighed and went upstairs to Brad's room. I listened at the foot of the stairs.

Hey pal, I heard Chuck say,

Hi Pop.

You coming up with any job leads? Any thoughts of what you want to do?

I'm going to check some things out tomorrow.

You got to think of your future.

I am, Pop. I got some applications out.

That's good. Keep putting them out there.

I will.

Don't worry your mother.

I won't.

There was a long pause. Then Chuck left his room without another word, and I hurried away from the stairs.

I don't know, Lorraine, he said. He mixed scotch and water in a tall glass. He poured me a glass of sherry. I just don't know.

Neither do I, Chuck. He has to do something.

Well, he says he has applications out. Maybe tomorrow.

Yes, maybe.

Lorraine, what's the matter? Chuck asked outside the bathroom.

Nothing.

Who was that?

Robocall, Chuck, I told you.

Lord, Lorraine. You're crying.

I'm not crying.

Lorraine, I heard you.

Before we were married, Chuck told me his maternal grandmother had lived with his parents when he was growing up in Chicago. It was very tense. He didn't elaborate and I didn't ask, but I imagine this older woman attempting to lord it over her daughter and son-in-law and the tension that could create. And Chuck as a boy negotiating all of that by remaining quiet and unnoticed. He has remained that to this day. He doesn't like to raise a fuss. He's never said all that, but that's what I think. My mother died when I was eight. After the funeral, my father, also not one to talk, told my older sister and me that it was time to stop crying and move on. Of course, we didn't stop crying, but we knew not to cry in front of our father. We had a spot in our backyard where bluebells grew and I would sit and think of my mother and cry, and when I did stop crying finally, I would still sit among the bluebells for the comfort I found there.

I'm alright, I said and opened the bathroom door. Chuck stood facing me biting his lower lip.

Lorraine?

It was about Brad.

What about Brad?

I brushed the fingers of his right hand with mine. I'd decided I'd call Katie, the social worker in the morning. If I said anything now he'd ask me a hundred questions I couldn't answer. I'd just scream. Really I would.

It was a robocall. I'm sorry. I'm tired.

In the morning, I called Katie. She had a soft voice that I found reassuring. Because of confidentiality, she said, she should not say anything to me about Brad. However, she and Nancy were good friends and she wanted to help. She suggested we get together at Davids, a restaurant near her office.

About twelve?

Yes, I said. Twelve. Thank you.

I wondered what I should wear into the Tenderloin and decided on blue jeans and an old sweater. I had a worn pair of sneakers I used for gardening and put them on. I didn't care if they got dirty. After I dressed and had coffee, I took an Uber into the city. A small TV on the back of the passenger seat played the news. Four people shot in Hunters Point, I read in the closed captioning, killed by a drive-by shooter. People lingered on a dark street in front of a house with a slanted roof. A bare bulb illuminated the porch where indistinct figures moved. Broken yellow police tape snapped against a tree. A police spokeswoman wearing a COVID mask told a reporter there had been an argument at the house between two brothers earlier in the day. The older brother had allegedly said something disrespectful to the younger one and one of them pulled a gun. She had no other details. Disrespectful? I thought. What did that mean? How many times has someone not held a door for me? I didn't shoot them. Disrespectful! Really. People have simply lost their minds. Hunters Point was just across the Bay from Walnut Creek yet it might as well be on the other side of the globe. Just the other day, I had clipped an article from a newspaper that offered safety tips for anyone going into the city.

Don't give money to beggars.

Avoid groups of teenagers.

Stay in lighted areas.

Chuck installed three locks on our front door and bars over the windows. It was like living in a zoo, I told Joanie, and we're the ones in a cage. I don't know. People ought to be able to live in their own home without this crazy nonsense. But we don't, and here I am going into the Tenderloin to see about Brad, who had become one of those people. All of it just frightened the daylights out of me.

The driver double-parked in front of what I presumed was Davids and I got out. A torn awning jutted over the door. Homeless men stood under a utility pole, smoking. If I hadn't known they were homeless I would have assumed they were workers on break. A dog sat in a shopping cart on top of a sleeping bag. People jostled around me, stepping onto the street to avoid clothes-filled plastic bags and pitched tents sheltering people who just sat and stared. A woman wearing three sweaters and a stained pair of sweatpants ranted. The shadow from a cloud moved over the block. I felt dirty just standing there and I hurried inside. Behind the counter, a man flipped a sandwich on grill. He pressed down on the bread with a spatula and cheese leaked out and the grill hissed and steam rose. Looking around, I saw a woman at a back table staring at me. She had long black hair pulled back from her face and sunglasses perched on top of her head. She was short and thin and wore a sweatshirt a little too large for her. Mid-thirties, certainly not older. I hope she knows something, I thought.

Are you … ? I mouthed.

She nodded and approached.

Mrs. Billington?

Yes.

Katie Smith. Please.

She led me to her table. A half-filled glass of Coke stood on a damp napkin. Off to the side, an empty aquarium stood on a shelf.

Would you like something?

No, I'm fine.

Songs that I did not recognize played from overhead speakers. The ranting woman came in and began shouting. The cook stepped around the counter and used his bulk to pressure her back outside. She continued shouting about cutting wiretaps beneath the sidewalk.

That's Betty, Katie said. She motioned for me to sit. When Betty gets off her meds, this is what happens. The owner here is very kind. He'll put her out but he always gives her a to-go box when he closes.

Thank you for meeting me, I said.

Of course, Katie said.

She glanced at the floor, toed a loose tile.

Well, as I said to you, I'm not supposed to give out information about clients to anyone, including family. We don't know the kinds of families people have, and if it's safe to share information. But I trust Nancy, so after you and I spoke I got ahold of Brad. He comes in every morning for a shower. I told him, You can do whatever you want to do but you don't have a right to torture your mother. She's worried about you. I convinced him to see you. He's going to be here soon. He's probably at St. Anthony's for lunch.

I would have bought him lunch.

After school, when he was small, Brad would always ask for two pieces of wheat toast and a glass of milk and he'd dunk the toast in the milk. He didn't want cookies or chips. He loved toast. Like he was already an old man. I would take him to the supermarket and he would sit in the passenger seat and wait for me while I went inside. He was never one of those children who would ride in the shopping cart. He always preferred to stay outside in the car and watch people coming and going.

Of course, he eventually reached that age when he didn't want to do anything with me. I'd come home with grocery bags in my arms and he'd just sit in the kitchen and look at me until I demanded he help me carry the bags in. Even if I only had one bag, I insisted he get out of his chair. The number of bags wasn't the point. And I'd always have other errands to run. I could have done them in one trip but every trip provided an opportunity to ask for help with a bag. I don't know. I just felt it was important. I deserved a little courtesy from my only child. My only child. Even now that hurts to say. When Chuck and I married we bought a four-bedroom house for the family we planned, but I was only able to have Brad. He used to explore the vacant bedrooms with a timidity that suggested he knew they were empty because of loss. One day, while he was still small, he closed the doors to the empty rooms as if to lock away the memory of lives that had never been. I would sometimes stand in the hallway, each shut door an affront to the expectations I'd had. Years spent trying to have children. Years of miscarriages until we quit trying. A sadness we didn't discuss. At least we had Brad, we would say—if we said anything. Now he was another child lost.

They only get coffee in the shelter before we put them out in the morning to set up for our day programs, Katie explained. They go to St. Anthony's at eleven for their first meal. By then they're pretty hungry. Everyone on the street knows about St. Anthony's. It's only open for an hour, so he should be here any time. Is he not in his car anymore?

I don't know anything about a car.

You said on the street.

That's where he stays or in our shelter.

On the street, I repeated to myself. I'd never heard it put like that.

He wanted me to be here when you two met. I hope you don't mind.

No, I said, I don't mind.

But I did. He had always come to me. If he got a bad grade on a test in math he'd talk to me about it and then after Brad went to bed, I would talk to Chuck when he was tired and not prone to pay too much attention. Is he not doing his homework? Chuck, he's doing his homework. He'll do better. Not everyone is good at math. Well, tell him to try harder. Alright. He will. Turn on the porch light and get me another glass of sherry? Often he wouldn't answer and I'd turn and see that he'd fallen asleep in his La-Z-Boy, arms folded, chin against his chest, frown on his face like a little boy. He'd roll his head against the wall and start to snore.

How do you know Brad?

I'm an alcohol intake counselor. I've put him in detox several times. We've talked. He told me about going to college and being in a fraternity.

Lambda Chi Alpha.

Yes, he told me.

I pulled my wallet from my purse and withdrew a photograph from a plastic sleeve. It showed Chuck, Lance, Brad, and me outside his dorm. We'd just dropped him off. He had never been away from home. Kindergarten through his senior year in high school. Summers, he attended a sports day camp. He was always home by five. His friends went to overnight camps and were away sometimes for as long as six weeks. I wonder if Chuck and I should have given him more rein. Maybe it would have helped in some way. Matured him.

This was Brad when we dropped him at college.

Katie held the picture.

Where was this?

Chico State.

She handed the photo back. I looked at it one more time before I put it back in my wallet. He hadn't been serious about his classes. His grades were all C's and D's. He joined Lambda Chi Alpha and I think he spent too much time playing around. Partying, if you will. I'm sure that's what happened. He was placed on probation for a semester before he was expelled after the third quarter of his sophomore year. He came home and worked in an animal shelter for a year. Sometimes, he would bring a dog home. Chuck had no patience for this, and told him to go back to school or find another job. A garden supply store hired him. He would come home smelling of dirt and his skin tanned so dark from being in the sun that I thought looked like someone from another country. He complained that he worked harder than any of his coworkers and quit. Just like college, Chuck said to him. Brad said nothing. He stayed in his room; went out at night. I'd hear him come back at two in the morning. Chuck told him to find another place to live if he was going to behave like that. Chuck, I said. Don't "Chuck me," he'd snap. We're not a hotel. I knew not to say anything more. It would just upset him further. We sat in the living room with our drinks and Chuck strummed his fingers against the arm of a chair driving me to distraction. He would pick up the remote and flip through sports stations, squinting his eyes, and then shut the TV off. He rested his chin in his right hand, legs crossed, his left foot tapping the air. Chuck, I'd say. What, Lorraine? But I didn't know what else to say. Then Larry helped Brad get a job and he moved in with him and I thought, Well, we got through that, thank goodness.

Do you have children?

No, Katie said. I spend all day with adults who need me for something, big things, little things. The idea of going home to a kid who'd need me would be too much. Maybe sometime but not now. But I get it. I drank. After work all the time. Then one day I saw my doctor for just a routine physical. He took blood for the tests they do and a few days later called me and said, Do you drink? No, I lied, why? Well, your liver enzymes are off the charts. I was working at Out of the Rain too. Not for a minute did I see myself in my clients. I was so embarrassed that I'd lied to my doctor. So, I stopped drinking. I just stopped. It's been four years now.

I wish Brad would do that.

Everyone's different, Mrs. Billington. He has to want to stop. I know it's hard.

No, I said, you don't. He's not your son.

You're right. I'm sorry.

She looked at me with such a sorrowful look I wanted to slap her. A police van parked across the street and two officers stepped out and approached the ranting woman. She got quiet and walked a little way away. A man without shoes curled on the street raised his head when one of the officers nudged him with his shoe. The man didn't move. The officer leaned down and shouted and the man sat bolt upright, the officer jumped back and the man fell to one side and curled up. The officer shook his head.

You know more about Brad than I do now.

I wouldn't say that, Katie said. It's nothing you did. He's chosen to drink. No matter what's going on with him, no one's holding a bottle to his mouth. You should know that.

He's not even thirty.

People don't start drinking in their fifties.

I think I want some water.

Of course, Katie said. Let me get it.

She stood and walked to a refrigerator. The glass doors caught a warped reflection of the street. I brushed tears from the corner of my eyes. Katie sat down and gave me water bottle.

Thank you, I said. Twisting off the top I took a small sip. She looked at her phone and put it back in her pocket.

I'm sorry, she said.

What?

Well, he should be here.

You don't think he's coming?

I don't know. It shouldn't take this long. St. Anthony's is only five blocks away. He might've gotten distracted or didn't want to face you. He's an alcoholic, Mrs. Billington. I'll ask him to call you when I see him. I'm sorry.

I turned the water bottle in my hands spinning it in circles.

I shouldn't even be talking about Brad with you. Please don't say anything.

Who other than my husband would I say anything to? I asked.

Katie stood.

I'm going to give him more time, I said.

Do you want me to wait with you?

No.

I feel bad.

So do, I said. Thank you for your time.

I'm sorry.

You said that, thank you.

Don't give up, Mrs. Billington. And don't beat yourself up.

I raised my hands for her to be quiet. Katie went out the door and the cook wiped his hands on a towel and stared after her. I don't know. Taking a napkin, I dabbed the corners of my eyes and took another sip of water. I let out a breath. I'll not speak to Chuck about today. What is there to say? Our son was in the hospital and now he is out God only knows where and I know no more about him now than I did yesterday? At some point, today will catch up with me. Perhaps Chuck will be asleep by then. I hope so.

The Distance Between
Then and Now

How're you going to do it?
Do it?

Gun, pills? Cut your wrist?

Jesus, man, those are some hella questions.

This is a suicide hotline. I have to ask.

Listen, I called because, well, I saw this number on YouTube. It said Advice Line. I was just like sitting here watching TV and thinking, I can heat a chicken pot pie or I could go out. I'm sick of pot pies. But I don't feel like going out. And this happens a lot. I get off work, come home, and then I go look in the fridge and all's I got is frozen pot pies. Maybe a can of Hormel Chili. And I don't care but I do. I care. I'm tired of eating the same shit every day. So, I called you.

Are you thinking of suicide, sir?

I'm thinking I want something different than chicken pot pie and chili.

What would you like?

Something else. You're not listening.

I'm not sure what you want. This is a suicide hotline. Are you thinking of killing yourself?

Forget it. I guess I'll go out.

He hangs up and stares at his feet. Crooked shadows stamp the faded blue carpet . Glancing out his kitchen window, he sees an old man in a long corduroy coat across the street tapping his cane into icy ridges of snow piled against the curb. The snow has formed a slushy dam at the curb, and large, shallow pools of brown water stretch from the sidewalk into the street. He watches people as they try to jump over the water, often unsuccessfully, or tiptoe through it until they reach an island of pavement on the other side of the street.

He assumes that the old man has taken it upon himself to clear the slush and drain the street. In the past, he would see him walking through the neighborhood picking up trash. He has never spoken to the old man. Maybe he'll talk to him tonight. He stands and takes his Army field jacket and shrugs it on. He puts an asthma inhaler in his pocket. A VA doctor diagnosed him with asthma after he had gotten back from Afghanistan. Probably from inhaling all that dust.

His dog, a Lab and German shepherd mix—at least that's what he assumes—watches him.

Not now, he says.

He picks up a pen and puts it in the breast pocket of his shirt. For a long time, he felt weird without a weapon. The dog jumps onto the sofa and turns its back to him. He had another dog but it died. He remembers how it looked at him when the vet put it down. Betrayed. After all these years, it seemed to say. He had a wife too, but they divorced a year ago. Little things that led up to big things and before they knew it, they couldn't stand the sight of each other. Maybe it wasn't that personal. Maybe they just wore each other down. Their love, if it had existed, now a distant thing. He hasn't seen her in months. No need to. No kids. No alimony. He watches YouTube movies most nights, the dog asleep at his feet. It's company enough but not enough. For either of them. Should get another dog. For the dog, at least.

Outside, he looks at the night sky. Despite the dark, he can see the heavy outline of clouds and the glow of skyscrapers downtown. When he was on patrol in Afghan villages, nights turned everything black. No glow of city lights anywhere on the horizon. Pitch black. He thought this must have been what nights were like at the beginning of time. Fires glowed inside of mud huts. Guys broke their ankles stepping into holes they couldn't see. He put a red protective lens over his flashlight to conceal his position from the bad guys.

A cold wind cuts against his face. His vapory breath bursts from his mouth. He pulls his collar against his neck. He'd heard it might snow again tonight. Feels like it. Well, he'll make this quick. Grab a bite at Donny's. Good as any and it's close.

He crosses the street and watches the old man working the slush with his cane. Something to do, he supposes. Why else would the old man waste his time this way? The old man taps out narrow channels to the storm sewer, draining the puddles. Shifting chunks of ice move with the water, blocking the flow again. The old man breaks it up once more. He raises a hand in greeting, but the old man doesn't see him.

He walks downhill to Broadway. A homeless man in a sleeping bag lies beside an overturned milk crate. An "open" sign flashes red at the corner. Above it, an unlit sign ringed with dead light-bulbs: Donny's Grill. He comes here so much, it's almost the same as staying home. He always takes a booth at the rear. The other regulars who prefer to sit at the counter call him Booth. He thinks they must know his real name by now. Then again, he doesn't know theirs.

Stamping his cold feet on the doormat, he opens the door and a blast of warm air lifts the hair off his forehead. A waitress looks at him and then finishes wiping a table. She takes the rag and hangs it off her apron.

What's going on, Booth?

I'm good, Marcia.

He sniffles from the cold.

Water?

Water.

He slides into the booth and rubs his hands. The usual crew sits at the counter. One young guy he doesn't know shouts, Hey, fuckface, to another young guy he also doesn't recognize. The second young guy laughs and waves him off. The other people at the counter talk in low voices, ignoring them. Dim light pales the room. He gets irritated at the young guy shouting, Hey, fuckface, over and over. That dude doesn't belong here. This isn't that kind of place. Or maybe it is. Maybe a new crowd is coming in. Everywhere he goes, a foreign land.

He takes a menu wedged between empty salt and pepper shakers and a napkin holder. The red-checkered tablecloth sticks to his elbows. He doesn't need the menu; he knows what he wants. Still, maybe there's something new. There isn't. When Marcia brings his water, he asks for his usual, a burger with chips. He watches the sway of her hips as she walks away and gives his order to the cook. The cook reads the slip of paper and clips it above the grill. He reaches into the refrigerator for a paper-wrapped meat patty.

He leans back and waits. The plastic seat cover crackles. In Kabul, all these Western-style restaurants popped up downtown. He liked a place called Yummies. He'd always order a burger because he just thought it was a trip to have a burger in Kabul. He and the other guys got out of their Humvee and stood with their M16s. He went inside and ordered for all of them, two burgers each. Afghans seated at tables stared at him. Conversations stopped. Sit in or take away. That's how Af-ghans said for here or to go. Sit in or take away. Take away, he said, waiting in the silence until the food was ready.

He rubs his face. Work, walk the dog, watch some shit on YouTube, read, go to bed, wake up, go to work, start all over again. He lives his life as if it were a drill. He doesn't think about it until he does. He called the 800 number after he saw an ad on YouTube. Struggling to get through the day? a young woman said, staring intently into the camera. Call The Talk Hotline. We're here for you. Nothing suggested it was for people considering offing themselves. Nothing. He had expected the chick in the ad to answer but the guy who did was nice enough. He wishes they had talked longer. Maybe he was a vet. He should have asked. He wishes he had stayed home and just eaten the damn pot pie instead of sitting in this booth thinking how he made an ass of himself by calling an 800 number for people thinking of doing themselves in.

Snow starts falling. Light at first, then big, wet flakes. He pictures the old man breaking up the slush and cursing the snow. The "open" sign casts a red glow and wind bounces the snowflakes across parked cars. A couple walking hand in hand turn their faces from the wind. They'll embrace when they get home, he thinks, and rub the chill off each other. Afghans wore sandals year-round, even when it snowed. Most of the ones he saw anyway. They wrapped themselves in prayer shawls, and he wondered how they didn't freeze. On medical missions, his unit would distribute blankets and men would take them, bow, thank the soldiers, and offer them tea.

Marcia turns a switch on the wall and the voice of Madonna rises out of two speakers above the coffee maker. He can't recall the name of the song. He'll wake up at two in the morning and remember it with no one to tell. He'll write it down to get it out of his head, fall asleep, then look at what he wrote in the morning and wonder, What's this? Then he'll remember. His wife would shake him in the middle of the night and tell him he was shouting in his sleep. I didn't know, he said. What'd I say? Nothing, she said, just shouting. She rolled on her side with her back to him and fell asleep again. He lay awake the rest of the night to avoid dreams he didn't remember.

Through the restaurant window, he notices two men step out of a white van. They turn their backs to the wind and snow, heads down. They wear ski masks. The snow clings to the fabric, turning their faces white.

I'll have to walk home in this shit, he thinks. And then let the dog out. He rubs his eyes. Tired. No reason, just tired. Arms sore. Stocking deliveries at Home Depot all day. February yet they were already receiving orders for spring. He pulled cart after cart loaded with boxes to the freight elevator, leaning forward, head down, his arms stretched out behind him.

The dignity of work, he told Phil, a coworker.

I'm thinking better of you already, Phil said.

Ski mask guys enter Donny's. Snow blows inside and then the door closes behind them. One of the men stays by the door while the other man looks around and then moves toward

Fuckface in long, fast strides and jerks him off his stool. Fuck-face flies backward, arms in the air, and collapses after striking the back of his head against a table and knocking it over. Fuck-face rolls to one side groaning. He clasps his head in his hands.

Stay down! the man shouts and kicks him.

Booth looks at Fuckface feeling far removed, as if he's looking at him through the wrong end of a telescope. He takes his pen in his right hand but doesn't move. Ski Mask, he presumes, knows Fuckface. Fuckface screwed him over some dumb shit and now it's payback time. He watches Fuck-face grope at the air, as if he's trying to grasp a rope to pull himself up. Ski Mask holds him down, his right foot against his chest, and pulls a pistol out of his coat pocket. He looks around the restaurant sweeping up everyone in his gaze.

Get on the ground and lie on your stomachs, bitches! he shouts. Close your eyes. This is a robbery.

Marcia starts shaking. The cook stands by the grill and raises his arms and then Marcia raises hers. Ski Mask steps away from Fuckface and goes behind the counter, knocking over glasses with a sweep of his arm. Booth understands now that Ski Mask has nothing against Fuckface. Fuckface was a random target. Ski Mask wants to instill fear, shock everyone into obedience to remain in control. He tells the cook to get on the fucking floor. He orders Marcia to open the cash register. She lowers her arms, opens the drawer, steps backward, and raises her arms again. Ski Mask tells her to lie down beside the cook.

You too, Ski Masks says to Booth. On the floor. Close your eyes.

At first, he doesn't move. He watches everyone, his eyes darting from Ski Mask behind the counter to Second Ski Mask by the door and makes an assessment. There could be civilian casualties if he chooses to get involved. He gets on the floor. He presses a cheek against the cool tile and closes his eyes. Once on a medical mission one hour south of Jalalabad, his patrol stopped by a school to give polio vaccine. Soldiers took up positions around the perimeter of the school. He stayed with the medics who would administer the vaccine. They had arrived moments before the teacher woke the children from a midday nap. About twenty boys and girls slept on rugs on opposite sides of the classroom. He squinted as the lights came on. The teacher shook them. They rolled on their backs, eyes closed, resisting the light. Whoever remained quiet, the teacher said, would get a piece of candy. He smiled at her bribe and the dazed look of the waking children and then he felt himself lifted in the air and falling to the floor, the noise of an explosion filling his head until he thought it might burst. He heard nothing but a muffled roar between his ears. Debris from a shattered wall fell on him. Screams, gunfire, shouting. He got up, stumbled. Overturned desks, arms, legs, blood black with dust. A car burned outside. He tried to focus. Another explosion. He fell forward, rolled onto his back, choking on dust, shorn clothing like confetti, like snow falling.

Close your eyes, Ski Mask says, standing above him.

He rifles through Booth's pockets and takes his wallet and asthma inhaler. Booth senses him pause. Then he places the inhaler on Booth's back. Booth doesn't move. He squeezes the pen. In his mind he stabs this man several times in the throat. He obeys to avoid killing him, while vividly remembering the smell of things dying, rotten stuff, vehicle fumes, shit burning, bodies torn open red as raw steak, that smell. The inhaler slips to the floor. Ski Mask puts it on his back again. Then he takes Booth's left hand and places the inhaler in it. If he notices the pen balled in his fist, he doesn't comment.

Breathe, he tells him.

He stands.

Breathe, he says again from somewhere above him. Let's go! he shouts. Second Ski Mask follows him to the door. Booth hears them leave, doesn't move, eyes closed. He lets his head clear in the silence, smells nothing but feels the cold rising off the floor.

They're gone, Marcia says.

He opens his eyes and stands. Whoever remains quiet will get a piece of candy. He looks at the other customers pushing themselves off the floor. Like zombies, they stagger, sit at the counter, resume their usual positions.

Are you alright? they ask one another.

The cook and Marcia help Fuckface off the floor and lead him behind the counter. The cook fills a plastic bag with ice and holds it against his head. The waitress calls the police.

He shoves his inhaler back in his pocket and pats his other pocket. Ski Mask has his wallet. Gone. He'll have to call the bank about his ATM card. He can't think of the name of the bank. He remembers how to get there. Take Broadway to Juniper. He'll go home and get his car, drive there, see the bank's name, write it down and go home and call. Crazy, he can't remember. What the hell? Drive in the snow, shit, just to get the name then drive home and call. Nuts.

I'm not hit, he tells himself.

He walks home. A hard wind is blowing the accumulating snow into drifts. He kicks the snow aside, shaking it off his boots. The cold constricts his lungs. He feels the inhaler in his pocket. He doesn't see the old man when he gets home. Poor bastard will have his work cut for him with this snow. He stops in a convenience store across from his apartment. The bright ceiling lights shine the scuffed tile floor a yellowish alien color. He sees the owner filling a shelf with cans of tuna and vegetable soup. He doesn't move until the owner looks over his shoulder and notices him.

Hey, he says.

Hey.

What's up? Your usual? A ham and cheese sandwich?

He shakes his head. The owner slaps his hands together and wipes them against his jeans. He has recently started serving food in the morning to day laborers. Pans for scrambled eggs float in a sink filled with soapy water.

I was robbed.

His voice feels overly loud in the empty store.

Robbed?

At Donny's. Two guys.

Really? Donny's?

Yeah.

Jesus.

Took my wallet. I have to call my bank.

Do you need a phone?

No, I can't remember the name of the bank.

You can't . . . where's it at?

Broadway and Juniper.

That's U.S. Bank.

Right. That's it. Jesus. Thank you. I was going to drive there to get the name.

The store owner reaches into a cooler and offers him a sixteen-ounce can of beer.

Take this.

I can't pay. I don't have my wallet.

Don't worry about it. Go home. You better call the bank.

I will.

He leaves with the beer, crosses the street and hurries up the steps of his building and unlocks the front door. At least they didn't take his keys. His hands shake. So cold, he thinks. I could've killed him. The dog greets him wagging its tail. He pats its head. I was robbed, he says, and lets it out. It runs down the steps and looks back at him. He closes his door, hurries down the steps to let the dog out, watches until it finishes peeing on a bush, and then he lets it back in and unlocks the door to his apartment. He sets the beer down, takes off his jacket, and drapes it around a chair. He tosses the pen, inhaler, and his keys on the counter. He feels a mounting rage that he didn't kill Ski Mask. It was good he didn't, but still. Now he's got to get a new ATM card.

He drops the beer in the trash beneath the sink. During a routine physical, his doctor said, Do you drink? Your blood tests show your liver enzymes are through the roof. No, he lied, I don't drink. The lie embarrassed him and he stopped drinking. Eight months now. Fell into a sloppy habit, drinking every night, that's all it was. Boy, those Aussies in Kandahar could drink. Sometimes a stereotype is true. Fucking Australians. Call the bank, he reminds himself. He sits down, the dog by his side. He thinks he should feel different. One swift jab to the Adam's apple with his pen and Ski Mask would be dead. Blood, that acrid smell. His stomach turns. Better call the bank, he tells the dog.

This one guy told me and everyone else to get on the floor. He took my wallet. Then he took my inhaler. He said breathe. He goes, breathe.

Wow. Strange. You're OK?

Yeah. Like he cared. Like he was giving me a message.

I don't know about that.

I don't know either. It made an impression is all. Why would he care?

I don't know. What matters is you're okay. You weren't hurt. But this is a suicide hotline. You don't sound like you're contemplating suicide. Maybe you just need to talk to someone?

Well, that's kind of what I'm doing. We're doing. Are you the person I spoke to earlier?

I don't think so. You better call the bank. Didn't you say they took your wallet with your credit card?

ATM card.

Right. And your license. You'll have to get another driver's license.

Yeah, right. I didn't think about that.

Okay. Good. I'm glad you weren't hurt.

He follows a number of voice prompts before he reaches a live person on the bank's 24-hour line. If you have an existing account, press two; if you have a question about your account, press three; if you are calling about a lost or stolen card, press five, or press zero for a customer service representative.

Pushing zero, he waits for the operator. A woman gets on and asks him his name and account information. He tells her what happened. She looks up his account using his Social Security number and cancels his debit card. She says he will receive a new one in five to ten business days. Is there anything else? No one was hurt, he tells her. I'm glad, she says. Is there anything else? No. Thank you for calling U.S. Bank.

He hangs up and faces the bare walls of his living room. A plumber who fixed his toilet a few weeks back told him he needed to hang some pictures. He thought that was a good idea. He still thinks it is.

The dog curls up at his feet and closes its eyes. Eight o'clock. If he had not gone out, he'd probably be in bed now. He'd have watched a YouTube movie and called it a night. Not even nine and he'd be in bed if this had been a normal night. If he'd just had a pot pie and stayed home, none of this would have happened. At least to him. Maybe Ski Mask has asthma. Maybe someone in his family does. He kneels beside the dog and rolls it on its back. The dog wags its tail and stretches its head expecting a neck scratch. He holds the dog's forelegs down. The dog squirms, whimpers.

Breathe, he says.

The dog whimpers louder.

Breathe, he says.

He releases the dog. It kicks its legs in the air, rolls to one side, stands and shakes. It licks his face desperately as if to say, Are we all right?

He dreams. He stands at the pharmacy window of CVS with his pen and orders an asthma inhaler. Ski Mask waits behind him and Booth spins around and stabs him. Ski Mask falls, his chest oiled in blood. Booth fumbles for the inhaler. He sticks it in Ski Mask's mouth although he's no longer Ski Mask but one of those Afghan schoolkids. Breathe, he says. He puts a hand behind kid's head. Breathe.

He clocks in at work at seven in the morning. Boxes stacked to the ceiling. A saleswoman is loading a cart. She tells him if he gets orders of potting soil to let her know. We've got a sale in the garden center, she says. I'll put it right out on the floor. Okay, he says. Good morning. Oh, yeah, good morning, she says.

He starts sorting boxes making room on some shelves. His coworker Phil clocks in.

Hey.

Hey, Phil says. Shit traffic.

He looks at his timecard.

Seven ten, not too late. I can work an extra ten minutes to make it up.

For the big money.

For the big money, yeah, Phil says. What's going on?

Nothing. Making room on the shelves. Did you hear about the robbery?

When? Phil says.

Last night. At Donny's.

Donny's?

On Broadway, Phil.

I don't have a goddamn clue. How'd you hear about it?

He considers saying, Because, Phil, I was there. I got robbed. He feels small somehow that Phil doesn't know. Sort of takes the oomph out of it. A few weeks ago when they overheard a customer telling one of the cashiers that his son just got back from Afghanistan, he had to remind Phil that Americans were still fighting over there. Really? Phil said. I thought we'd left. Fucking Phil. He doesn't know he's a vet. What could an ignorant fuck like him say? What was it like? He can't even begin to answer that question.

I just heard about it, he tells Phil.

After work, he drives home, lets the dog out, and walks to Donny's.

We made the 10 o'clock news last night, Marcia tells him.

He takes a booth. The regulars are all here at the counter like nothing happened. That bugs him. Something did happen.

Marcia wipes his table and gives him a glass of water.

The cops think it's the same guys have hit almost a dozen restaurants, she says.

What happened to the guy they roughed up?

Fuckface? Haven't seen him or his friend, Marcia says.

You okay?

Yeah, thanks for asking, Booth. You eating?

A burger, please.

She laughs. He smiles. She has a pleasant face. Her brown hair stops just at her shoulders, and she has enough buttons on her blouse open to hint at cleavage. He feels an urge to run a finger over the curve of her full mouth. He imagines asking her on a date.

After you left, the police came and then Channel Five, Marcia says.

Did you talk to them?

The police but not Channel Five. You should've stayed. The cops wanted to talk to witnesses.

Rain check.

Marcia laughs again.

Here we still are, she says.

It's when you're away and alone you think about it.

After he eats, he goes home. He sees the old man standing on the sidewalk watching him.

Hey, Booth shouts.

The old man raises his chin.

I always see you out here. I thought it was about time I said hello.

The old man smiles and raises a hand. Booth doesn't think he heard him. He sees the convenience store owner mopping the floor. He thinks of saying hello but keeps going.

A clear, cold night sky. Stars. The dead schoolchildren were lined up in rows under white sheets paled blue by moonlight. Wailing parents. Piercing like the screams of cats. He lets his dog out.

In the morning, he'll buy a book to make himself stop watching YouTube movies every night. And another dog. He'll stop at the animal shelter for a dog to keep his dog company and see. Just see. He called the wrong number the other night, never meant to dial a suicide hotline. You want to come up for coffee? he should have asked the old man. I live just over there. He can ask him tomorrow. He sighs and chews on the tip of his pen. Tomorrow. He's got things to do. A vast distance between then and now. If he can just hang on.

Borders

Hieu catches the same shit from his dad that I get from mine. His folks were born here in El Paso after their parents moved to Texas from Vietnam during the war, when you had like American soldiers over there fighting. Hieu'll imitate his dad going on about how his mother and father worked two, three jobs sometimes to support the family, making a long face and talking deep and serious, sounding like I don't know who, his dad or his grandparents, I guess, and it doesn't matter because I always bust up laughing. Then I'll talk like my dad and how he goes on about Afghans living here and not helping in the war on terror. You are Americans now, he shouts, not Afghans. Then I'll wag a finger in Hieu's face and go like my dad; Never forget that! and Hieu cracks up.

A lot of people think me and Hieu look Mexican. Lots of people here don't like Mexicans. They say they're not legal and steal jobs, but me and Hieu don't care. People'll speak Spanish to us, like this one lady at a taco stand. She'll go, *Buenas noches, Qué le gustaría?* Hieu doesn't get her, but I've picked up enough Spanish to know what she's saying: What would you like? So, yeah, I think I could be Mexican if I get good enough at Spanish, and then I'd go live in Juarez where I could stop dealing with my dad's bullshit.

Most days, me and Hieu walk home after school. Sometimes he'll come with me to my mom's house and sometimes I'll go to his house. When Hieu's at my house, we'll sit in my room, do our homework and then get on my Xbox. Before, when my dad'd be home from Afghanistan and him and my mom were still together, we'd hear them yelling at each other. Usually about how he was never around and he had no right to bad-mouth how she did things at the house. Hieu'd look at me and I'd like shrug. Now that I'm living with just my mom, I don't worry about her and my dad embarrassing me in front of Hieu.

My mom left my dad when he went back to Afghanistan for, I don't know, the hundredth time. Not that many, but he'd been going back like a lot. She told him she was done one night in a Skype call. Because of the time difference, I was asleep. The next morning she goes, Your father and I have decided not to live together. We think it's for the best. You'll still see him when he's home, but he won't be staying with us. I looked at her and I didn't know what to say. I'd just woken up on a Saturday morning. At least I didn't have school. I thought of calling Hieu but I really didn't want to talk to him or anybody. My heart beat faster and I felt like all alone and I wanted to cry—a part of me did—but I couldn't, I guess, because not all of me wanted to. I knew everything had just changed on me but I wasn't feeling the change. I mean even when he was home, it was like he wasn't. He'd sit alone in the living room and be like really quiet but he'd also be real intense to everything going on around him. I mean, I couldn't walk up behind him without him spinning around and giving me this look like I was a stranger and he'd caught me at something, but it was just me. He spent a lot of time on the phone with other Afghans he knew in El Paso, getting mad at them for not having gone to Afghanistan like him and helping with the war. You are Americans now, he said. Serve your country.

After the divorce, my dad lived with his parents between deployments. I'd stay with him Thursday night to Sunday night. One morning, we ran out of eggs and my grandmother asked us to go to the store. In the checkout line, he saw a woman wearing a burqa. You are still living in the old country, he shouted at her. I have lost my wife for this country. I would lose them a thousand times if I had to for America!

People stared at us. He wiped tears from his eyes and stormed out, and I hurried after him. We got in the car, he slammed his door, and we drove to another store. He gave me ten dollars and told me to get a carton of eggs. When I came out, I found him parked beneath a tree, his forehead resting against the steering wheel. I tapped on the window. He jerked upright, gave me a hard look, and then slumped back in his seat.

Get in, he said, his voice catching and his eyes glossy with tears again.

Back at my grandparents', he took out six eggs and placed them on the counter. His mood began to change and he became like almost happy as if nothing had happened. He greased a frying pan and added salt, oregano, and chopped tomato. This is how you make an Afghan omelet, he said. He let it cook for a few minutes and added diced potatoes and chopped onions. He cracked the eggs over the mixture without breaking the yolks. When the eggs were half-cooked, he added some red chili flakes and chopped coriander. Then he covered the pan and let it cook for seven minutes.

I opened a cabinet and took out four plates and set the table. He let me remove the cover from the pan. Steam clouded my face, and I inhaled the spicy aroma. The yolks were round and orange in a sea of egg white accented by all the other ingredients. I imagined the yellow circles in that old video game Pac-Man chasing each other and laughed, and for no reason my dad laughed too.

When we finished eating, my grandfather told us to save our napkins for the next meal. Waste not, want not, he said. Money doesn't grow on trees. He loved these corny expressions. I'd look at my dad and he'd nod and I knew that meant I was to do what my grandfather said. I cleared the table, and my dad walked into the living room with a newspaper. He read some of it and then lowered it to his lap and stared at nothing. He never asked about my mother.

My dad was born in Kabul in 1965. The Soviets invaded fourteen years later. He was thirteen when he and his parents left for Pakistan. They applied for a humanitarian visa for the United States and with the help of an NGO moved to El Paso, where my grandfather's brother was already living. Difficult years followed. My grandfather drove a taxi twelve to fifteen hours a day; my grandmother cleaned houses. After school, my dad cut lawns and delivered newspapers. He gave his paychecks to his father. My grandfather would always celebrate Thanksgiving by throwing a party for their neighborhood to express his appreciation for living in America. He grilled lamb and chicken kabobs and served them with nan. After a while, he only made hamburgers and hot dogs because that was more American. Eventually, my dad got him to bake turkeys. However, he never stopped speaking Dari, the language of northern Afghanistan, to my grandmother and dad.

After he graduated from high school, my dad found work as a janitor. He took side jobs on weekends and met my mother while installing a kitchen counter at her parent's house. She was working at a casino. Her parents were from Poland. Practicing Catholics, they were leery of a Muslim boy dating their daughter. My dad went to a mosque on Fridays because his parents insisted, but he didn't pray five times a day or spend time thinking about Allah.

On their dates, my mother would ask him about Afghanistan, but he refused to talk about it. We lost everything when we left, he told her. Those years are very far away. San Antonio is my home now. My mother held his hand and said nothing. She knew little about Poland, but she had grown up speaking Polish and my dad picked it up from her. She learned some Dari from him. When she was little, she went with her mother to church every day. But as she got older she attended only on Sundays, and after a while only on Christmas and Easter. To avoid pissing off their parents for marrying outside their faiths, my mom and dad did a city hall wedding with a judge.

Then 9/11 happened. My dad gave up his job and contracted with the U.S. Army as a translator. I was six, and I remember him and my mom getting into it. She told him he was crazy. What if you get killed? she asked. What would I do? You're always saying we don't have enough money, and now you do this? He said his family would help. My grandfather told her, He's an American. He must do this. He's my husband first, my mom said. She wouldn't talk to him for days. She still doesn't talk to my grandfather.

He flew to Kabul four weeks later. Then it started. He would be gone for months at a time before he'd come home for a minute and leave again. He never talked about the war. In those first few years, I'd stand in the driveway and wait for him until my mother called me inside.

My dad just got back from a deployment, and I can't help but think back to those days. They seem a long time ago. He and my mom have been divorced for six years. I'm about to graduate from high school, class of 2013. I got a part-time job at a restaurant. My dad told me I better make that full-time if I want to go to college. Your grandparents got ahead without help, he said, and so did I. I rolled my eyes. I'll talk to my mom. She'll help me out, I think. This morning, I wake up, go into the kitchen and decide to make an omelet. I break the eggs against the side of the bowl with one hand, differently from my dad who cracks the eggs open by tapping the shell with a fork and then prying them apart with both hands. He doesn't break the yolks but I do, whisking the eggs just enough to create a yellow pond floating in the bowl. Then I add the other ingredients.

My dad comes out of his room. He watches me. That's not how you make an Afghan omelet, he says. I make a face. You're still living in the old country, I say, imitating him. You're an American now. Never forget that. He stares at me. The sun comes through the curtains in patches. A shadow pools between us. Get out, he says, in a hard voice that doesn't sound like him, like it's coming from some place deep and far away. Get out. I drop the fork in the bowl and go outside through the garage. I call Hieu but he doesn't answer.

I think I'll go see the taco lady, get something to eat. She doesn't correct my Spanish but she does Hieu's. When he tries to roll his R's he sounds like he's gargling, and she says, No, no, no, pissing him off. I'm Vietnamese, he tells her. I still think it'd be cool to take a bus to Juarez and be Mexican for a while. Hieu doesn't want to anymore. He doesn't like Mexicans now. I figure I'll go alone.

Acknowledgments

Versions of some of these stories first appeared in the following publications:

Apple Valley Review ("The Distance Between Then and Now," "Solo Act"), *BULL* ("Becoming Them," "The Last One"); *Chagrin River Review* ("Fledgling"); *Cholla Needles* ("About Brad," "The Company I Keep," "Touring," "The Wait," "Rebel", "The Cleavers"); *Collateral* ("Dependents"); *Green Hills Literary Lantern* ("On Deck"); *Kansas City Noir* ("Missing Gene"); *I-70 Review* ("Borders"); *Litro Magazine* ("A Father's Wish"); *The Massachusetts Review* ("Carpet Deals," "Having Once Served," "Strangers"); *New Letters* ("Hridi's Dilemma,"); *Wrath-Bearing Tree* ("An Arrangement," "Love Engagement," "The Guest," "Pleasantries")

Thanks to the staff of Cornerstone Press, especially director and publisher, Dr. Ross K. Tangedal, and my editor, Eva Nielsen and her colleagues, for taking on this manuscript. My thanks to everyone at the publications in which some of these stories first appeared. Without you this book would not exist.

I also want to acknowledge Roland Sharrillo, Bruce Janssen, and Jesse Barker for critiquing early drafts of this manuscript.

J. Malcolm Garcia is the award-winning writer of several books of journalistic nonfiction, as well as the novel, *Out of the Rain* (2024), a finalist for the 2025 Mark Twain American Voice in Literature Award. Garcia is a recipient of the Studs Terkel Prize for writing about the working classes and the Sigma Delta Chi Award for excellence in journalism. His work has been anthologized in *Best American Travel Writing*, *Best American Nonrequired Reading*, and *Best American Essays*. He lives in San Diego.